Messalina of the suburbs

E.M. Delafield

Messalina of the suburbs

ISBN: 979-8-88830-569-0

DEDICATED

TO

M. P. P.

My Dear Margaret,

We have so often agreed that causes are more interesting than the most dramatic results, that I feel you are the right person to receive the dedication of my story about Elsie Palmer, in which I have tried to reconstruct the psychological developments that led, by inexorable degrees, to the catastrophe of murder. These things are never "bolts from the blue" in reality, but merely sensational accessories to the real issue, which lies on that more subtle plane of thought where only personalities are deserving of dissection.

For what it is worth, I offer you an impression of Elsie Palmer's personality.

E. M. D.
August, 1923

CONTENTS

MESSALINA OF THE SUBURBS

PART I

I

"Elsie, I've told you before, I won't have you going with boys."

"I don't, mother."

"Yes, you do. And don't contradict. Surely to goodness you're aware by this time that it's the heighth of bad manners to contradict. I've taken trouble enough to try and make a lady of you, I'm sure, and now all you can do is to contradict your mother, and spend your time walking the streets with boys."

"Mother, I never."

"Now don't tell lies about it, Elsie. Mother knows perfectly well when you're telling a lie, and you don't take her in by crocodile tears either, my lady. Don't let me have to speak to you again about the same thing, that's all."

Elsie began to cry, automatically and without conviction. "I'm sure I don't know what you mean."

"Yes, you do, miss. I mean Johnnie Osborne, and Johnnie Osborne's brother, and Stanley Begg and the rest of them. Now, no more of it, Elsie. Go and give the gurl a hand with washing up the tea-things, and hurry up."

Elsie went away, glad that it was so soon over. Sometimes mother went on for ages. Thank the Lord she was busy to-day, with two new paying guests coming in. As she went past the drawing-room door Elsie looked in.

"Hallo, little girl!"

"Hallo, Mr. Roberts! Can't stay, I've to go and help the girl wash up or something."

"You've been crying!"

"I haven't, then!" She went further into the room and let him see the downward droop of her pouting mouth and her wet eyelashes. She had not cried hard enough to make her nose turn red.

"I say, what a shame! What have they been doing to you?"

"Oh, nothing. Mother's on the warpath, that's all. It isn't anything."

1

"How rotten of her! Fancy scolding you! I thought you were always good, Elsie."

"And who said you might call me Elsie, if you'll kindly answer me that, Mister Impertinence?"

She shook her short, bobbing curls at him and laughed, suddenly good-tempered.

"You witch! Elsie, shall you miss me a tiny bit when I'm gone?"

"Oh, you're going, are you?" She pretended to consider. "Let me see, there's a single gentleman coming, who'll have your room, and a married lady and gentleman for the front bedroom. I don't really suppose, Mr. Roberts, there'll be time to miss you much, with the house full like that." She looked innocently up at him.

"Little devil!" he muttered between his teeth, causing her to thrill slightly, although she maintained her pose of artlessness without a visible tremor.

"Who's the bounder who's going to have my room after to-night?"

"Mis-ter Roberts!" She affected a high key of indignation. "He isn't a bounder. You know very well that mother's awfully particular. She wouldn't take anyone without he was a perfect gentleman in every way. Now I can't wait another minute. I should get into an awful row if mother caught me here."

"What's the harm? Don't run away, Elsie. Just tell me this: are you coming to the pictures to-night—for the last evening?"

"Oh, are you going to take me and Geraldine? I don't suppose Geraldine'll be able to—she's ill."

"Can't we go without her?"

"Mother wouldn't let me."

"Well, look here, Elsie—come without telling anyone. Do, just for the lark. I swear I'll take the greatest care of you."

"Oh, how could I? Besides, mother'd want to know where I was."

"Can't you say you're going somewhere with that eternal friend of yours—that Irene Tidmarsh girl, or whatever her name is?"

"I'll thank you to remember you're speaking of a friend of mine, Mr. Roberts. And the idea of suggesting I should do such a thing as deceive my mother! Why, I'm surprised at you!"

"Don't rot, Elsie. Say you'll come. Slip out after supper, and meet me at the bottom of the road. There's a jolly good programme on at the Palatial."

"I hope you'll enjoy the pictures, Mr. Roberts," said Elsie demurely. She sidled backwards to the door.

"I shall wait for you—eight o'clock sharp."

"Don't catch cold waiting," she mocked.

2

"Look here, kid——"

"That's mother! She'll skin me alive, if I give her half a chance!" She flew out into the hall and down the passage to the kitchen.

The servant Nellie was there, and Elsie's sister Geraldine.

"Where've you been, Elsie?"

"With mother. I didn't know you were here; I thought you were s'posed to be ill."

"So I am ill," returned Geraldine bitterly. "But as you were out, someone had to do some work."

Elsie looked critically at her sister. Geraldine did look ill, sallow and with black rims round her eyes, but then she had something altogether wrong with her digestion, and often looked like that.

"Bilious again?"

"'M. I think it was that beastly pudding we had last night. I've been awfully sick."

"Poor wretch!"

Neither of them paid any attention to Nellie Simmons, who went on plunging and clattering greasy spoons and plates about in the water that steamed from a chipped enamel basin.

"Can't you take this rag, Elsie, and wipe a bit, and let me get upstairs? I'm sure I'm going to be sick again."

"I suppose I must, then—poor me!"

"Poor you, when you've been out since dinner! I should like to know what for. If it was me, now——Oh, Lord, my head!"

"Well, go on upstairs again. Have you tried the new medicine that Ireen's aunt did the testimonial for?"

"Yes, and I don't believe it's a bit better than any of the others. I feel like nothing on earth. I say, where were you all the afternoon?"

"Curiosity killed the cat," said Elsie, wiping the plates.

"I'm sure I don't want to know."

"That's all right then, we're both satisfied, because I don't mean to tell you."

Geraldine looked angrily at her sister and walked away, her thin plait of dark hair flapping limply between her angular, slouching shoulders.

"What is there for supper to-night, Nellie?" said Elsie presently.

"The 'am."

"Oh, goodness, that old ham! Why can't we ever have anything nice, I should like to know! And I s'pose the cold tart's got to be finished up, and that beastly cold shape?"

"That's right," Nellie said laconically.

"Well, there'll be no cooking to do, that's one thing."

"She wants some soup put on, because of the new people, but I've left it all ready. I'm off at six sharp, I can tell you."

3

"What's the hurry, Nellie?" asked Elsie amicably. She saw that Nellie wanted to be asked, and she felt good-humoured because there was no cooking to be done, and she could lay the supper and ring the bell earlier than usual, so as to be able to keep her appointment with Mr. Roberts.

"I've got someone waiting for me, I 'ave," Nellie said importantly. "Couldn't be kept waiting—oh dear, no!"

Elsie looked at the ugly, white-faced Cockney woman, whose teeth projected, decayed and broken, and round the corners of whose mouth and nostrils clung clusters of dry pimples, and burst out laughing.

"It's true!" said Nellie, offended. "And I'm off now."

She went to dry her chapped hands on the limp and dingy roller-towel that hung beside the cold-water tap.

Elsie laughed again, partly to tease Nellie Simmons and partly because it really amused her to think that her own projected diversion with Mr. Roberts should be parodied by this grotesque Nellie and some unknown, equally grotesque, companion.

Nellie pulled down her hat and coat from the peg on the kitchen door, put them on and went away, although it was quarter of an hour before her time. She knew well enough that none of them would say anything, Elsie reflected. Girls were too difficult to get hold of, when one took in guests.

As soon as the side door had slammed behind Nellie, Elsie flew into the scullery. A broken piece of looking-glass hung there, where she had nailed it up herself long ago.

She pulled down the thick, dust-coloured wave of hair that fell from a boyish, left-hand parting, until it lay further across her forehead, deepening the natural kink in it with her fingers, and loosening the black ribbon bow that fell over one ear. The soft, flopping curls fell to her shoulders on either side of her full, childish face. She rubbed hard at her cheeks for a moment, without producing very much visible effect on their uniform pale pinkiness, starred all over with tiny golden freckles. The gold was repeated in her eyelashes and pale eyebrows, but Elsie's eyes, to her eternal regret, were neither blue nor brown. They were something between a dark grey and a light green, and the clear blue whites of them showed for a space between the iris and the lower lid.

Her nose was straight and short; her wide mouth, habitually pouting, possessed a very full underlip and a short, curving upper one. When she showed her teeth, they were white and even, but rather far apart. The most salient characteristic of her face was that its high cheek-bones, and well-rounded cheeks, gave an odd

4

impression of pushing against her underlids, so that her eyes very often looked half shut, and small. Elsie saw this in herself, and it made her furious. She called it "a Japanese doll look."

She realised that her soft, rounded neck was really beautiful, and was secretly proud of the opulent curves of her figure; but to other girls she pretended that she thought herself too fat, although in point of fact she wore no stays.

She thought with pride that she looked more like eighteen than sixteen years old, although she was not, and knew that she never would be, very tall.

Dragging a black velveteen tam-o'-shanter from her pocket, Elsie pulled it rakishly on over her curls, her fingers quickly and skilfully pouching the worn material so that it sagged over to one side. The hands with which she manipulated the tam-o'-shanter were freckled too, like her face, and of the same uniform soft pink. The fingers were short, planted very far apart, and broad at the base and inclining to curve backwards.

She wiped them on the roller-towel, as Nellie Simmons had done, only far more hurriedly, and then went quietly out at the side door. It opened straight into a small blind alley, and Elsie ran up it, and into the road at a corner of which her home was situated. Turning her back on No. 15, from which she had just emerged, she kept on the same side of the road, hoping to escape observation even if Mrs. Palmer were to look out of the window.

Very soon, however, she was obliged to cross the road, and then she rang the bell of a tall house that was the counterpart of the one she lived in, and indeed of all the other hundred and eighty yellow-and-red brick houses in Hillbourne Terrace.

Irene Tidmarsh opened the door, a lanky, big-eyed creature, with two prominent front teeth and an immense plait of ugly brown hair. Her arms and legs were thick and shapeless.

"Hallo, Elsie!"

"Hallo, Ireen. Look here, I can't stay. I only want to ask you if you'll swear we've been to the pictures together to-night, if anyone ever asks. Quick! Be a sport, and promise."

"What's up?" Irene asked wearily.

"Oh, only my fun. I don't particularly want mother to know about me going out to-night, that's all. If I can say I was with you if I'm asked, it'll be all right, only you'll have to back me up if she doesn't believe me."

"Oh, all right, I don't care. You're a caution, Elsie Palmer—you and your made-up tales. Don't see much difference between them and downright lies, sometimes."

5

"Well, what am I to do? I can't ever go anywhere, or have any amusement, without mother and Geraldine wanting to know all about it, and if I've been behaving myself, and 'cetera and 'cetera."

"Who is it this time, Elsie?"

"Only this fellow who's leaving to-morrow, the one that's been P.G. with us such a time, you know."

"Oh, Roberts?"

"'M. Well, so long, dear. Thanks awfully and all that. Ta-ta. Don't forget."

"Ta-ta," repeated Irene. "You'll have to tell me all about it on Sunday, mind."

"Awright."

Elsie turned and hurried homeward again, shrugging her shoulders up to her ears as the wind whistled shrilly down the street.

It was September, and cold.

When she was indoors again, she pulled off her tam-o'-shanter and stuffed it once more into the pocket of her serge skirt. Then she went upstairs to the room at the top of the house that she shared with Geraldine.

"I wish you'd knock."

"Whatever for? It's my room as much as yours, isn't it?" Elsie said without acrimony.

"Have you been washing up all this time?"

"Nellie went off early."

"The slut! Whatever for? Did you tell mother?"

"No. It wouldn't be a bit of good. She won't say anything to Nellie just now, whatever she does, with these new people just coming in."

"Oh, my head!" groaned Geraldine, not attending.

She lay on her bed, her white blouse crumpled, and a machine-made knitted coat, of shrimp-pink wool, drawn untidily over her shoulders. Her black Oxford shoes lay on the mat between the two beds, and her black stockings showed long darns and a hole in either heel.

Elsie began to arrange her hair before the looking-glass in a painted deal frame that stood on the deal chest-of-drawers. Presently she pulled a little paper bag from one of the drawers and began to suck sweets.

"No good offering you any, I suppose?"

"Don't talk of such a thing. Elsie, I can't come down to supper to-night. Do be a dear and bring me up a cup of tea—nice and strong. I've got a sort of craving for hot tea when I'm like this, really I have."

6

"You don't want much, do you, asking me to carry tea up four flights of stairs? I'll see what I can do." Elsie began to hum, in a small, rather tuneful little voice. She let her skirt fall round her feet as she sang and pulled off her blouse, revealing beautifully modelled breasts and shoulders. Her arms were a little too short, but the line from breast-bone to knee was unusually good, the legs plump and shapely, with slender ankles and the instep well arched. She wore serge knickerbockers and a flimsy under-bodice of yellow cotton voile over a thick cotton chemise.

"Are you going out again?" asked Geraldine in a vexed, feeble voice.

"I may go round and sit with Ireen for a bit, after supper. I think she wants to go to the pictures, or something."

"How's Mr. Tidmarsh?"

"Going to die, I should think, by all accounts," glibly replied Elsie, although as a matter of fact she had forgotten to make any enquiry for Irene's father, who had for months past been dying from some obscure and painful internal growth.

"Why doesn't he go to a hospital?"

"Don't ask me. Ireen's always begging him to, but he won't."

"Old people are awfully selfish, I think," said Geraldine thoughtfully.

"Yes, aren't they? Look, I'm going to put this collar on my Sunday serge. That ought to smarten it up a bit."

She pinned the cheap lace round the low-cut V at the neck of an old navy-blue dress, and fastened it with a blue-stoned brooch in the shape of a circle. Her throat rose up, fresh and warm and youthful, from the new adornment.

"Isn't it time I put my hair up, don't you think?"

"No. You're only a kid. I didn't put mine up till I was eighteen. Mother wouldn't let me."

Elsie dragged a thick grey pilot-cloth coat from behind the curtain of faded red rep that hung across a row of pegs and constituted the sisters' wardrobe, caught up the black tam-o'-shanter again and ran downstairs.

All the time that she was laying the table in the dining room, which was next to the kitchen on the ground floor, Elsie hummed to herself.

The tablecloth was stained in several places, and she arranged the Britannia-metal forks and spoons, the coarse, heavy plates and the red glass water-jug so as to cover the spots as much as possible. In the middle of the table stood a thick fluted green glass with paper chrysanthemums in it.

Elsie added the cruet, two half-loaves of bread on a wooden

7

platter with "Bread" carved upon it in raised letters, and put a small red glass beside each plate. Finally she quickly pleated half a dozen coloured squares of Japanese paper, and stuck one into each glass.

"Mother!" she called.

"What?" said Mrs. Palmer from the kitchen.

"It's ready laid."

"What are you in such a hurry for? Miss M. and Mr. Williams haven't turned up yet."

"Mr. Roberts wants his supper early, I know."

"You've no business to know, then. Well, put the ham on the table and the cold sweets, and he can go in when he pleases. This is Liberty Hall, as I call it."

Elsie carried in the ham, placing the dish on the table beside the carving-knife and fork that were raised upon a "rest" of electro plate. The glass dishes containing a flabby pink decoction of cornflour, and the apple tart, with several slices of pastry gone from the crust, she laid at the other end of the table.

"Supper's in, Mr. Roberts," she cried through the open door of the drawing-room, but this time she did not go in, and flew back to the kitchen before Mr. Roberts appeared.

"Geraldine's asking for tea, mother."

"There's a kettle on. She can come and fetch it."

"I'll take it up," Elsie volunteered.

"You're very obliging, all of a sudden. I'm sure I only wish you and your sister were more like sisters, the way Aunt Ada and Aunt Gertie and Mother were. There wasn't any of this bickering between us girls that I hear between you and Geraldine."

"You've made up for it later, then," said Elsie pertly. "The aunts never come here but they find fault with things, and Aunt Ada cries, and I'm sure you and Aunt Gertie go at it hammer and tongs."

"Don't you dare to speak to me like that, Elsie Palmer," said her mother abstractedly. ("Give me a spoon, there's a good gurl.") "What you gurls are coming to, talking so to your own mother, is more than I can say. What's at the bottom of all this talk about carrying tea to Geraldine? What are you going to do about your own supper?"

"Have it in here. I don't want much, anyway. I'm not hungry. Tea and bread-and-jam'll do."

"Please yourself," said Mrs. Palmer.

She was a large, shapeless woman, slatternly and without method, chronically aggrieved because she was a widow with two daughters, obliged to support herself and them by receiving boarders, whom she always spoke of as guests.

8

"Where are these what-you-may-call-'ems—these Williamses—coming from?" Elsie asked, while she was jerking tea from the bottom of a cocoa-tin into a broken earthenware tea-pot.

"Ask me no questions and I'll tell you no lies," said her mother.

She had no slightest reason to conceal the little she knew of the new people who were coming, but it was her habit to reply more or less in this fashion, semi-snubbing, semi-facetious, whenever either of her daughters asked a question.

"I'm sure I don't want to know," said Elsie, also from habit.

She made the tea, poured out two cups-full and took one upstairs. As she had expected, the alarm clock on the wash-stand showed it to be eight o'clock.

Almost directly afterwards, she heard the front door slam.

No. 15 was a narrow, high house, with very steep stairs, but Elsie was used to them, although she grumbled at the number of times she went up and down them, and she and Geraldine and Mrs. Palmer all kept numerous articles of toilet and clothing in the kitchen, so as to save journeys backwards and forwards.

She now went down once more, and sitting at a corner of the newspaper-covered kitchen table, drank tea and ate bread-and-jam deliberately.

"That's the bell!"

Mrs. Palmer hoisted herself out of her chair, from which she had been reading the headlines of an illustrated daily paper, commenting on them half aloud with: "Fancy!... Whatever is the world coming to, is what I say...."

"That'll be the Williamses, and about time too. You'll have to give me a hand upstairs with the boxes afterwards, Elsie, but I'll give 'em supper first."

She went out into the hall, and Elsie heard the sounds of arrival, and her mother's voice saying: "Good evening, you've brought us some wet weather, I'm afraid.... You mustn't mind me joking, Mrs. Williams, it's my way.... Liberty Hall, you'll find this...."

Elsie ran to the back kitchen, donned the pilot-cloth coat and the tam-o'-shanter, and slipped out through the side door into the wet drizzle of a cold autumn evening.

"Ooh!" She turned up the collar of the coat, and pushed her gloveless hands deep into her pockets as she hurried along the pavement. It shone wet and dark, giving blurred reflections of the lamps overhead. Every now and then a tram jerked and clanged its way along the broad suburban road.

Only a few shops were lit along the road. Most of the buildings on either side were houses that displayed a brass sign-plate on the door, or a card with "Apartments" in one of the windows. Right at the end of the street, a blur of bluish light streamed out from the Palatial Picture House.

"I thought you weren't coming," said young Roberts, reproachfully. "It's long after eight." He wore a light overcoat and he, also, had turned up his collar as a protection against the rain.

"I had to help mother, of course. And if you want to know, I ought to be there now." She laughed up at him provocatively.

"Come on in," he said, pulling her hand through his arm.

II

This was Elsie's real life.

Although quite incapable of formulating the thought to herself, she already knew instinctively that only in her relations with some man could she find self-expression.

In the course of the past two years she had gradually discovered that she possessed a power over men that other girls either did not possess at all, or in a very much lesser degree. From the exercise of unconscious magnetism, she had by imperceptible degrees passed to a breathless, intermittent exploitation of her own attractiveness.

She did not know why boys so often wished to kiss her, nor why she was sometimes followed, or spoken to, in the street, by men. At first she had thought that she must be growing prettier, but her personal preference was for dark eyes, a bright colour, and a slim, tall figure, and she honestly did not admire her own appearance. Moreover, her looks varied almost from day to day, and very often she seemed plain. She had never received any instruction in questions of sex, excepting whispered mis-information from girls at school as to the origin of babies. The signs of physical development that had come to her early were either not commented upon except in half-disgusted, half-facetious innuendo from Geraldine, or else dismissed by Mrs. Palmer curtly:

"Nice gurls don't think about those things. I'm ashamed of you, Elsie. You should try and be nice-minded, as mother's always told her gurls."

A sort of garbled knowledge came to her after a time, knowledge that comprised the actual crude facts as to physical union between men and women, and explained in part certain violent bodily reactions to which she had been prone almost since childhood.

10

She had not the least idea whether any other girl in the world ever felt as she did, and was inclined to believe herself unnatural and depraved.

This thought hardly ever depressed her. She thought that to remain technically "a good girl" was all that was required of her, and admitted no further responsibility.

Geraldine and she quarrelled incessantly. Geraldine, with her poor physique and constant indispositions, was angrily jealous of Elsie's superb health and uninterrupted preoccupation with her own affairs. She had only just begun to suspect that Elsie was never without a masculine admirer, and the knowledge, when it became a certainty, would embitter the relations between them still further on Geraldine's side.

On Elsie's side there was no bitterness, only contempt and unmalicious hostility. She disliked her elder sister, but was incapable of the mental effort implied by hatred. In the same way, she disliked her mother, almost without knowing that she did so.

Her home had always been ugly, sordid, and abounding in passionless discord. Elsie's real life, which was just beginning to give her the romance and excitement for which she craved, was lived entirely outside the walls of No. 15, Hillbourne Terrace.

To-night, as she entered the hot, dark, enervating atmosphere of the cinema theatre, she thrilled in response to the contrast with the street outside. When she heard the loud, emphasised rhythm of a waltz coming from the piano beneath the screen, little shivers of joy ran through her.

A girl with a tiny electric torch indicated to them a row of seats, and Elsie pushed her way along until the two empty places at the very end of the row were reached. It added the last drop to her cup of satisfaction that she should have only the wall on one side of her. Human proximity almost always roused her to a vague curiosity and consciousness, that would have interfered with her full enjoyment of the evening.

She settled herself in the soft, comfortable seat, slipping her arms from the sleeves of her coat, and leaning back against it.

Roberts dropped a small box into her lap as he sat down beside her.

"Thanks awfully," she whispered.

A film was showing, and Elsie became absorbed at once in the presentment of it, although she had no idea of the story. It came to an end very soon, and a Topical Budget was shown. Elsie was less interested, and pulled the string off her box of chocolates.

"Have one?"

"I don't mind. Thanks."

11

"They're awfully good." She chewed and sucked blissfully.

"Ooh! Look at that ship! Isn't it funny?"

"Makes you feel seasick to look at it, doesn't it?" whispered Roberts, and she giggled ecstatically.

Words appeared on the screen.

"'Hearts and Crowns,' featuring Lallie Carmichael."

"How lovely!" said Elsie.

The story was complicated, and as most of the characters were Russian, Elsie did not always remember whether Sergius was the villain or the lawyer, and if Olga was the name of the "vampire" or of the soubrette. But the beautiful Lallie Carmichael was the heroine, and a clean-shaven American the hero. Elsie watched them almost breathlessly, and after a time it was she herself who was leaning back in the crowded restaurant, in a very low dress, and waving an ostrich-feather fan, torn between passion and loyalty. The American hero assumed no definite personality, other than that which his creator had endowed him. The scenes that she liked best were those between the two lovers, when they were shown alone together, and the American made passionate love to the princess.

At the end of the First Part, the lights went up.

Elsie turned her shining eyes and rumpled curls towards her escort.

"It is good, isn't it?" he said, with a critical air.

"Isn't it good? Have another sweet?"

"Well, thanks, I don't mind. Are you enjoying yourself, kiddie?"

"Awfully. I like pictures."

"What about me? Don't you like me a little bit too, Elsie, for bringing you?" His voice had become low and husky.

Still under the emotional influence of the story, the music, and the relaxation produced by bodily warmth and comfort, she looked at him, and saw, not the common, rather negligible features of sandy-haired Mr. Roberts, but the bold, handsome American hero of the film.

"Of course I like you," she said softly.

"You won't forget me when I've gone?"

"No."

"You will, Elsie! You'll let some other fellow take you to the pictures, and you won't give me another thought."

"Of course I shall, you silly! I shall always remember you—you've been awfully sweet to me."

"Will you write to me?"

"We'll see about that."

"Promise."

"Promises are like pie-crusts, made to be broken."

12

"Yours wouldn't be. I bet anything if you promised a chap something, you'd stick to it. Now wouldn't you?"

"I daresay I should," she murmured, flattered. "Mother says I've always been a terrible one for keeping to what I've once said. It's the way I am, you know."

No fleeting suspicion crossed her mind that this was anything but a true description of herself.

"Elsie, do you know what I should like to do?"

"What, Mr. Roberts?"

"Call me Norman. I should like to make a hell of a lot of money and come back and marry you."

"You shouldn't use those words."

"I'm in earnest, Elsie."

"You're making very free with my name, aren't you?"

"You don't mind."

"No," she whispered.

"You're a little darling."

The lights went out again, and his hand fumbled for hers in the darkness. Warm and unresisting it lay in his, and presently returned pressure for pressure.

The story on the screen began to threaten tragedy, and Elsie's body became tense with anxiety. She pressed her shoulder hard against that of Roberts.

He, too, leant towards her, and presently slipped one arm round her waist. Instantly her senses were awake, and although she continued to gaze at the screen, she was in reality blissfully preoccupied only with his embrace, and the sensations it aroused in her.

Intensely desirous that he should not move away, she relaxed her figure more and more, letting her head rest at last against his shoulder. She began to wonder whether he would kiss her, and to feel that she wanted him to do so. As though she had communicated the thought to him, the man beside her in the obscurity put his disengaged hand under her chin and tilted her face to his.

She did not resist, and he kissed her, first on her soft cheek and then on her mouth.

Elsie had been kissed before, roughly and teasingly by boys, and once or twice, furtively, by an elderly lodger of Mrs. Palmer's, whose breath had smelt of whisky.

But the kisses of this young commercial traveller were of an entirely different quality to these, and the pleasure that she took in them was new and startling to herself.

"Elsie, d'you love me?" he whispered. "I love you. I think you're the sweetest little girl in the whole world."

13

Elsie liked the words vaguely, but she did not really want him to talk, she wanted him to go on kissing her.

"Say—'I love you, Norman.'"

"I won't."

"You must. Why won't you?"

"It's so soppy."

"Elsie!"

She felt that the magnetic current between them had been disturbed, and made an instinctive, nestling movement against him.

He kissed her again, two or three times.

Reluctantly, Elsie forced herself to the realisation that the film must soon come to an end, and the lights reappear. She looked at the screen again, and when the lovers, in magnified presentment, exchanged a long embrace, responsive vibrations shook her, and she felt all the elation of conscious and recent initiation.

The lights suddenly flashed out, a moment sooner than she expected them, and she flung herself across into her own seat, pressing the backs of her hands against her flushed, burning cheeks and dazzled eyes.

She knew that Norman Roberts was looking at her, but she would not turn her head and meet his eyes, partly from shyness, and partly from coquetry.

"Isn't this the end?" she said, knowing that it was not, but speaking in order to relieve her sense of embarrassment.

"No, it isn't over till half-past ten; there's another forty minutes yet." He consulted his wrist-watch elaborately. "I expect they'll have a comic to finish up with."

Elsie sensed constraint in him, too, and in sudden alarm turned and faced him. As their eyes met, both of them smiled and flushed, and Roberts slipped his arm under hers and possessed himself of her hand again.

"Did you like that?" he whispered, bending towards her.

"The picture?"

"You know I don't mean that."

She laughed and then nodded.

"Elsie, tell me something truly. Has any other fellow ever kissed you?"

Her first impulse was to lie glibly. Then her natural, instinctive understanding of the game on which they were engaged, made her laugh teasingly.

"That's telling, Mr. Inquisitive."

"That means they have. I must say, Elsie, that considering you're only sixteen, I don't call that very nice."

Elsie snatched away her hand. "I get quite enough of that sort

14

of thing at home, thank you, Mr. Norman Roberts, Esquire. There's no call for you to interfere in my concerns, that I'm aware of."

His instant alarm gratified her, although she continued to look offended, and to sit very upright in her chair.

"Don't be angry, Elsie. I didn't mean to offend you, honour bright. Make it up!"

The pianist began some rattling dance-music and the lights went out again.

Elsie immediately relaxed her pose, feeling her heart beat more quickly in mingled doubt and anticipation.

The doubt was resolved almost within the instant. Roberts pulled her towards him, bringing her face close to his, and whispered:

"Kiss and be friends!"

All the while that the last film was showing, Elsie lay almost in his arms, seeing nothing at all, conscious only of feeling alive as she had never felt alive before.

Even when it was all over and they rose to go, that sense of awakened vitality throbbed within her, and made her unaware of fatigue.

"Follow me," said Roberts authoritatively, and took his place in front of her in the gangway. There he waited, meekly and like everybody else, until the people in front should have moved. But to Elsie there was masculinity in the shelter of his narrow, drooping shoulders, as he stood before her in his crumpled light overcoat, every now and then shifting from one foot to the other.

She followed him step by step, pulling her hair into place under the tam-o'-shanter, and settling it at its customary rakish angle.

It was no longer raining, and a watery moon showed through a haze.

They dawdled as soon as they were out of the crowd, with linked arms and clasped hands.

"Swear you'll write to me, Elsie."

"All right."

"Lordy, to think of all we might have done together these three months I've been here, and I've never had more than a word with you here and there!"

"I was at school all the time, till last week."

"You aren't going back to school again?"

"No, that's over, praise be! I'm supposed to be taking up typing and shorthand, some time, though there's plenty for two of us to do at home, I should have said."

The faint reverberations of a church clock striking came to them.

"Goodness, that's never eleven o'clock striking! Well, you will get me into a row and no mistake!"

She began to run, but stopped under a lamp just before No. 15 was in sight.

He had kept pace with her high-heeled, uneven steps easily, and stopped beside her.

"Say good-night to me properly, then."

"How, properly? Good-night, Mr. Roberts, and thank you ever so much. Oh, and bonne voyage to-morrow, in case I don't see you. Will that do?"

"No, it won't. I want a kiss."

"You don't want much, do you?" she began half-heartedly, and looking up and down the street as she spoke.

It was empty but for themselves.

Roberts caught hold of her and kissed her with violence. Unresisting, Elsie put back her head and closed her eyes.

"Kiss me—you shall kiss me," he gasped.

At the sense of constriction that came upon her with the tightened grasp of his arms, Elsie gave a fluttering, strangled scream and began to struggle.

"Let me go! You're hurting me!"

He loosened his hold so abruptly that she nearly fell down.

She began to hurry towards home, moving with the ugly, jerking gait peculiar to women who walk from the knees.

"Shall I see you to-morrow before I go?" His voice sounded oddly humble and crestfallen.

"I'll come to the drawing-room for a minute—no one's ever there in the mornings."

"What time, Elsie? I ought to be off at nine."

"Oh, before that some time, I expect. I say, you've got your key, haven't you?"

A sharp misgiving assailed her as he began to fumble in his pockets.

"Yes, all right." He put it into the lock.

Elsie, relieved, stood on tiptoe and put her arms round his neck. "Good-night, you dear," she whispered. "Now don't begin again. Open the door and go in first, and if the coast isn't clear, just cough, and I'll wait a bit. I'll see you to-morrow."

When he signed to her that the house was quiet, and that she could safely enter, Elsie slipped past him like a shadow while he felt about for matches, and flew upstairs. Her mother slept in the back bedroom on the third floor, and Elsie saw that her door was shut and that no streak of light showed under it. Satisfied, she went up the next flight of stairs to the bedroom.

16

Geraldine, of course, was bound to know of her escapade, but Geraldine would either believe, or pretend to believe, that Elsie had been with Irene Tidmarsh, and the two Palmer girls always combined with one another against the sentimentalised tyranny that Mrs. Palmer called "a mother's rights."

Geraldine was lying in bed, reading a paper novelette by the light of a candle stuck into an empty medicine bottle that stood on a chair beside her. She looked sallower than ever now that she had undressed and put on a white flannelette nightgown with a frill high at the neck and another one at each wrist.

Her lank hair was rolled up into steel waving-pins. It was one of Geraldine's grievances that she should be obliged to go to bed in curlers every night, while Elsie's light curls lay loose and ruffled on her pillow. Sometimes, when they were on friendly terms, she and Elsie would speculate together as to how the difficulty could be overcome when Geraldine married, and could no longer go to bed and wake up "looking a sight."

She rolled over as Elsie cautiously opened the door. "You've come at last, have you? How did you get in?"

"Mr. Roberts let me in. He knew I'd be late to-night," said Elsie calmly, beginning to pull off her clothes.

"You've got a nerve, I must say. Mother thinks you were in bed ages ago. She came up after supper and said you were in the kitchen. She was in the drawing-room nearly all the evening, doing the polite to the Williamses."

"Did she find out that supper hadn't been cleared away?"

"I suppose she didn't, or she'd have been up here after you. You're in luck, young Elsie."

"I shall have to go down and do it first thing to-morrow before she's down," said Elsie, yawning.

"Where have you been?"

"Pictures."

"With Ireen?"

"'M."

"I shall ask her what they were like, next time I see her," said Geraldine significantly.

Elsie pulled the ribbon off her hair without untying it, shuffled her clothes off on to the floor from beneath a nightgown that was the counterpart of her sister's, and dabbed at her face with a sponge dipped in cold water. She carefully parted her hair on the other side for the night, and brushed it vigorously for some moments to promote growth, but the worn bristles of her wooden-backed brush were grey with dust and thick with ancient "combings."

At the bedside Elsie knelt down for a few seconds with her face

17

hidden in her hands, as she had always done, muttered an unthinking formula, and got into bed.

"You're very sociable, I must say," Geraldine exclaimed. "Out half the night, and not a word to say when you do come up!"

"I thought you had a headache."

"A lot you care about my headache."

"I'm going to put the light out now."

"All right."

They had always shared a bedroom and never exchanged formal good-nights.

In the dark, a tremendous weariness suddenly came over Elsie. She felt thankful to be in her warm, narrow bed, and blissfully relived the evening's experience.

She found that she could thrill profoundly to the memory of those ardent moments, and even the bodily lassitude that overwhelmed her held a certain luxuriousness.

Dimly, and without any conscious analysis, she felt that for the first time in her sixteen years of life she had glimpsed a reason why she should exist. It was for this that she had been made.

No thought of the future preoccupied her for a moment. She did not even regret that Norman Roberts should be going away next day.

"I must get up in good time to-morrow, and get a word with him in the drawing-room before he's off," was her last waking thought.

But she was sleeping profoundly, her head under the bedclothes, when Mrs. Palmer's customary bang at the door sounded next morning soon after six o'clock.

"Wake up, girls."

"Awright!" Geraldine shouted back sleepily. If one or other of them did not call out in reply, Mrs. Palmer would come into the room in her grey dressing-gown and vigorously shake the bed-posts of either bed.

They could hear her heelless slippers flapping away again, and Elsie reluctantly roused herself.

"I simply must clear that supper-table before mother goes down," she thought. Still half asleep, and yawning without restraint, she put on her thick coat over her nightgown, and ran downstairs with bare feet.

The broken remains of supper, even to Elsie's indifferent eyes, looked horrible in the grim morning light.

She huddled everything out on a tray, pushed it out of sight in the back kitchen, and ran upstairs again, her teeth chattering with cold.

The still warm, tumbled bed was irresistible, and tearing off her coat, Elsie buried herself in it once more.

She slept through Geraldine's sketchy, scrambled toilet and muttered abuse of her sister's laziness, and did not stir even when her senior, as the most unpleasant thing she could do, opened her window, which had been closed all night, and let in the damp, raw, foggy morning air.

Elsie did not stir again until the door was flung open and Geraldine pulled the bedclothes off her roughly, and said angrily:

"Get up, you lazy little brute! I had to wash all the beastly things you left over last night, and mother and I had to do the breakfasts, and see that young Roberts off and everything."

"Has Roberts gone?"

"Yes, of course he has. It's past nine, you lazy pig, you——"

"Oh," said Elsie indifferently, stretching herself.

III

For a little while after Norman Roberts had gone away, Elsie was bored. She received a letter from him, reproaching her for not having been downstairs on the morning of his departure, and giving her an address in Liverpool. He begged her to write to him, and the letter ended with half a dozen pen-and-ink crosses.

"That's for you, Elsie."

Elsie, who hated writing, collected with some difficulty a pen, ink, and a coloured picture postcard of the Houses of Parliament.

"Thanks for yours ever so much," she wrote. "I expect you're having a fine old time in Liverpool. All here send kind remembrances."

Then, because she could not think what else to put, she filled in the remaining space on the card with two large crosses. "From your's sincerely, Elsie."

Roberts, after an interval, wrote once more, and this letter Elsie did not answer at all. She was out nearly every evening, walking, or lounging round the nearest public park, with Irene Tidmarsh, Johnnie and Arthur Osborne, and Stanley Begg.

Arthur Osborne was nominally Irene's "friend," but he, as well as Johnnie and Stanley, always wanted to walk with Elsie, or to sit next her at the cinema, and their preference elated her, although the eldest of the three, Arthur, was only twenty, and not one of them was earning more than from fifteen to twenty shillings a week.

19

At last Irene and Elsie quarrelled about Arthur, and Irene, furious, went to Mrs. Palmer.

"It's no more than my duty, Mrs. Palmer," she virtuously declared, "to let you know the way Elsie goes on. The fellows may laugh and all that, but they don't like it, not really. I know my boy doesn't, for one."

Mrs. Palmer, on different grounds, was quite as angry as Irene.

She worked herself up, rehearsing to Geraldine all that Irene had said, and a great deal that she alleged herself to have replied, and she summoned her two unmarried sisters, Aunt Ada and Aunt Gertie Cookson, to No. 15.

"What I want," she explained, "is to give the gurl a fright. I'm not going to have her making herself cheap with young rag-tag-and-bobtail like those Osborne boys. Why, a pretty gurl like Elsie could get married, as easily as not, to a fellow with money. Nice enough people come to this house, I'm sure. It's on account of the gurls, simply, that I've always been so particular about references and all. I'm sure many's the time I could have had the house full but for not liking the looks of one or two that were ready to pay anything for a front bedroom. But I've always said to myself, 'No,' I've said, 'a mother's first duty is to her children,' I've said, especially being in the position of father and mother both, as you might say."

"I'm sure you've always been a wonderful mother, Edie," said Aunt Ada.

"Well," Mrs. Palmer conceded, mollified.

When Geraldine came in with the tea-tray to the drawing-room that Mrs. Palmer was for once able to use, because the Williamses, her only guests, had a sitting-room of their own, the aunts received her with marked favour.

"Mother's helpful girlie!" said Aunt Gertie, as Geraldine put down the plate of bread-and-butter, the Madeira cake on a glass cake stand, and another plate of rock-buns.

"Where's Elsie?" Mrs. Palmer asked significantly.

"Cutting out in the kitchen."

"Tell her to come along up. She knows your aunties are here."

"I told her to come, and she made use of a very vulgar expression," Geraldine spitefully declared.

"I don't know what's come over Elsie, I'm sure," Mrs. Palmer declared helplessly. "She's learnt all these low tricks and manners from that friend of hers, that Ireen Tidmarsh."

Mrs. Palmer was very angry with Irene for her revelations, although she was secretly rather enjoying her younger daughter's notoriety.

20

"Get that naughty gurl up from the kitchen directly," she commanded Geraldine. "No—wait a minute, I'll go myself."

With extraordinary agility she heaved her considerable bulk out of her low chair and left the room.

"And what have you been doing with yourself lately?" Aunt Gertie enquired of Geraldine.

She was stout and elderly-looking, with a mouth over-crowded by large teeth. She was older than Mrs. Palmer, and Aunt Ada was some years younger than either, and wore, with a sort of permanent smirk, the remains of an ash-blond prettiness. They were just able, in 1913, to live in the house at Wimbledon that their father had left them, on their joint income.

"There's always heaps to do in the house, I'm sure, Aunt Gertie," said Geraldine vaguely. "And I'm not strong enough to go to work anywhere, really I'm not. Now Elsie's different. She could do quite well in the shorthand-typing, but she's bone idle—that's what she is. Or there's dressmaking—Elsie's clever with her needle, that I will say for her."

Mrs. Palmer came back with Elsie behind her. The girl reluctantly laid her face for a moment against each of the withered ones that bumped towards her in conventional greeting.

"Hallo, Aunt Gertie. Hallo, Aunt Ada," she said lifelessly.

Mrs. Palmer began to pour out the tea, and whilst they ate and drank elegantly, the conversation was allowed to take its course without any reference to the real point at issue.

"What are these Williamses like, that have got the downstairs sitting-room, Edie?"

"Oh, they are nice people," said Mrs. Palmer enthusiastically. "A solicitor, he is, and only just waiting to find a house. I believe they've ever such a lot of furniture in store. They lived at Putney before, but it didn't suit Mrs. Williams. She's delicate."

Mrs. Palmer raised her eyebrows and glanced meaningly at the aunts.

Aunt Ada gazed eagerly back at her.

"Go and get some more bread-and-butter, Elsie," commanded Mrs. Palmer, and when the girl had left the room she nodded at Aunt Ada.

"You know, Mrs. Williams isn't very strong just now. She's been unlucky before, too—twice, I fancy."

"But when? Surely you aren't going to have anything like that here?"

"Oh dear, no! I told her it was out of the question, and she quite understood. It isn't till April, and they hope to move into their new

21

house after Christmas. She must be about fifteen years younger than he is, I imagine."

"How strange!" said Aunt Gertie.

Both she and Aunt Ada were always intensely interested in any detail about anybody, whether known or unknown to them personally.

"Rather remarkable, isn't it, that there should be an event on the way——" Aunt Ada began.

Mrs. Palmer frowned heavily at her as Elsie came back into the room. "It's ever so long since we've seen you, as I was just saying," she remarked in a loud and artificial voice, making Elsie wish that she had waited outside the door and listened. She thought that they must have been talking about her.

After tea was over, they did talk about her. Mrs. Palmer began: "You can let Geraldine take the tea-things, Elsie. It won't be the first time, lately, she's done your share of helping your poor mother as well as her own."

"I'm sorry to hear that," from Aunt Gertie.

"Geraldine's health isn't as strong as yours, either. She looks to me as though she might go into consumption, if you want to know," said Aunt Ada.

They looked at Elsie, and she looked sulkily back at them.

It was one of the days on which she was at her plainest. Her face looked fat and heavy, the high cheek-bones actually seemed to be pushing her lower lids upwards until her eyes appeared as mere slits. Her mouth was closed sullenly.

"Elsie's not been a good gurl lately, and she knows it very well. Her own mother doesn't seem to have any influence with her, so perhaps ..." said Mrs. Palmer to her sisters, but looking at her child, "perhaps you'll see what you can do. It's not a thing I like to talk about, ever, but we know very well what happens to a gurl who spends her time larking about the streets with fellows. To think that a child of mine——"

"What do you do it for, Elsie?" enquired Aunt Gertie, in a practical tone, as though only such shrewdness as hers could have seized at once upon this vital point.

"Do what?"

"What your poor mother says."

"She hasn't said anything, yet."

"Don't prevaricate with me, you bad gurl, you," said Mrs. Palmer sharply. "You know very well what I mean, and so do others. The tales that get carried to me about your goings-on! First one fellow, and then another, and even running after a whipper-snapper that's already going with another gurl!"

"This is a bit of Ireen's work, I suppose," said Elsie. "I can't help it if her boy's sick of her already, can I? I'm sure I don't care anything about Arthur Osborne, or any of them, for that matter."

The implication that Elsie Palmer, at sixteen and a half, could afford to distinguish between her admirers, obscurely infuriated the spinster Aunt Ada.

She began to tremble with wrath, and white dents appeared at the corners of her mouth and nostrils. "You're not the first gurl whose talked that way, and ended by disgracing herself and her family," she cried shrilly. "If I were your mother, I'd give you a sound whipping, I declare to goodness I would."

Elsie shot a vicious look at her aunt out of the corners of her slanting eyes. "Are the grapes sour, Aunt Ada?" she asked insolently.

Aunt Ada turned white. "D'you hear that, Edie?" she gasped.

"Yes, I do," said Mrs. Palmer vigorously, "and I'm not going to put up with it, not for a single instant. Elsie Palmer, you beg your auntie's pardon directly minute."

"I won't."

The vast figure of Mrs. Palmer in her Sunday black frock upreared itself and stood, weighty and menacing, over her child. She had never hit either of her daughters since childhood, but neither of them had ever openly defied her.

"Do as I say."

"N-no."

Elsie's voice quavered, and she burst into tears. Mrs. Palmer let out a sigh of relief. She knew that she had won.

"Do—as—I—say."

"I'm sure I'm very sorry, Aunt Ada, if I said what I didn't ought."

"It isn't what you said, dear," said Aunt Ada untruthfully. "It was the way you said it."

There was a silence.

Then Mrs. Palmer pursued her advantage. "You may as well understand, Elsie, that this isn't going on. I haven't got the time, nor yet the strength, to go chasing after you all day long. I know well enough you're not to be trusted—out of the house the minute my back's the other way—and coming in at all hours, and always a tale of some sort to account for where you've been. So, my lady, you've got to make up your mind to a different state of things. What's it to be: a job as a typewriter, or apprenticed to the millinery? Your kind Aunt Gertie's got a friend in the business, and she's offered to speak for you."

"I'd rather the typing," said Elsie sullenly.

"Then you'll come with me and see about a post to-morrow

23

morning as ever is," said Mrs. Palmer. "It's your own doing. You could have stayed at home like a lady, helping Mother and Geraldine, if you'd cared to. But I'm not going to have any gurl of mine getting herself a name the way you've been doing."

"I suppose I can go now?"

"You can go if you want to," said Mrs. Palmer, flushed with victory. "And mind and remember what I've said, for I mean every word of it."

It was only too evident that she did, and Elsie went out of the room crying angrily. She did not really mind the idea of becoming a typist in an office or a shop in the very least, but she hated having been humiliated in front of her aunts and Geraldine.

As she went upstairs, sobbing, she met Mrs. Williams coming down. She was a gentle, unhealthy-looking woman of about thirty, so thin that her clothes always looked as though they might drop off her bending, angular body.

"What's the matter, dear?"

"It's nothing."

"Come into the sitting-room, won't you, and rest a minute?"

"Well, I don't mind."

Elsie reflected that there would probably be a fire in the sitting-room, and in her own room it was cold, and she knew that the bed was still unmade.

She followed Mrs. Williams into the sitting-room, where Mr. Williams sat reading a Sunday illustrated paper.

"Horace, this poor child is quite upset. Give her a seat, dear."

"It's all right," said Elsie, confused.

She had only seen Mr. Williams half a dozen times. He always breakfasted and went out early, and Elsie, of late, had eaten her supper in the kitchen. They had met at meal-times on Sundays, but she had never spoken to him, and thought him elderly and uninteresting.

Mr. Williams was indeed forty-three years old, desiccated and inclined to baldness, a small, rather paunchy man.

His little, hard grey eyes gleamed on Elsie now from behind his pince-nez.

"No bad news, I hope?" His voice was dry, and rather formal, with great precision of utterance.

His wife put her emaciated hand on the girl's shoulder. "Two heads are better than one, as they say. Horace and I would be glad to help you, if we can."

"It is silly to be upset, like," said Elsie, sniffing. "Mother and I had a few words, that's all, and I'm to get hold of a job. I'm sure I

24

don't know why I'm crying. I shall be glad enough to get out of this place for a bit."

"Hush, dear! That isn't a nice way to speak of your home, now is it? But about this job, now. Horace and I might be able to help you there."

She hesitated and looked at her husband. "What about the Woolleys, dear?"

"Yes—ye-es."

"These are some new acquaintances of ours, and they've a lovely house at Hampstead, but Mrs. Woolley isn't any too strong, and I know she's looking out for someone to help her with the children and all. It wouldn't be going to service—nothing at all like that, of course; I know you wouldn't think of that, dear—but just be one of the family at this lovely house of theirs."

"It isn't in the country, is it?" Elsie asked suspiciously.

"Oh no, dear, Hampstead I said. Only three-quarters of an hour by 'bus from town. Don't you like the country?"

"Too dead-alive."

"Well, these people that I'm telling you about, this Doctor and Mrs. Woolley, they're youngish married people, and most pleasant. Aren't they, Horace? And they've two sweet kiddies—a boy and a girl. Don't you think you'd like me to speak to Mrs. Woolley, now, dear?"

Elsie was not sure. She felt that Mrs. Williams was going too fast. "I don't know," she said ungraciously.

"She's right," said Mr. Williams. "We mustn't be in too great a hurry. Write to your friend Mrs. Woolley by all means, my dear, and let this young lady think it over, and have a talk with her mother and sister. She may not care to live away from home altogether."

"Horace is always so business-like," said Mrs. Williams admiringly. "I expect he's right, dear. But you'd like me to write, just to see if there's any chance, now wouldn't you?"

"What should I have to do there?"

"Why, just help look after the kiddies. I'm sure you love children, now don't you?—and perhaps make a dainty cake or two for afternoon tea, if Mrs. Woolley's busy, or do a bit of sewing for her—and keep the doctor amused in the evening if she has to go up early."

It was the last item that decided Elsie. "I don't mind," she said in her usual formula of acceptance.

Mrs. Williams was delighted. "I'm going to write off this very evening," she exclaimed enthusiastically. "Horace and I have to go out now, but I shan't forget. It'll be a lovely chance for you, dear."

Elsie rather enjoyed telling her mother and Geraldine that

evening that "Mrs. Williams was wild" to secure her services for a lady friend of hers, who had a lovely house at Hampstead.

"This Mrs. Woolley is delicate, and she wants a young lady to help her. Of course, there's a servant for the work of the house."

"If she's counting on you to help her, the same as you've helped your poor mother since you left school, she's got a disappointment in store," said Mrs. Palmer grimly. "I don't know that I'd let you go, even if you get the chance."

In the end, Geraldine, who wanted the top bedroom to herself, and who thought that Elsie, and the problem of Elsie's behaviour, were occupying too much attention, persuaded Mrs. Palmer that it would never do to offend the Williamses.

"Besides," she argued, "it'll be one less to feed here, and we can easily move her bed into the second-floor back room and use it, if we want to put up an extra gentleman any time."

Mrs. Palmer gave in, contingent on a personal interview with Mrs. Woolley.

This was arranged through Mrs. Williams. She one day ushered into the dining-room of No. 15 a large, showily-dressed woman, who might have been any age between thirty-eight and forty-five.

Her rings, and her light, smart dress impressed Elsie, and her suggestion of paying twenty-five pounds a year for Elsie's services satisfied Mrs. Palmer.

"My hubby's a frightfully busy man," Mrs. Woolley remarked. "He isn't at home a great deal, but he likes me to do everything on the most liberal scale—always has done—and he said to me, 'Amy, you're not strong,' he said, 'even if you have a high colour'—so many people are deceived by that, Mrs. Palmer—'and you've got to have help. Someone who can be a bit of a companion to you when I'm out on my rounds or busy in the surgery, and who you can trust with Gladys and Sonnie.'"

"I'm sure Elsie would like to help you, Mrs. Woolley, and you'll find her to be trusted," Mrs. Palmer replied firmly. "I've always brought up my gurls to be useful, even if they are ladies."

"She looks young," said Mrs. Woolley critically.

"She'll put her hair up before she comes to you. It may be a mother's weakness, Mrs. Woolley, but I'm free to confess that Elsie's my baby, and I've let her keep her curls down perhaps longer than I should."

Elsie remained demure beneath what she perfectly recognised as a form of self-hypnotism, rather than conscious humbug, on the part of her mother.

There was at least no sentimentality in her leave-taking a week later.

"Good-bye, Elsie, and mind and not be up to any of your tricks, now. Mother'll expect you on Sunday next."

"Good-bye, Mother," said Elsie indifferently.

She had that morning washed her hair, which made it very soft and fluffy, and had pinned it up in half a dozen fat little sausages at the back of her head. She was preoccupied with her own appearance, and with the knowledge that the newly-revealed back of her neck was white and pretty. She wore a blue serge coat and skirt, a low-cut blouse of very pale pink figured voile, black shoes and stockings, and a dashing little hat, round and brimless, with a big black bow that she had herself added to it on the previous night.

In the Tube railway, a man in the seat opposite to her stared at her very hard. Elsie looked away, but kept on turning her eyes furtively towards him, without moving her head. Every time that she did this, their eyes met.

The man was young, with bold eyes and a wide mouth. Presently he smiled at her.

Elsie immediately looked down at the toes of her new black shoes, moving them this way and that as though to catch the light reflected in their polish.

At Belsize Park Station she got out, carrying her suitcase.

As she passed the youth in the corner, she glanced at him again, then stepped out of the train and went up the platform without looking behind her. Although there was a crowd on the platform and in the lift, and although she never looked round, Elsie could tell that he was following her.

The feeling that this gave her, half fearful and half delighted, was an agreeable titilation to her vanity. She had experienced it before, just as she had often been followed in the street before, but it never lost its flavour. When she was in the street, she began to walk steadily along, gazing straight in front of her.

She heard steps on the pavement just behind her, and then the young man of the train accosted her, raising his hat as he spoke:

"Aren't you going to give me the pleasure of your acquaintance?" he suavely enquired.

His voice was very polite, and his eyes looked faintly amused.

"Oh!" Elsie cried in a startled tone. "I don't think I know you, do I?"

"All the more reason to begin now. Mayn't I carry that bag for you?"

He took it and they walked on together.

"Perhaps you can tell me where Mortimer Crescent is," Elsie said primly.

"It will be my proudest privilege to escort you there," he replied in mock bombastic tones.

It was a form of persiflage well known to Elsie, and she laughed in reply. "You are silly, aren't you?"

"Not at all. Now if you called me cheeky, perhaps...."

"I'll call you cheeky fast enough. A regular Cheeky Charlie, by the look of you!"

"I think I was born cheeky," he agreed complacently. "D'you know what first made me want to talk to you?"

"What?"

"That pink thing you've got on with all the ribbon showing through it."

He put out his hand and, with a familiar gesture, touched the front of her blouse just below her collar-bone.

"You mustn't," said Elsie, startled.

"Why not?"

"I don't allow liberties."

"We'll have to settle what liberties are, miss. Come for a walk this evening and we can talk about it."

"Oh, I couldn't! I'm just going into a new job."

She purposely used the word "new," because she wanted him to think her experienced and grown-up.

"What can a kiddie like you do?"

"Why, I'm private secretary to a duke, didn't you know that?"

"Lucky duke! Where does he live?"

"Oh, that'd be telling. This isn't Mortimer Crescent?"

"It is, very much so indeed, begging your pardon for contradicting a lady."

"Well, don't come any further," begged Elsie. "Ta-ta, and thanks for carrying the bag."

"When do I see you again?"

"I dunno! Never, I should think."

"Seven o'clock to-night?"

"No, I can't, really."

"To-morrow, then? I'll be outside the Belsize Park station, and we'll go on the razzle-dazzle together. I'd like to show you a bit of life. Seven o'clock, mind."

"You and your seven o'clock! You'll be somewhere with your young lady, I know."

"Haven't got one."

"Wouldn't she have you?" scoffed Elsie. "No accounting for tastes, is there?"

"I'll make you pay for this to-morrow night, you little witch— see if I don't!"

Elsie had caught hold of her suitcase, and began to walk away from him.

"Which number are you going to?"

"Eight."

"I'll ring the bell for you."

He did so, rather to her fright and vexation. She urged him in low tones to go away, but he continued to stand beside her on the doorstep, laughing at her annoyance, until a capped and aproned maid opened the door.

Then he lifted his hat, said "Good-night" very politely, and went away.

She never saw him again.

IV

Elsie found the life at 8, Mortimer Crescent, a pleasant contrast to that of her own home.

Mrs. Woolley herself never came downstairs before half-past nine or ten o'clock, and then she was very often only partly dressed, wearing a stained and rumpled silk kimono and a dirty lace-and-ribbon-trimmed boudoir cap. Elsie's only duty in the morning was to keep the two children quiet while their mother slept. This she achieved by the simple expedient of letting them go to bed so late at night that they lay like little logs far on into the morning.

Elsie shared a bedroom with Gladys, and Sonnie's cot was in a dressing-room opening into theirs.

The children were rather pallid and unwholesome, never quite free from colds or coughs, and seeming too spiritless even to be naughty. They went to a kindergarten school from eleven to four o'clock every day, and Elsie took them there and fetched them away again.

During the daytime she was supposed to dust the dining-room, drawing-room, and Mrs. Woolley's bedroom, but she soon found out that no accumulation of dust, cigarette ends, or actual dirt would ever be noticed by the mistress of the house.

There was a general servant, who was inclined to resent Elsie's presence in the house, and who left very soon after her arrival. Another one came, and was sent away at the end of a week's trial because Mrs. Woolley said she was impertinent, and after an uncomfortable interim, during which Elsie nominally "did" the

29

cooking, and they lived upon tinned goods and pressed beef, there came a short-lived succession of maids who never stayed.

At first, Doctor Woolley was seldom seen by Elsie. He went out early, and both he and his wife were out nearly every night.

Mrs. Woolley told Elsie that they adored the theatre. Elsie, who adored it too, had on these occasions, after putting the two children to bed, to remain sulkily behind while Dr. and Mrs. Woolley, after an early meal, walked away together to the Underground station. Sometimes Dr. Woolley was sent for, and could not go, and Mrs. Woolley rang up one of her friends on the telephone—always another woman—and took her instead. One evening after this had happened, the doctor returned unexpectedly early, just as Elsie had finished putting Gladys and Sonnie to bed.

She was coming downstairs, some needlework in her hands, as the doctor slammed the hall door behind him. Instantly the prospect of a dreary evening, probably to be spent in sucking sweets and surreptitiously looking over everything on Mrs. Woolley's untidy writing-table, disappeared.

"Hallo! And how was you to-morrow, Miss Elsie?" cried the doctor genially.

He was a stout, middle-aged man, jocose and very often foul-mouthed, with nicotine stains on his fingers and grease spots on his waistcoat.

He affected a manner of speech that Elsie found intensely amusing.

"You and I all on our ownie own, eh? Where's the missus?—and the kids?"

"The children are in bed, and Mrs. Woolley's gone to the play with Miss Smith, Doctor."

"And haven't you got a drink of cocoa and a bit of bread for a poor man, kind lady?"

Elsie burst out laughing. "You're so silly, I can't help laughing!"

"'Silly,' says she, quite the lady. 'How's that?' says I; to which she says, 'Not at all,' says she, and the same to you and many of them," was the doctor's reply.

Elsie giggled wildly.

"Come along now, tell that slut in the kitchen to stir her stumps and bring some food to the dining-room. Have you had your supper yet?"

"No, Doctor."

"Then you and I will make a party-carry, otherwise a tête-à-tête, otherwise a night of it. Run along and I'll get out something that will make your hair curl."

Elsie had heard this formula before, and understood that the doctor would unlock the door of the tiny wine-cellar and bring out a bottle.

She told the maid to bring supper for Doctor Woolley to the dining-room, but she herself carried in her own plate and cup and saucer, knowing that Florrie was quite aware she had already eaten her evening meal with Mrs. Woolley.

The doctor was drawing the cork out of a bottle as she came into the room. The electric light was turned on, and the small dining-room, with drawn red curtains, and the gas-fire burning, was bright and hot.

The doctor ate heavily of cold meat and pickles, prodding with a fork amongst the mixed contents of the glass jar until he had annexed all the pickled onions that it contained.

He made Elsie sit down and eat too, but he made no demur to her assurance that she wasn't hungry and only wanted some cake and a cup of cocoa.

At first the doctor gave all his attention to the food and warmth of which he stood in need, and Elsie felt self-conscious, and as though she were out of place.

She ceased to answer his occasional facetious interjections, and threw herself back in her chair, gazing down at her own clasped hands.

Gradually the atmosphere of the room altered, and Elsie's instinct told her that the current of magnetism that had never failed her yet was awakening its inevitable response in the man opposite.

At once she felt confident again, and at her ease.

"I say, why didn't the missus take you to the theatre when she found I was busy?" he queried suddenly.

"Oh, I don't know. I suppose she never thought of such a thing."

"Wanted someone nearer her own age, eh? You won't find the ladies running after someone younger and prettier than themselves, you know. Too much of a contrast."

Elsie laughed self-consciously.

"All the better for me, eh? I'm not often allowed to get you all to myself like this, eh? Ah, when I was a gay young bacheldore things was different, they was."

Elsie laughed again, this time in spontaneous tribute to the humour of wilful mis-pronunciation.

"Now, what about this bottle that you made me get out, eh? Where are the glasses?"

He found two in the cupboard of the carved walnut sideboard, and poured a liberal allowance of port from the bottle into each.

"Oh, I couldn't, Doctor! You must excuse me, really you must. I simply couldn't."

31

"Oh, couldn't you, really, awfully, truly couldn't?" he mimicked in exaggerated falsetto. "Well, you've got to—so that's that!"

"Who says so?"

"I say so. I. Moi. 'Je,' replies I, knowing the language. Come along now, be a good girl."

He laid his big coarse hand on hers, and at the contact the familiar thrill of sensuous excitement and pleasure ran through her.

"Are you going to drink it?" he said masterfully.

"Oh, I suppose I must try it. I've never tasted wine before," Elsie added truthfully.

"High time you began, then."

He went back to his place, and drank in long gulps, first saying:

"Our hands have met—our lips not yet—
Here's hoping!"

Elsie sipped at her glass, choked, and put it down again. "How beastly!" she said, shuddering.

"You'll get used to it."

"No, I shan't, because I'm not going to touch the horrid stuff again."

"We'll see about that."

He came round beside her again, and held her with one arm while he tried to force the glass to her lips.

Elsie turned her head aside, struggling and laughing.

"You young monkey!" said the doctor, and forced her face upwards with his free hand.

His breath was in her face, and his inflamed eyes gazing into hers. Instinctively Elsie ceased to struggle and closed her eyes.

He kissed her mouth violently. "God! You haven't got much to learn. Who's been teaching you?" he asked her roughly.

"Oh, you oughtn't to have done that," said Elsie feebly.

"Rubbish! You know I've been thinking of nothing else since you've been here."

He sat down and pulled her on to his knee. "Now tell me all about it," he commanded. His manner was no longer facetious, and he had dropped his jocosities of speech.

"Let me go," said Elsie.

"Sit still."

"Suppose someone were to come in?"

"No one will."

She wriggled a little, half-heartedly, and he gripped her more firmly round the waist. The scene degenerated into a sort of scrambling orgy of animalism.

32

Elsie, although she was frightened, was also exhilarated at the evidence that she possessed power over a man—and a married man—so much older than herself.

She knew that if at any moment he became unmanageable, she had only to threaten to call the servant, and she fully intended to do so as a last resort. But in the meanwhile there was an odd and breathless fascination in feeling that she stood so close to a peril in which lay all the lurking excitement of the unknown.

A sudden wail from the room overhead startled them both.

"That's Sonnie!" gasped Elsie.

"Oh, blast the kid!"

But he let her go and she flew upstairs, glad, and yet disappointed, at her release.

She dismissed Sonnie's nightmare with sharp injunctions not to be silly, tucked him up and decided to go to her own room and not to return downstairs.

"That'll show him," she murmured, simulating to herself a conventional indignation.

In reality, she was intensely excited, and she had been tossing about her bed restlessly for nearly an hour before reaction overtook her, and she became prey to a strange, baffled feeling of having been cheated of the climax due to so emotional an episode.

When at last Elsie slept, it was after she had heard Mrs. Woolley come in and the doctor bolt the hall door and both of them go upstairs to their bedroom, on the other side of the landing.

Every day now held the potentialities of amorous adventure.

Sometimes Elsie did not see the doctor all day long, sometimes they met in the evenings, with Mrs. Woolley present, and he talked in the old facetious style, watching Elsie furtively as she giggled in response.

He very often made excuses for passing things to her at meals, so that their hands touched, and he pressed her foot under the table with his big one, or rubbed it up and down her ankle.

There were moments, however, when they were alone together, and then he pulled her to him and kissed her roughly all over her face and neck, pushing her abruptly away at the first possibility of interruption. Once or twice, at the imminent risk of being discovered, he had snatched hasty and provocative kisses from her lips in a chance encounter on the stairs, or even behind the shelter of an open door.

The perpetual fear of detection, no less than the tantalising incompleteness of their relations, was a strain upon Elsie's nerves, and she was keyed up to a pitch of unusual sensitiveness when the inevitable crisis came.

33

Mrs. Woolley, in a new blue dress that looked too tight under the arms, had taken the children to a party.

The maid Florrie was out for the afternoon. Elsie, restless and on edge, terribly wanted an excuse to go down to the surgery. At last she found one, and after listening at the door to make certain that no belated patient was with the doctor, she knocked.

"Come in!"

He was sitting at the writing-table, rapidly turning over the leaves of a big book.

"Elsie!"

"Oh, if you please, Doctor," she minced, "they've all gone out, and Mrs. Woolley left a message to say if you could go and fetch her and the children from 85, Lower Park Avenue, about seven o'clock-"

"Stow it, Elsie! D'you mean to say you and I are the only people left in the place? Where's that damned slut in the kitchen, eh?"

"It's Florrie's afternoon out, Doctor, but——"

"Florrie be damned! Look here, Elsie, this sort of thing can't go on."

She backed until she stood against the wall, feeling the warm blood surge into her face and looking at him through half-closed eyelids.

"What sort of thing?"

"You know very well what I mean. Look at me. D'you think I'm a man?"

He thrust out his chest and doubled up his arms, standing with his legs wide apart. In spite of his grossness and unwholesome fat, Elsie thrilled to the suggestion of his masculine strength.

"Yes," she murmured.

"Well, I tell you no man's going to stand what you're making me stand. Elsie, you little devil! Don't you know you're driving me mad? God, if I could tell you the sort of dreams I get at night, now!"

"About me?" she asked curiously.

"Shut up!" His voice was savage, and she suddenly saw sweat glistening on his upper lip and round his nose.

Elsie decided to begin to cry. "It frightens me when you shout at me like that. Perhaps I'd better go," she said sobbingly.

"No, no, no! I say, what a brute I am! Come here and be comforted, little girl."

He sat down heavily in the revolving chair before the writing-table and held out his hand.

Elsie advanced slowly, without looking at him, until she came within reach of his arm. Then he caught hold of her and drew her on to his knee, gripping her tightly until her weight sank against his shoulder.

34

"Let me kiss all the tears away. What a hound I am to make you cry! Was'ums very mis'mis?"

He petted and soothed her, kissing the back of her neck and her dust-coloured curls, murmuring absurd, infantile phrases.

Presently he whispered: "D'you love me?"

Elsie laughed and would not answer, and he struggled with her playfully, pulling her about, and grasping at her with his big hands.

After the horse-play, she put both arms round his neck and lay still.

"I want to know something," said Doctor Woolley slowly.

"What's that?"

"Don't you know more than a good little girl ought to know?"

"What about?"

"About—life. About being kissed, for instance. I'm not the first, my girl, not by a long, long way. You're the sort that begins early, I know."

"You've a nerve!" Elsie ejaculated, not knowing what to say.

"Well, it's true what I'm saying, isn't it? I mean, you've let fellows kiss you?"

"Just boys, perhaps."

"Hasn't anyone taught you anything besides kissing, eh?"

"Of course not! What do you take me for, I'd like to know? Mother brought up me and my sister like ladies, let me tell you. Besides, I don't know what you're driving at, I'm sure."

"Yes, you do."

"No, I don't."

"Then I'll show you."

"No!" screamed Elsie in a sudden, only half-assumed, panic.

She sprang up, but he pulled her back again.

"You silly little fool! You don't suppose I'd really say or do anything to frighten you, do you? Why, you're much too precious."

He kissed her again and again.

"Tell me one thing, though. You did know what I meant, didn't you?"

"I suppose so."

"Of course you did! A girl like you couldn't help knowing. My God, I wish I'd known you ten years ago. I wasn't married then."

"You oughtn't to talk like that."

"Why not? It's true. Amy's as cold as ice—not a real woman at all. And she's as jealous as the devil. I've always wondered why she let anyone like you come into the house at all. It's a miracle she hasn't spotted us yet."

"It'd be all up with me being here if she did," said Elsie shrewdly.

35

"If you go, I swear I'll go with you," said Doctor Woolley, but he said it without conviction, and Elsie knew it. "Can't do without you, little one, at any price, now. But you've got to be even sweeter than you've been to me yet."

Elsie shivered a little, excited and disturbed, and in part genuinely shocked.

"When will you, Elsie?"

His breath on her neck was hot and hurried.

She jumped off his knee. "Oh, look, it's getting on for half-past six! You'll have to be off."

"Come back! You haven't told me what I want to know yet." He grabbed at her dress.

"Listen!" cried Elsie.

In the second during which he turned, arrested, she slipped out of the room.

Her heart was beating very fast, and her face burning.

She half expected him to follow her, but he did not do so; and she was partly relieved and partly disappointed.

She saw him again at supper, which the Woolleys always called dinner, and the consciousness between them caused a singular constraint to pervade the atmosphere. Mrs. Woolley, for the first time, seemed to be aware of it, and every now and then turned sharp, bulging brown eyes from her husband to Elsie, compressing her thin lips until they formed a mere hard line in her red face.

When the meal was finished, she told Elsie to go upstairs and fetch one of her evening dresses. "I want to see if I can't smarten it up a bit," she explained. "I'm in rags, not fit to be seen."

"I'll stand you a new frock, Amy," said the doctor suddenly. "How much d'you want, eh?"

"Oh! Why, whatever's up, Herbert? I'm sure it's ages since I've had a thing, and I'd be only too delighted——"

She broke off.

"Run up, Elsie, will you? The primrose dress, with the black lace, in the left-hand corner of my wardrobe...."

Elsie went, envious of the new dress, and at the same time thinking mockingly of Mrs. Woolley's mottled skin and the lines that ran from her heavy nostrils to her sagging chin. Dresses and jewellery ought to be for girls who were young and pretty, not married women, plain and stout, like Mrs. Woolley. When Elsie came down again the doctor had gone, and Mrs. Woolley was in high good humour.

"I'll get some tulle to-morrow, Elsie, and we can freshen it up round the neck and sleeves. You'd better rip off all this old stuff. And look here—you're handy with your fingers—you can take the

36

lace off and put it on that old navy blouse of mine, that's got no collar. You know the one I mean ... you can drape it a bit...."

Elsie assented rather sulkily.

"Doctor Woolley's so generous," said Mrs. Woolley complacently. "He's for ever giving me things, me and the children. If you knew more of the world, Elsie, you'd realise how lucky a woman is when she gets a hubby like mine who's never so much as looked at another woman since he married. Some men aren't like that, I can tell you. The tales I could let out, if I cared to, that I've heard from some! But if Doctor Woolley's manner sometimes puts ideas into people's heads, why, they've only themselves to blame is what I always say. He wouldn't give a thought to anyone but me, not really."

She looked full at Elsie as she spoke, and Elsie stared back at her.

The girl was puzzled and angry, not feeling certain that she knew whether Mrs. Woolley really believed her own words, or was using them to convey an oblique warning.

"If she really imagines that, she must be a fool," thought Elsie contemptuously, only to veer round uneasily a moment later to the conviction that Mrs. Woolley had been talking at her.

It was the latter unpleasant belief that prevailed, without possibility of mistake, in the course of the next few days. Whenever the doctor was in the house, Mrs. Woolley made a point of remaining at his side, and during the hours when he was in the surgery she kept Elsie employed with the children, every now and then coming to look in on her with excuses that were always transparently flimsy.

The tension in the atmosphere pervaded the whole house.

At last one afternoon, when Gladys and Sonnie were at school, and Mrs. Woolley in the drawing-room with an unexpected caller, Elsie and the doctor met upon the stairs.

She knew that she was looking her worst, strained and overwrought, and with the odd Japanese aspect of her eyes and cheek-bones intensified. Even her hair felt limp and unresilient.

She looked at the doctor rather piteously, envisaging to herself her own unprepossessing appearance, and wishing that she had at least powdered her face recently.

"Where's Amy?"

"In the drawing-room, with a lady visitor."

"Thank God! I've been hag-ridden for the last week. What the devil's up, Elsie?"

"I don't know," she murmured. "At least, I know Mrs. Woolley's been horrid to me lately, that's all."

37

"She has, has she?" he muttered furiously. "Here—come in here."

He drew her into the shelter of the nearest doorway.

"Elsie, I'm mad about you. This sort of thing can't go on—it's simply hell."

"Oh, hush, someone'll hear...."

"I don't care who hears!" But he lowered his voice. "I haven't had a kiss from you for days—quick!"

Their lips met.

"You dear little girl! Is she being a beast to you?"

Elsie, in his embrace, started violently. "Someone coming upstairs!" she hissed.

He stood motionless to listen, waited a second too long, and then sharply shut the door.

"Florrie!" Elsie whispered in a frightened voice. "Did she see us?"

"No, no—not a chance. Or, if she did, she only saw me. She won't think anything of that."

"She's gone upstairs—I must go."

"No, don't. I tell you it's all right. Hang it, Elsie, when am I going to get a word with you again?"

"Oh, I don't know. I think I shall go home again." She was half crying.

"Elsie, d'you know Amy's going out to-morrow night? She's going to see her friend, that Williams woman, who's ill."

"What, the one that was at mother's place?"

"Yes—yes—but they're in their own house now. It'll take her all the evening to get there and back, pretty nearly."

"She won't go."

"Yes, she will. I shall tell her I'm going off to a case at Roehampton or somewhere, and that I shan't be back till late."

"Oh, don't. It simply isn't safe."

"It's quite safe, you little fool. You and me have got to come to an understanding, I can't stand this life another minute. Look here, we'll go out somewhere together."

"No, no! That'd be much worse. Sonnie always wakes up, and he'll scream himself into a fit if I'm not there, and then Florrie would know——"

"I forgot the kids. Elsie—Gladys sleeps in your room doesn't she?"

"Yes," said Elsie, suddenly flushing scarlet.

He laughed abruptly, scanning her face with hungry eyes. "I'll have a fire in the surgery. We'll go down there. Florrie knows better than to put her foot inside it," said Doctor Woolley significantly.

V

It was two days later.

Florrie and Mrs. Woolley were talking in the kitchen. Elsie hung about in the diminutive passage, trying desperately to hear what they were saying. An awful intuition gripped her that they were talking of her.

Florrie's voice was indistinct, almost inaudible, but snatched phrases rose occasionally from the angry monotone that was Mrs. Woolley's.

"... My innocent children ... turn my back ... the gutter ... don't you talk to me ... the gutter ... out of the gutter...."

Elsie tried wildly to persuade herself that Mrs. Woolley was abusing Florrie. Sometimes she lost her temper with her servants, and shouted at them.

On the evening that Mrs. Woolley had gone to see her friend Mrs. Williams, who was reported very ill, Elsie, in her best frock, had boldly gone into the surgery, where a fire blazed, and there was a sofa newly piled with cushions. On the table had been placed a bottle and glasses and a dish of biscuits. Doctor Woolley had locked the door behind her, in spite of Elsie's half-meant protests, but at first he had been entirely jovial, using catch-phrases that had made her laugh, and drinking heartily.

She herself had begun to feel rather affronted and puzzled at his aloofness, before it suddenly came to an end.

The remembrance of her own surrender rather bewildered Elsie. She had never consciously made up her mind to it, but the doctor's urgency, her own physical susceptibility, and an underlying, violent curiosity had proved far too strong for her feeble defences, based on timidity and on the recollection of certain unexplained, and less-than-half-understood, arbitrary axioms laid down during her childhood by her mother.

She supposed that that one half-hour in the surgery had made "a bad girl" of her, but the aspect of the case that really preoccupied her was her terror that Mrs. Woolley should have found it out.

She felt sick with fright as the kitchen door opened, and, turning round, pretended to be looking for something in the housemaid's closet under the stairs.

She heard Mrs. Woolley brush past her and go into the drawing-room, slamming the door violently behind her.

Elsie, her knees shaking, went upstairs to fetch Gladys and Sonnie and take them to their kindergarten.

39

She dawdled on the way back, being unwilling to go into the house again, and alternately hoping and dreading that the doctor would be at home for the midday meal.

At one o'clock, however, Mrs. Woolley and Elsie sat down without him.

Mrs. Woolley did not speak to Elsie. She kept on looking at her, and then looking away again. Her hard face was inscrutable, but Elsie noticed that her hands, manipulating her knife and fork, shook slightly. The doctor came in before the meal was over, jaunty and talkative.

"Hallo! Is this Wednesday, or Piccadilly, or what? Which I mean to say is, has the cold meat stage been passed and the rice pudding come on, or contrarywise?"

Elsie burst into nervous laughter, the strident sound of which caused the doctor to glance at her sharply, and Mrs. Woolley said:

"Nonsense, Herbert! The way you talk, sometimes! The girl has got your meat and vegetables keeping hot in the oven, and I'm sure you haven't seen rice pudding at the table for a fortnight. There's a nice piece of cheese on the side, too."

The doctor ate in silence, voraciously, as he always did, and his wife presently said in a thin, vicious voice:

"Of course, you've nothing to say to your wife, Herbert. It's easy enough to talk and be amusing with strangers, isn't it?—but I suppose it isn't worth while in your own home."

"What's up, Amy?" he growled. He did not look at Elsie, who found herself fixing apprehensive eyes on him, although she knew it was a betrayal.

"Why should anything be up, as you call it? But as it isn't very amusing for me to sit here all day while you eat, and as I happen to be rather busy, strange though it may seem, I think I'll ask you to excuse me."

She turned her head towards Elsie, but spoke without looking at her. "I'll thank you to come and find that paper pattern for Gladys's smock. The child isn't fit to be seen."

Mrs. Woolley pushed Elsie out of the room in front of her, making it obvious that she meant her to have no opportunity of exchanging a look with the doctor.

Throughout the afternoon she never let the girl out of her sight until Elsie had actually left the house to go and fetch the two children from school.

It was abundantly evident that a crisis impended. The atmospheric tension affected everyone in the house, and Elsie, her nerves on edge, became frantic.

She said, immediately after supper, that she was tired, and

should go to bed, and Mrs. Woolley laughed, shortly and sarcastically.

Elsie went up to her room and cried hysterically on her bed until Gladys woke and began to whine enquiries.

It seemed impossible, to Elsie's inexperience, that the horrors of that day should repeat themselves, but the next one was Sunday, and brought its own miseries.

The doctor, who did not go to church as a rule, announced his intention of accompanying his family, and they set out, a constrained procession: Gladys, in tight black boots and with fair hair crimped round her shoulders, holding her father's hand, Mrs. Woolley, walking just a little faster than was comfortable for Sonnie's short legs, clutching the boy's hand, and Elsie slouching a pace or two behind, cold and wretched.

At the bottom of the Crescent they met an elderly couple who often came to see them, and whom Elsie knew well by name as Mr. and Mrs. Loman.

The encounter broke up the procession, and caused a readjustment of places. Mrs. Woolley was at once claimed by the sallow, spectacled Mrs. Loman, and the children, with shrill acclamations, ran to her husband, Sonnie's godfather and the purveyor of many small treats and presents.

The doctor, after a loud and boisterous greeting, boldly joined Elsie, and both of them dropped behind the others.

"Oh, I've wanted so to speak to you!" gasped Elsie.

"Shut up—don't make a fuss now, there's a good girl. Keep a cheery face on you, for God's sake, or we shall give the show away worse than we've done already."

Mrs. Woolley turned round. "Herbert, Mrs. Loman is just saying that she hasn't set eyes on you for ages. Come and give an account of yourself."

She spoke in a thin, artificial voice, but her eyes blazed a command at him.

The doctor stared back at her, insolent security in his manner. "Thankee, Amy, but I wouldn't interrupt a ladies' confab. for the world. Go on about your sky-blue-purple Sunday-go-to-meeting costumes, and I'll keep Elsie company."

Mrs. Loman laughed and the doctor grinned back at her.

White patches had appeared on the mottled surface of Mrs. Woolley's face, but she made no rejoinder.

Doctor Woolley turned to Elsie again, the merriment dropping from his manner. "That'll shut her up for a bit," he said between his teeth. "Has she been giving you gyp, Elsie?"

"Oh, it's been awful. I'm certain she's found out."

41

"How?"

"That Florrie, I suppose."

"Damn Florrie and her mischief-making! Well, kiddie, the fat's in the fire. I'm afraid there's only one thing for it."

"What?"

"Why—why, my dear child, don't you see for yourself—you'll have to clear out of here. No use waiting for Amy to make a bloody row, now is there? If you simply say you're going home again, she won't have a leg to stand on. And if it wasn't for—for the kids, I'd go with you."

"You wouldn't," said Elsie bitterly. "I may be a bit green, but I'm not green enough to swallow that."

"Don't talk like that," said Doctor Woolley. He slipped his hand under her arm, and at the contact, jaded and miserable as she was, her pulses leapt. His fingers squeezed her arm.

"We've had some happy times together, little girl, eh?" he murmured in a sentimental voice. "And don't you see that when you're on your own again we can meet ever so much more freely. I want—you know what I want, don't you, Elsie?"

She did not respond. "What I want, is to know what'll happen to me if I go back to mother and say I've left Mrs. Woolley. You don't suppose she, and my sister and my aunts, aren't going to ask what's happened, do you?"

"Well, you can tell them something," said the doctor impatiently. "A clever girl like you, Elsie, surely you can think of something. Besides, everybody knows that a pretty girl doesn't always hit it off with a woman older than herself. There's nothing wonderful in that. Damnation, they're stopping!"

"Here we are," said Elsie.

He withdrew his arm hastily from hers after a final pressure.

Mrs. Woolley and her friend were already standing at the church steps, and both of them fixed their eyes on Elsie and the doctor as they came up. Elsie saw Mrs. Woolley touch the other woman's elbow, and guessed at, rather than heard, the words coming from between her teeth:

"Look at that, now—look at that."

On Mrs. Loman's face was an expression of mingled eagerness, curiosity, and disgust. It was evident that Mrs. Woolley had spoken freely of her wrongs.

Elsie spent her time in church in wondering whether it would yet be possible to blunt Mrs. Woolley's suspicions, or whether she dared face her mother with a made-up story to account for her return.

She was still young enough to have a furtive dread that her

42

mother must be omniscient in her regard, and she was afraid that Mrs. Palmer would somehow guess at her lapse and tax her with it.

Elsie had very often lied to her mother before, but not with any conspicuous success, and she felt just now strangely shaken and unnerved, physically and morally.

When they came out of church, the Lomans hospitably pressed their friends to return with them, share the hot Sunday dinner, and spend the afternoon. The children were specifically included, but Mrs. Loman glanced in Elsie's direction, and then looked back at Mrs. Woolley, raising her eyebrows.

"You'd better go and see your mother this afternoon," said Mrs. Woolley coldly. "Go home first and tell Florrie we shall be out, and she can lock up the house and go out for a bit herself. Tell her she must be back by five."

"All right," said Elsie lifelessly.

She turned on her heel, when a sudden shout stopped her.

"Post those letters of mine, will you?" said Doctor Woolley very loudly. "You'll find them in"—he came nearer to her—"wait in till I come," he muttered almost inaudibly, and rejoined his wife before Elsie had taken in the meaning of his words. It came to her afterwards, and the renewed sense of intrigue very slightly relieved the dull misery pervading her.

At No. 8, Mortimer Crescent, the hot joint was taken out of the oven and left to grow cold, but Florrie had made a Yorkshire pudding, and she and Elsie ate it for their dinner, and added pickles and bread and cheese and cake to the meal. Very soon afterwards, Florrie announced that she was going off at once.

"So am I," said Elsie. "I told her I'd lock up the house. Mind you're in by five."

"That's as it may be," haughtily said Florrie, with a venomous glance. Elsie felt far too tired to quarrel with the maid, as she had often done before, and when Florrie was actually gone she went upstairs and lay down on her bed. It was nearly three o'clock before a cautious sound from below betrayed the return of the doctor.

Elsie rose and automatically glanced at herself in the looking-glass. One side of her face was flushed, her eyes looked small and swollen-lidded, and her hair was disordered. She dabbed powder on her face and pulled her wave of hair further down over her forehead before going downstairs.

The doctor was hanging up his hat on the crowded hooks that lined one side of the wall in the tiny entrance lobby.

"Coast clear?"

Elsie nodded.

"Sure?"

43

"Absolutely." She held out the key of the house door. "I've locked up at the back."

"Then I'll lock up at the front," said Doctor Woolley, and did so.

"My God, we're in a bloody mess," he began, turning round and facing Elsie.

Desperate, she ran forward and threw herself into his arms, instinctively seeking the only reassurance she knew, that of physical contact.

The doctor suddenly buried his face in her hair, then forced her face upwards and kissed her passionately.

They clung to one another.

At last he released his clasp, only keeping one arm round her waist.

"Where can we go? We'll have to settle something, and Lord knows when I shall get another chance of speaking to you, with that hell-cat on the warpath. I've had the deuce and all of a time getting here now, and we must both clear out of the place before she and the kids get back. Put on your hat and coat, old girl, and come along."

"Where to?"

"Where I take you," said the doctor brusquely.

When she came down again, he hurried her out of the house, locking the door again behind them, and putting the key under the scraper, where it was always looked for on Sunday.

"Taxi!"

The doctor hailed a passing taxi and made Elsie get into it.

He gave the address of a hotel in a street of which she had never heard.

"Where are we going to?"

"Somewhere where I can talk to you."

He passed his arm round her again, and she made no pretence of resistance, but lay against him, letting him play with her hand and occasionally bend his head down to kiss her lips.

Elsie had slept very little for the past three nights; she had shed tears, and she had been subject to a continual nervous strain. By the time that the taxi stopped she was almost dozing, and it was in a half-dazed state that she followed Dr. Woolley into the dingy hall of a high building and, after a very short parley with a stout man in evening dress, to an upstairs sitting-room.

She asked nothing better than to sink on to the narrow couch in a corner of the room and let herself be petted and caressed, but after a time her wearied senses awoke, and told her that the man beside her was becoming restive and excited.

"Look here, Elsie," he said finally, "you're a beguiling little

44

witch, you are—but we've got to come down to hard facts. I'm going to order you a pick-me-up, and have one myself, and then we can talk about what's to be done next. I've got to be home again, worse luck, by seven o'clock. I'm supposed to have had an urgent call to Amy's friend, Mrs. Williams. She's ill enough, poor soul, in all conscience, and I'll have to go there before I go home. Now then, what'll you have?"

"Tea," said Elsie.

He laughed. "Women are all alike! You can have your tea—poisonous stuff, tincture of tannin—and I'll order what I think's good for you to go with it. Wait here till I come back."

He went out, and Elsie, already revived and stimulated, flew to the spotted and discoloured looking-glass, and took out her pocket-comb to rearrange her curls.

She actually enjoyed the hot, strong tea when it came, and her spirits suddenly rose to a boisterous pitch.

They both laughed loudly at the faces that Elsie made over the bottle that the doctor had obtained, and from which he repeatedly helped himself and her, and although they kept on telling one another that they must talk seriously, their hilarity kept on increasing. At last he began to make violent love to her, and Elsie responded coquettishly, luring him on by glance and gesture, while her tongue uttered glib and meaningless protests. Very soon, her flimsy defences gave way altogether, and she had ceded to him everything that he asked.

Then the inevitable reaction overtook her, and she cried, and called herself a wicked girl, and finally sank limply into a corner of the taxi that Dr. Woolley had summoned to the door of the hotel.

He got in beside her. "Buck up, little girl!" he cried urgently. "You'll be at No. 8 in no time, and we don't want Amy asking awkward questions. Look here, I'll put you down at the corner of the Crescent, and you can walk to the house. The air'll do you good, and besides, we can't be seen together. I'm off to that wretched Williams woman, and I'm not going to be in till late."

Elsie continued to sob.

"Come, come, come—pull yourself to pieces," Doctor Woolley tried to make her laugh. "We've not settled anything, but we've had our time together. Ah, a little love is a great thing in a world like this one, Elsie. Thank you for being so sweet to me, little girl."

He kissed her hastily, with a perfunctoriness of which she was aware.

When the taxi stopped in the main thoroughfare, a little way before the turning into Mortimer Crescent, he almost shoved her on to the pavement.

"Don't forget—you've been out ever since dinner-time, and you imagine me to have been in the buzzim of my family enjoying back chat with the old Lomans. Don't say anything about that, though, unless you're asked. Tell the man to drive like blazes now, will you?"

Elsie mechanically obeyed.

Then she dragged herself to No. 8. Her ring was answered by Florrie.

The little servant girl was grinning maliciously. "She's in the d—'s own temper and all, and you're going to catch it hot and strong for leaving her to put the children to bed."

"Mind your own business, Florrie," said Elsie, pushing past her.

She affected not to hear the single word that the servant flung at her back, but it made her wince.

In the bedroom she found Gladys already in bed, wide awake.

"Mother put us to bed. She was awfully cross, and she slapped Sonnie twice and me once."

"What for?"

"Oh, because I whined, she said. And she slapped Sonnie when he told her about Dadda being so funny with you. You didn't know we saw one day," giggled Gladys.

"Saw what?"

"One day when Dadda kissed you and Sonnie and I saw, over the banisters, and we laughed, but you didn't hear us."

"You little viper!" muttered Elsie between her teeth. "I'd like to kill you, I would."

Gladys alternately giggled and whined, and Elsie was quite unable to distinguish whether the child was really malicious or simply amused by something to which she attached no meaning.

"Anyway, if she's told her mother, it's all up," thought Elsie.

She saw that there was nothing for it but to leave Mortimer Crescent, and spent a miserable night wondering what to say to her mother and sister.

At midnight she heard the sound of the doctor's key in the front door and his heavy foot on the stairs. He paused outside her door for some seconds, then she heard him go into his wife's room.

Elsie tossed about in her narrow bed. Her present dilemma frightened her, and she had a vague, irrational idea that some awful and horrible penalty always descended sooner or later upon girls who had done as she had done. These fears, and her lack of any vivid imagination, had dulled her emotional susceptibilities, and she scarcely felt regret at the thought of no longer seeing the doctor. He now stood to her for the symbol of an assuaged desire, the fulfilment of which had brought about her present miseries. Nevertheless, at the back of her consciousness was latent the conviction that never again would she be satisfied with the clumsy demonstrations and meaningless contacts of her intercourse with the boys and youths whom she had known at home.

It seemed to her next morning that she was wholly ugly. Her complexion looked sodden and her eyes were nearly invisible. Her mouth, in some odd way, seemed to have swollen. No one could have called her pretty, and to anyone who had seen her in good looks she would have been almost unrecognisable. Mrs. Woolley, coming downstairs at ten o'clock, eyed her with a malignant satisfaction.

"Perhaps," she said, "you won't be altogether surprised to hear that I'm going to make some changes. You'd better pack your box, and go home to your mother, I think."

"I was going to tell you that I couldn't stay on here any longer," said Elsie swiftly. "The ways of the house aren't what I've been used to, Mrs. Woolley."

In a flash, Mrs. Woolley had turned nasty, and Elsie had seen her own unwisdom.

"Oh, aren't they indeed? Perhaps you'd be so kind as to tell me what you are used to—or shall I tell you?"

Then she suddenly raised her voice almost to a scream and poured out a torrent of abuse and invective, and the two children crept in from the hall and began to cry, and to make faces at Elsie, and demonstrations of hitting her with their little hands, and the servant Florrie held the door half open, so that she might see and hear it all.

Elsie screamed back again at Mrs. Woolley, but she had neither the fluency nor the determination of the older woman, and she was unable to prevent herself from bursting into tears and sobs.

Finally Mrs. Woolley drove her out of the room, standing at the foot of the stairs while Elsie ran up to pull on her best hat and coat, and forbidding the children to follow her.

"Don't go near her, my pets—she's a wicked girl, that's what she is—not fit to be in the same house as innocent little children. Now then, out you go, miss, before I send for the police."

"I'll go," said Elsie, shaking from head to foot, "and I'll never set foot in your filthy house again. And I'll send for my trunk and for every penny you owe me, and I'll have the law on you for insinuations on my character."

Then she dashed out of the house and into the street.

Elsie's return home caused far less sensation than she had feared. Mrs. Palmer, indeed, was very angry, but principally at Elsie's folly in having come away without her trunk or the money due to her.

When a week had elapsed, and nothing had come from Mortimer Crescent, Mrs. Palmer declared her intention of going to a solicitor.

"However you could be such a fool, young Elsie—and I don't half understand what happened, even now. What was the row about?"

Elsie had decided upon a half-truth. "Oh, she was a jealous old fool, and couldn't bear her hubby to look the same side of the room as anyone else. That's all it was, really. She spoke to me very rudely, I consider—in fact she was decidedly insulting—so I simply up and said: 'Mrs. Woolley,' I said, 'that's not the way I'm accustomed to be spoken to,' I said, 'and what's more I won't stand it.' Quite quietly, I said it, looking her very straight in the face. 'I won't stand it,' I said, quite quietly. That did for her. She didn't know how to take it at all. But, of course, I wasn't going to stay in the house a moment after that, and I simply walked straight upstairs and put on my things and left her there. She knows what I think of her, though."

"Yes, and she knows what she thinks of you," remarked Mrs. Palmer shrewdly, "and it probably isn't so far out, either. She may be jealous as you say—those fleshy women often are, when their figures come to be a perpetual worry, so to speak—but there's no smoke without a fire, and I know you, Elsie Palmer. I suppose this doctor fellow was for ever giving you sweets and wanting to take you out at nights, and sit next you in the 'bus coming home, with his wife on the other side of him as like as not. You were a young fool, let me tell you, to lose a good place like that for a man who can't be any use to you. What you want to look out for is a husband. I shan't have a minute's peace about you till you're married."

"Why?" asked Elsie, rather gratified, and very curious.

"Never you mind why. Because Mother says so, and that's enough. Now you can get on your hat and come with me to Mr. Williams' office and see what he can do to get this trunk of yours away from that woman. She's no lady, as I saw plainly the very first time I ever laid eyes on her."

On the way to the City, Mrs. Palmer questioned Elsie rather half-heartedly. "You've not been a bad girl in any way while you've been away from Mother, have you?"

"No, of course not. I don't know what you mean," Elsie declared, sick with sudden fright.

"I should hope you didn't. Because mind, Elsie, any gurl of mine who disgraced herself wouldn't get any help from me. And though I don't object to a bit of fun while a gurl's young, skylarking may lead to other things. I hope there's no need for me to speak any plainer. I've brought you gurls up innocent, and I intend you shall remain so. Not that Geraldine's ever given me a moment's worry."

"Oh, Geraldine!" Elsie was profoundly relieved at seeing an opportunity for changing the subject indirectly. "She's a sheep."

"You've no call to speak like that of your elder sister, miss. I wish you were half as steady as she is. She's the one to help her widowed mother, for all she has such poor health."

"What do you suppose is the matter with her, Mother?"

"Bile," said Mrs. Palmer laconically. "Your father was the same, but it doesn't matter so much in a man."

"Why ever not?"

"It doesn't interfere with his prospects. Now I often think Geraldine won't ever get a husband, simply because of the bad colour she sometimes goes, and the way her breath smells. She can't help it, poor gurl."

Elsie felt contemptuous, rather than compassionate. When they came to the office, a very young clerk, who stared hard at Elsie, explained that Mr. Williams was away. He had suffered a family bereavement.

"His wife?" gasped Mrs. Palmer, greatly excited.

"I am sorry to say that Mrs. Williams died yesterday morning. Mr. Williams was not at the office, and a telephone message came through later to the head clerk, giving the melancholy intelligence. I believe Mrs. Williams had been ill for some time."

"Why, goodness me, we knew her ever so well, my daughter and I! They stayed with us in the autumn.... Elsie, fancy poor Mrs. Williams dying!"

"Fancy!"

"Would you care to see the head clerk, Mr. Cleaver, madam?" said the youth politely, still gazing at Elsie.

"Yes, yes, I think I'd better. He may be able to tell us something more, Elsie," cried Mrs. Palmer gloatingly.

But when the clerk had gone away to see whether Mr. Cleaver was disengaged, Mrs. Palmer remarked to her daughter:

"Not that he'll be able to say much, naturally not. It's an awkward subject to enter on at all with a gentleman, poor Mrs. Williams being in the condition she was."

"I heard Doctor Woolley say she was very ill."

49

"It's a funny thing, Elsie, but many a time I've felt a presentiment like. I've looked at Mrs. Williams, and seen death in her face. And that Nellie Simmons, she told me she'd had a most peculiar dream about Mrs. Williams one night. Saw her lying all over blood, she said, and it quite scared her. I knew then what it meant, though I told Nellie not to be a silly gurl. But dreams can't lie, as they say, not if they're a certain sort."

Elsie shuddered, as a thrill of superstitious terror went through her. Dreams played a large part in her life, and Mrs. Palmer had always shown her children that she "believed in dreams," especially in those of a macabre nature.

The young clerk came back, and took them into a small room where a bald-headed, pale-faced man sat at a writing-table. Mrs. Palmer's delicacy ran no risk of affront from him, for he was monosyllabic on the subject of Mrs. Williams' death, and only said that Mr. Williams would not be back until the following week.

Mrs. Palmer, looking disappointed, launched into a voluble story of Elsie's trunk and its non-return.

Mr. Cleaver said that the firm would write a letter to Mrs. Woolley that evening. He seemed disinclined to enlarge on that, or any other subject.

"It's been a great worry, as you can imagine," Mrs. Palmer said, reluctant to terminate an interview which was anyhow to cost her money. "However the girl could have been so silly, I don't know. But we mustn't look for old heads on young shoulders, I suppose."

"I suppose not."

For the first time, Mr. Cleaver glanced at Elsie as though he really saw her. "Your young lady will be looking for another post, no doubt?"

"By-and-by," said Mrs. Palmer with a sudden languor. "I'm afraid if I had my way, Mr. Cleaver, I'd keep both my girlies at home with their mother. And this one's my baby, too. I really only let her go to that Mrs. Woolley to oblige poor Mrs. Williams, who was a dear friend of mine. My daughter has been trained for the shorthand-typing, really, haven't you, Elsie?"

"M."

"I see. Well, Mrs. Palmer, the letter shall go off to-night, and I am very much mistaken if the lady does not——"

"Don't call her a lady, Mr. Cleaver. She's no——"

Mrs. Palmer had said all this before, and Mr. Cleaver held open the door for her, and compelled her to pass through it before she had time to say it all over again.

Elsie and Mrs. Palmer were in the omnibus that was to take

50

them back to their own suburb very much earlier than they had expected to be.

"I'll tell you what, we'll stop at the corner shop and have a wreath sent in time for the funeral. I've got some money on me," said Mrs. Palmer.

They chose a wreath and were given a black-edged card upon which Mrs. Palmer inscribed the address of Mr. Williams and: "With true sympathy and every kind thought from Mrs. Gerald Palmer, Miss Palmer and Miss Elsie Palmer."

"I'd meant to say a few very sharp words to them about introducing that Mrs. Woolley to me, and persuading me to let you go to her, but of course, it'll have to be let drop now. I daresay poor Mrs. Williams was taken in by the woman herself."

For two or three days Elsie lounged about at home, obliged by her mother to help in the house, but spending as much time as she could with Irene Tidmarsh, whose old father was still living, although suffering from incurable disease. Sometimes when Elsie and Irene were gossiping in the dining-room, they would hear the old man roaring with pain overhead, and then Irene would run up to him, administer a drug, and come down again looking rather white. A desiccated spinster aunt made occasional appearances, and took Irene's place whilst Irene went to the cinema with Elsie. But Irene never mentioned Arthur Osborne, and Elsie saw neither him nor his brother.

She told herself that she did not care, and that she was sick of men and their beastly ways.

She one evening repeated this sentiment to Geraldine, whom she suspected of disbelieving her version of the quarrel with Mrs. Woolley.

"So you say. I s'pose that's because there isn't anyone after you. If that Begg boy turned up again, or Johnnie Osborne or any of them, you'd sing quite a different song."

"You're jealous," said Elsie candidly.

Her sister laughed shrilly. "That's a good one, young Elsie. Me jealous of a kid like you! I should like to know what for? Why, you're not even pretty."

The taunt enraged Elsie, because she knew that it was true, and that she was not really pretty. What she did not yet realise was that she would always be able to make men think her so.

"Your trunk's come, Elsie," Mrs. Palmer screamed at the door. "Carter Paterson brought it, carriage to pay, of course. You'd better that there was a letter lying just under the newspaper spread over see there's nothing missing out of it."

51

Elsie made a perfunctory examination, noticing nothing but her untidily packed belongings.

"It's all right."

Mrs. Palmer had gone back into the kitchen again, and Elsie, who did not care what Geraldine thought of her, pulled out the note and read it. It was from Doctor Woolley, as she had expected.

"My Own Dear Little Girlie,

"What a rotten world it is, kiddie, and what a shame you being turned away like that. Believe me, dear little girlie, if I had been at home it would never have happened. Now, Elsie, you and I have had a very nice friendship, and I know you will understand what I mean if I say that it must come to an end for the present. Burn this letter, dear, won't you, and don't answer it on any account. The letters that come for me to this house are not safe from interference, so you see what trouble it might make. With all best wishes for your future, and thanking you for your sweet friendship, which I shall never forget,

"Yours,

"H."

"The cad!" said Elsie disgustedly.

She had not really expected Doctor Woolley to write to her at all, although there had been in her mind a vague anticipation of seeing him again very soon. But the letter, with its perfunctory endearments and cautionary injunctions, suddenly made it clear to her that the whole episode of their relationship was at an end.

"The swine," said Elsie, although without violent emotion of any kind.

She felt that life, for the moment, was meaningless, but rather from the familiar and sordid surroundings of her home, and from her own listlessness and fatigue, than from the defection of Doctor Woolley.

It failed to excite her when a letter arrived for Mrs. Palmer, from the office of Mr. Williams and written by himself, saying how much he regretted that Mrs. Woolley, the merest acquaintance of his dear late wife, should have failed to make Miss Elsie happy in her house. If Miss Elsie desired to find an appointment in the clerical line, as he understood, then Mr. Williams would be most happy to make a suggestion. Could Mrs. Palmer, with Miss Elsie, make it convenient to call at the office any afternoon that week?

52

"He may want to take you into his own office, Elsie, as like as not. He'd feel he ought to do something, I expect, considering they sent you to those people, those Woolleys, as they call themselves, in the first place."

"I'm not sure I want to go into an office, Mother."

"Now look here, Elsie, let me and you understand one another," said Mrs. Palmer with great determination. "I've had enough of your wants and don't wants, my lady. One word more, and you'll get a smack-bottom just exactly as you got when you were in pinafores, and don't you forget it. If you think you're going to live at home, no more use in the house than a sick headache, and wasting your time running round with God-knows-who, then I can tell you you've never made a bigger mistake in your life. Off you pop this directly minute, and get on your hat, and come with me to Mr. Williams. If he's heard of a job for you, we'll get it settled at once."

"I suppose," said Geraldine bitterly, "I'll have to see to the teas and everything else, while you're out. It seems to me it's always Elsie that's being thought about, and sent here, and taken there, and the rest of it."

"More shame for her," said Mrs. Palmer sombrely. "I declare to goodness I don't know how I'm to face your aunties next time they come here, unless there's something been settled about Elsie. I'm sick and tired of being told I spoil that girl."

"Whatever job she gets, she'll be home in a month," said Geraldine.

"She'll get something she won't relish from me if she is," Mrs. Palmer retorted. She pinned on her hat and pulled a pair of shiny black kid gloves out of a drawer in the kitchen dresser.

Elsie, rather sulky and unwilling, was obliged to follow her mother once more to the dingy office, but it cheered her to see the pleased, furtive smile on the face of the young clerk who had admitted them before. It was very evident that he had not forgotten her. Elsie thought more about him than about the desiccated, wooden-faced little solicitor, with the crêpe band round his arm, who responded to all Mrs. Palmer's voluble condolence with solemn little bows and monosyllables.

Mrs. Palmer was evidently disappointed at extracting from him no details about his wife's illness and death, and at last she turned the subject and began to speak of Elsie's qualifications as a typist.

"You see, Mr. Williams, I always felt it was waste, her going to be a kind of mother's help to that Mrs. Woolley. 'It's not what you've been trained for, my dear,' I said, 'but still, if you want to, you shall try it for a bit.' I've always been a one to let my girlies try their own wings, Mr. Williams. 'The old home nest is waiting for you when you're tired of it,' is what I always say. You've heard mother tell you that many and many a time, haven't you, Elsie?"

"Yes," said Elsie, bored.

She had often heard her mother make the like statements, in order to impress strangers, and she had no objection to backing her up, since it was far less trouble to do so than to have a "row" afterwards.

Mr. Williams bowed again. "I am sorry that Miss Elsie was exposed to unpleasantness of any sort, through an introduction of mine, and I may add that I entirely agree with you, Mrs. Palmer, in thinking that the—the domestic duties embarked upon were quite unworthy of her. Now, I am in want of a confidential clerk in this office."

Elsie saw her mother's eyes glistening behind the coarse fibre of her mended veil, and felt that her fate was sealed.

"Yes, Mr. Williams?"

"If I could persuade you to allow Miss Elsie to come to me.... Nine to six, and twenty-five shillings a week to begin with. Her duties would be light, simply to take down, type, and file my personal letters."

"It would be a very good beginning for her," said Mrs. Palmer, firmly, but with no undue enthusiasm. Elsie knew that her mother's mind was quite made up, but that she did not want to seem eager in the eyes of Mr. Williams.

"You'd like to give it a trial, Elsie?"

"I don't mind," said Elsie. She met the eyes of Mr. Williams and managed to smile at him, and for an instant it seemed to her that an answering pin-point of light appeared behind the pince-nez.

"It would be quite usual," said Mr. Williams gravely, "for me to give you a short test. Take this pencil and paper, please, and take this down."

He handed Elsie a shorthand pad and a pencil. She took down in shorthand the brief business letter that he dictated to her, and then, more nervously, read it aloud, stumbling over the pronunciation of one or two words, and once substituting one word for another, of which the shorthand outlines were similar, without any perception of the bearing of either upon the context.

Mr. Williams corrected her. "It's always the same," he told Mrs. Palmer in a low, rather melancholy voice. "These young people are wonderfully clever at taking dictation—eighty words a minute, a hundred words a minute—but you can't depend upon them to transcribe correctly."

Mrs. Palmer looked offended. "I'm sure Elsie will tell you that she wasn't doing herself justice, Mr. Williams. I'm sure she's as accurate as anybody, when she's not nervous. But if you think she won't do the work well enough, of course...."

Mrs. Palmer's lips were drawn together, and her intonation had become acidulated.

"Not at all," said Mr. Williams quietly, "not at all. You misunderstand my meaning altogether. I have no doubt that Miss Elsie will suit me very well indeed, when she has fallen into my little routine. What about next week?"

"Very well," Mrs. Palmer answered swiftly. "I'll let her come to you on Monday morning, Mr. Williams, and I'm very much obliged to you for thinking of us. It'll be a relief to me to know Elsie is in a good post. You see, I'm in the position of both father and mother to my girlies, and this one's my baby, as I always say——"

As Mr. Williams opened the door for them he said: "I hope that little affair about the trunk was satisfactorily concluded? It was perhaps a shade awkward, having the letter written from this office, in view of the fact that we were personally acquainted with the parties—but my head clerk, Mr. Cleaver, could hardly be expected to appreciate that.... A very worthy man indeed, and an able one, but the finer shades are rather beyond him. Good morning, Mrs. Palmer—good morning, Miss Elsie. Nine o'clock on Monday morning, then."

Mrs. Palmer went away in high spirits, and commented to Elsie and to Geraldine so enthusiastically upon Elsie's good fortune, that she began to believe in it herself.

"Are there any other girls there?" Geraldine asked.

And Elsie said quickly, "Oh dear, no! Both the other clerks are men."

She began to think that perhaps after all the hours spent in the office might not be without amusement.

Besides, all sorts of people came to see a solicitor.

Elsie spent the week-end in cutting out and making for herself a blue crêpe blouse, which she intended to wear on Monday morning. She also made a pair of black alpaca sleeves, with elastic at the wrist and at the elbow, to be drawn on over the blouse while she was working.

She put the sleeves, her shorthand pad and pencil, a powder-puff, mirror, pocket-comb, and a paper-covered novel in a small attaché case on Monday morning, pulled on the rakish black velvet tam-o'-shanter, and went off to Mr. Williams' office.

Her first day there was marked by two discoveries: that Mr. Williams expected to be called "sir" in office hours, and that the name of the youth who shared with her a small outer room where clients waited, or left messages, was Fred Leary.

55

A high partition of match-boarding separated the waiting-room from an inner office where Mr. Cleaver sat. And if Elsie and Fred Leary spoke more than a very few words to one another, Mr. Cleaver would tap imperatively against the wood with a ruler. He was also apt to walk noiselessly round the partition and stand there, silently watching Elsie, if the sound of her typewriter ceased for any undue length of time.

She learnt from Fred Leary that there had never been a female typist in the office before, and that Mr. Cleaver had been greatly opposed to the introduction of one.

"The Old Man always gets his way in the end, though," said Fred Leary, alluding to Mr. Williams.

"I knew him before," Elsie asserted, to give herself importance. "Him and his wife were in our house for a bit. I knew Mrs. Williams too."

"They said he led her a life," remarked Leary.

"What sort of way?"

"Oh, I couldn't tell a kid like you."

"What rubbish! As though I didn't know as much as you, any day."

He laughed loudly. "Girls always think they know everything, but they don't—not unless some fellow has——"

The sharp tap of Mr. Cleaver's pencil sounded against the matchboard, and silenced them.

The fact that their conversations had to be more or less clandestine added zest to them, and although Elsie was not in any way attracted by young Leary, who was spotty and unwholesome-looking, she several times went to a cinema with him on Saturday afternoons, and once to a football match. After the latter entertainment, however, they quarrelled.

Elsie had disliked the mud, the cold, the noise, the standing about and the crowds. She had been bored by Leary's enthusiasm, which was utterly incomprehensible to her, and secretly annoyed because, of the multitude of men surrounding her, not one had paid any attention to her, or to anything but the game and the players.

"I wasn't struck on that outing of yours," she remarked critically to her escort the following Monday morning. "Another time we'll give the football matches a miss, thank you."

Leary's admiration for Elsie, however, was less strong than his desire to see a league match, and he offended her by going by himself to the entertainment that she despised.

Elsie resented his defection less for his own sake than for that of the excitement that she could only experience through flirtation, and without which she found her life unbearably tedious.

She had been in the office nearly three months when Mr. Williams asked her suddenly if she liked the work there.

"I don't mind it," said Elsie.

She was in reality perfectly indifferent to it, and merely went through the day's routine without active dislike, as without intelligence.

"Now that you are used to our ways," said Mr. Williams deliberately, "I think you had better remove your table into my room. The sound of your machine will not disturb me in the least, and if clients desire a private interview, you can retire."

Elsie looked up, astonished, and met her employer's eyes.

His face was impassive as ever, but there was a faint, covetous gleam in his fish-like eyes.

Elsie, at once repelled and fascinated, gazed back at him, and felt her heart beginning to beat faster with a nervous and yet pleasurable anticipation.

VII

"When do you want to take your holiday, Elsie?"

"I'm not particular."

"Your mother will want you to get a breath of sea-air, I suppose."

"Oh, I don't know," said Elsie. "Mother's not awfully struck on going away."

It was late July, and between Elsie and her employer a curious, secret relationship had been established, at present only symbolised by occasional furtive touches of his hand on her neck or her dress, and a continual exchange of glances, steady and compelling on Williams's side, and responded to by Elsie almost against her own will.

Her typewriting table had been moved into his office, and she sat there nearly all day.

He spoke to her very little, but she was now always intensely conscious of his presence, and of her own effect upon him.

At first she did not understand to what his questions about the holidays were leading.

Next day, he spoke about them again.

"Shouldn't you like to go to Brighton—some place like that?"

"Rather."

"I often run down there myself from Saturday to Monday."

Mr. Williams looked at her more attentively than ever, and Elsie felt the blood creep up into her face. She knew that she blushed easily and deeply, and that men enjoyed seeing her blush.

"That hasn't got anything to do with me," she stammered, at once excited and confused.

"Hasn't it?"

"Mr. Williams!"

He glanced cautiously at the door, and then lowered his voice. "Look here, my dear child, I'm old enough to be your father and—and my dear late wife took quite a fancy to you. Surely you and I understand one another well enough to take a little holiday jaunt together without anyone but our two selves being any the wiser."

Elsie had not really expected the suggestion, and she was startled, but also triumphant.

"Whatever do you mean, Mr. Williams?"

He smiled, a small, thin-lipped smile, that held a suggestion of cynical mockery at her transparent pretence.

"Only what I say. I'm a poor, lonely fellow, with a little bit of money and no one to spend it on, and if I go to a nice hotel for the week-end I want someone to keep me company. Think over it, Elsie. You quite understand that I'm not asking anything of you—you're as safe with me as if I were your father. Just a pretty face opposite me at meals, and a smartly dressed little companion to take out for a walk on the front or to the theatre on Saturday night—that's all I want."

"Oh, I daresay," said Elsie.

His face stiffened, and she felt immediately that she had made a mistake.

"It's awfully kind of you to think of such a thing, Mr. Williams, but I really couldn't dream of it. Why, I don't know what mother would think——"

"Of course, it's a very conventional world," said Mr. Williams gravely. "You and I would know well enough that our little adventure was most innocent, but we don't want anyone to think or say otherwise. So I propose, Elsie, that we should keep it to ourselves. I presume it would be easy to tell your mother that you were staying with a friend?"

"Well—there's Ireen Tidmarsh, a young lady I often go with. I could say I was going to her."

"Just so. After all, you're of an age to manage your own affairs."

Elsie swelled with gratified vanity. She loved to be told that she was grown up.

"Well, what about the August Bank Holiday week-end? I could

58

meet you at the booking office at Victoria Station on the Saturday, and we could travel back together on the Tuesday morning. I'd like to show you something of life, Elsie."

He moistened his lips with his tongue as he spoke the words.

Elsie wished desperately that she could feel attracted by him, as she had been by Doctor Woolley. But Mr. Williams, physically, rather revolted her.

"Oh, I couldn't!" she repeated faintly.

He was very patient. "No expense, of course. And if you'd like a new hat or an evening frock, Elsie, or a pretty set of those silk things that girls wear underneath, why, I hope you'll let me have the privilege of providing them. You can choose what you like and bring me the bill—only go to a West End shop. Nothing shoddy."

Elsie was breathless at his munificence, and she longed wildly for the evening dress, and the silk underwear. Pale pink crêpe....

Perhaps it would be worth it.

"I'm sure you wouldn't ask me to do anything that wasn't perfectly right, Mr. Williams," she said demurely.

"I am glad you feel that. I'm glad you trust me," he solemnly replied.

"Of course I do."

"Then that's our secret. We need take no one into our confidence, Elsie, you understand. The arrangement is a perfectly innocent and natural little pleasure that you and I are going to share, but people are very often coarse-minded and censorious, and I would not wish to expose either of us to unpleasant comments. You'll remember that, and keep it to yourself?"

"Oh, yes," said Elsie.

That night as she was going to bed, she critically examined her own underwear. Her chemise and drawers were coarse, she wore no stays, and the garters that held up her transparent lisle-thread stockings were plain bands of grimy white elastic. Her short petticoat was white, with a torn flounce, and only the camisole, which showed beneath her transparent blouses, was trimmed with imitation Valenciennes lace and threaded with papery blue ribbons.

"What you doing, Elsie?" grumbled Geraldine from her bed. "Get into bed, do; I want to go to sleep."

"Have you seen those things they sell in sets, Geraldine, in some of the High Street shops? Sort of silk combinations and a princess petticoat and nightgown, all to match like?"

"I've seen them advertised at sale times, in the illustrateds, and beastly indecent they are, too. Why, you can see right through that stuff they're made of."

Elsie became very thoughtful.

59

Her sister's words had brought before her mind's eye an involuntary picture that both startled and repelled her.

"Anyway, the prices are something wicked. What's up, young Elsie?"

"Nothing. I heard something to-day that set me wondering, that's all."

"What?"

"Oh, some girl that wanted a pink silk rig-out, that's all."

"You must have some queer friends. No decent girl would wear those things—only tarts do, unless it's fine ladies that aren't any better than they should be, from what the Society papers say."

Geraldine, in her curling-pins and her thick nightgown, looked rigidly virtuous. "Get into bed, do."

"It's too hot," sighed Elsie.

The room was like a furnace, but neither of them would have dreamed of opening the window after dark.

Elsie tossed and turned about for a long while, unable to sleep. She visualised herself in new clothes, in evening dress, which she had never worn, and she thought of the excitement of staying in a big hotel where there would very likely be a band in the evenings and, of course, late dinner every night.

If only it had been anyone but Mr. Williams! But then, he was the only rich man she knew.

"It's a shame," thought Elsie, "that I shouldn't have opportunities of meeting other men like him, only different. I wish I'd gone in for manicure—I'd have met all sorts then."

For a moment she wondered whether her friendship with Williams might not lead to his introducing her to his wealthy friends, but she was shrewd enough to perceive that his first preoccupation would be to keep their connection secret, and that he was of far too cautious a temperament to risk her meeting with men younger and more attractive than himself.

Her last waking thought was of the silk set of underclothes, cool and lovely and transparent against her skin.

The following morning Mr. Williams behaved exactly as usual, and made no reference whatever to his suggestion of a holiday. Elsie, rather anxious and affronted, took advantage of a late call from a client to leave the office at six o'clock exactly, without returning into her employer's room to announce her departure as she usually did.

On her way to the crowded Tube station she was followed and accosted by a strange man. This adventure had become a common one to Elsie, but a certain recklessness pervaded her that evening, and when he urged her to come and sit in the park, under the cool of

60

the trees, she went with him. He was a man of thirty-five or so, with a miserable, haunted, disease-ravaged face, and he began almost at once to pour out to her a long story of his wife's treachery, of which he had just made the discovery.

"I've never looked at another girl," he kept on saying. "I've never spoken to one the way I've spoken to you to-night. But you remind me of her, in a way, and I knew you'd be all right, and sorry for a poor devil who's been fooled."

Elsie hardly listened to him, but she let him put his arm round her waist, and as his caresses became more violent and eager, she again felt that instinctive conviction that it was to such an end that she had been created. These physical contacts only, brought her to the fullness of self-expression. At last she realised that her companion was muttering a request that he might go home with her.

"What do you take me for?" Elsie asked furiously. "I'm a respectable girl, I am."

He became maudlin and begged her to forgive him, and she sank back again into his embrace, appeased at once.

At last, when the park gates were closing, she roused herself and insisted that if he wanted to go on talking to her they must go somewhere and have supper.

The man seemed too dazed and wretched to understand her, but when Elsie, rendered prudent by certain previous experiences, asked whether he had any money, he drew out a handful of loose silver.

"That's all right, then," she said, relieved, and took him to a cheap and very popular restaurant.

Elsie drank cocoa and ate sweet cakes, and her escort, leaning heavily on the marble-topped table, continued his low, maundering recitation of self-pity.

She had very little idea of what he was talking about.

She liked the restaurant and enjoyed her cakes, and the occasional contact between herself and the unknown man satisfied her for the time being.

When they left the restaurant, Elsie directed him to the omnibus that would take her nearest to her own suburb, and they climbed to the top of it, and sat in close proximity on the narrow seat all through the long drive.

It was with real difficulty that she tore herself away in the end, physically roused to a pitch that rapidly amounted to torment. She was frightened and disgusted by her own sensations, but much less so than she had been in the days of her technical innocence, before

61

she had known Doctor Woolley. She decided that she would go to Brighton with Mr. Williams.

And she would buy the silk underclothes—pink silk—and a real evening dress, cut low, that should reveal her shoulders and the full contour of her bust, and perhaps he would give her enough money for a string of imitation pearl beads as well.

"After all, he can afford to be generous," Elsie thought complacently. "An old man like him! I expect I'm a fool to look at him, really."

She meant that her attraction for men was sufficiently potent to ensure her ability to cast her spell wherever she chose, but common sense reminded her that the number of men within her immediate sphere was limited. Even men who followed her, or addressed her casually in the street, were mostly of the bank-clerk type, and of her own actual acquaintance scarcely one reached the level of the professional class to which Williams belonged.

At Hillbourne Terrace, Elsie found the front door locked, and realised that it must be late. She understood what had happened. Mrs. Palmer, angry at her daughter's tardiness, had probably decided to give her a fright, and was waiting in her dressing-gown, angry and tired, for Elsie to try the side door.

"I just won't, then," muttered Elsie angrily. "I'll jolly well go to Ireen."

She had seen a light in the house opposite as she came up the street, and it would not be the first time that she had called on Irene Tidmarsh for hospitality.

Her friend opened the door in person, and Elsie explained her position, giving, however, no specific reason for her lateness.

"Come in," said Irene indifferently. "You can sleep with me if you want to. I often thank God I've no mother."

The two girls went up to Irene's large, untidy bedroom in the front of the house, and began to undress, and Elsie was unable to resist the topic of the pink silk underclothes that obsessed her imagination.

"Geraldine says only tarts wear them."

"What does she know about it?" Irene enquired. "Ladies of title wear them—that Lady Dorothy Anvers, that's always being photographed, she goes in for black silk nightgowns—black, if you please!"

"I'd rather have pink, a great deal. I think black'd be hideous."

"Depends on one's skin, I suppose," said the sallow Irene thoughtfully. "Who wants to give you a silk nightie, young Elsie?"

Elsie deliberated. She was not usually communicative about her own affairs, but the notice of her employer had gratified her vanity, and she very much desired to boast of it to someone. Irene, at least, would be safe, and she sometimes offered shrewd pieces of advice that were not the outcome of experience, of which, by comparison with Elsie herself, she had little, but of a natural acumen.

Elsie, when the gas had been turned out, and the two girls were lying in Irene's bed, after extracting giggling oaths of secrecy, recounted to Irene the whole story of her adventure with Mr. Williams. She represented herself as still entirely undecided as to the sincerity of his assurance that their relationship was to be purely friendly.

"Rats!" was Irene's unvarnished comment. "It isn't very likely the old fool would have told you to get silk nighties and things unless he meant to see them himself. But I wouldn't do it, Elsie. It's too risky."

"Why, who's to find out? It isn't as if his wife was alive," said Elsie, with a recollection of the household in Mortimer Crescent.

"I don't mean that at all. But it's a beastly risk for you. He's your boss, after all. Suppose he gives you the sack, once this week-end business is over? Men are like that—they get sick of a girl directly they've had their fun, and then they don't want to be for ever reminded of it."

"It's quite as likely he'd be for ever pestering me to go with him again," Elsie declared, not at all desirous of supposing that her attractions could be provocative of such speedy satiety. "And even if he did sack me, there are plenty of other jobs going."

"You young fool! Don't you see what I mean? Suppose he landed you with a baby?"

"Oh!" Elsie was startled.

Like a great many other girls of her class and upbringing, although she possessed a wide and garbled knowledge of sex, she was singularly unable to trace the links between cause and effect. "A baby," in this connection, was to her nothing but an isolated catastrophe, that she had never particularly connected with the physical relations between a man and a girl.

"It couldn't, Ireen."

"Why not? Of course it could happen. A girl I know got caught, only luckily she had some sense, and went to one of these doctors that can stop it for you——"

"Can they?"

"Some can," said the well-informed Irene. "But mind you, it's an expensive business, and a jolly dangerous one. Why, the doctor can be had up for doing it, I believe. So don't you go and get yourself into any mess of that sort, now."

"I should think not," murmured Elsie.

"How old did you say this fellow, this Williams, was?"

"I don't know. About forty or forty-five, or something like that. He was years older than his wife, and she wasn't a chicken."

"And she's dead, is she?"

"Of course she is. I told you all about that ages ago."

"I know. Look here, Elsie, I've an idea. Why don't you marry this fellow?"

"Ireen Tidmarsh, are you dotty or what?"

"I'm giving you jolly good advice, and you'll be a young fool if you don't take it. He's rich, and you'd have a splendid position, and after a year or two you'd probably find yourself free to go your own way. He wouldn't live for ever, either."

"Don't," said Elsie.

"Well, it's true. You can bet he's on the look-out for a second wife already—widowers of that age always are."

"He wouldn't think of marrying me."

"Only because he can get what he wants without," said Irene curtly. "You show him he can't, and set him thinking a bit. If he's half as keen on you as you say he is, anyway, the idea's bound to cross his mind."

Elsie was rather bewildered, and disposed to be incredulous. She was incapable of having formulated so practical an idea for herself, and it held for her a sense of unreality. "Anyhow, I couldn't marry an old man like that. I don't even like him."

"Whoever you marry, young Elsie, you won't stick to him," said Irene cynically. "And if you ask me, the quicker you get a husband the better."

"That's what mother says."

"She wasn't born yesterday. Well, do as you like, of course, but it's the chance of a lifetime. I'm sure of that. Just hold out for a month—tell him you couldn't think of going anywhere with him—and see if he doesn't suggest your becoming the second Mrs. Williams."

"You're mad, Ireen," said Elsie, entirely without conviction.

She was in reality very much impressed both by Irene's worldly wisdom and by the sudden realisation it had brought to her of the possibilities latent in Mr. Williams' admiration.

She disliked having to work, and she knew that marriage was her only escape from work. To be married very young would be a triumph, and she thought with malicious satisfaction of how much she would enjoy asking Aunt Gertie and Aunt Ada to visit her in her own house.

"Well, good-night," said Irene's voice in her ear. "I'm going to

64

sleep. If you want to get over to your place early in the morning, don't wake me, that's all."

"All right."

Elsie turned over, gave a fleeting thought to the memory of the man she had met that evening, and fell asleep almost at once.

The next morning, after huddling on her clothes, and washing her face very hastily just before putting on her hat over her unbrushed hair, Elsie crossed the street and went home.

Mrs. Palmer was on the doorstep.

She was very angry.

"How dare you stay out all night like that, you good-for-nothing little slut? I haven't closed my eyes for wondering what'd happened to you. Where have you been?"

"At Ireen's."

"Why didn't you tell me you were going there?"

"I never thought of it, till I got here and found the door locked."

"It wasn't locked till nearly eleven o'clock, miss, and you could have come in by the side door, as you very well knew. And what were you doing out till eleven o'clock, I should like to know?"

"Nothing," said Elsie, beginning to cry.

Her mother promptly boxed her ears. "Elsie Palmer, you're nothing but a liar, and you'll break your widowed mother's heart and bring her to disgrace before you're done. However you've managed to grow up what you are, so particular as I've been with the two of you, is more than I can understand. Tell me this directly minute, who you were with last night?"

Elsie maintained a sullen silence, dodging as her mother aimed another heavy blow at her.

"I declare you'll make me lose my temper with you!" said Mrs. Palmer violently. "Answer me this instant."

"I went to the cinema."

"Who took you?"

"That fellow in the office—that Leary boy."

"Why couldn't you come in last night and say where you'd been, then? The fact is, Elsie, you're telling me a pack of lies, and I know it perfectly well. You can't take your mother in, let me tell you, whatever you may think, I'm sure I don't know what to do with you. I sometimes think you'd better go and live with your aunties; you'd find Aunt Gertie strict enough, I can tell you."

Elsie knew this to be true, and was fiercely resolved never to put it to the test.

"What you want is a thorough good whipping," said Mrs. Palmer, already absent-minded and preoccupied with preparations for breakfast. "Put that kettle on, Elsie, and be quick about it. And I

65

give you fair warning that the very next time I have to speak to you like this—(see if that's the girl at the door—it ought to be, by this time)—the very next time, I'll make you remember it in a way you won't enjoy, my lady."

Mrs. Palmer's active display of wrath was over, and Elsie knew that she had nothing to do but to keep out of her mother's way for the next few days.

She helped to get the breakfast ready in silence. She was too much used to similar scenes to feel very much upset by this one; nevertheless it influenced her in favour of acting upon Irene Tidmarsh's advice.

She knew very well that it would not be as easy to hoodwink Mrs. Palmer over a week-end spent out of London as she had pretended to Mr. Williams. Elsie was still afraid of her mother, and believed that she might quite well carry out her threat of sending her daughter to live with the two aunts.

Her chief pang was at relinquishing the thought of the pink silk underclothes, but she endeavoured to persuade herself that they might still be hers, when she should be on the point of marrying Mr. Williams. After all, it would be more satisfactory to own them on those terms than to be obliged to put them away after two days into hiding, in some place—and Elsie wondered ruefully what place—where they should not be spied out by Geraldine.

She went to the office as usual and was a good deal disconcerted when Fred Leary announced that "the Old Man" had telephoned to say that he was called away on business, and should not be back for two days.

Elsie, rather afraid that her own determination might weaken, decided to write to him, sending the letter to his home address.

Her unformed, back-sloping hand, covered one side of a sheet of notepaper that she bought in the luncheon hour.

"Dear Mr. Williams,

"One line to tell you that I have thought over your very kind suggestion about a holiday, but do not feel that I can say yes to same. Dear Mr. Williams, it is very kind of you, but I cannot feel it would be right of me to do as you ask, and so I must say no, hoping you will not be vexed with me. I do want to be a good girl. So no more, from

"Your little friend,
"Elsie."

VIII

It took Elsie exactly three months to bring Mr. Williams to the point predicted by Irene Tidmarsh.

During that time she was quiet, and rather timid, scrupulously exact in saying "sir" and very careful never to be heard laughing or chattering with Fred Leary.

Williams at first made no allusion to her note. When at last he spoke of it, he did so very much in his ordinary manner.

"I was sorry to get your little note the other day, Elsie, and to see that you don't quite trust me after all."

"Oh, but I do," she stammered.

He shook his head. "I'm afraid not. I'm afraid my little friend isn't quite as staunch as I fancied. It doesn't matter. Perhaps some day you'll know me better."

"It wasn't anything like that. It was just that I—I thought mother wouldn't like it," simpered Elsie. "It didn't seem to me to be quite right."

"It would have been quite right, or I shouldn't have asked you to do it," he replied firmly. "I'm a man of great experience, Elsie, a good many years older than you are, and you may be quite sure that I should never mislead you. But I see I made a mistake, you are not old enough to have the courage to be unconventional."

He looked hard at her as he spoke, but Elsie's vanity was not of the sort to be wounded at the term of which he had made use. She merely drooped her head and looked submissive.

A month later he asked her, in thinly veiled terms, whether she had yet changed her mind.

"I shan't ever change it," Elsie declared. "I daresay I've sometimes been rather silly, and not as careful as I ought, but I know very well that it wouldn't do for me to act the way you suggest. Why, you'd never respect me the same way again, if I did!"

She felt that the last sentence was a masterpiece. Williams shrugged his shoulders.

"Come, Elsie, let's understand one another. You're not ignorant, a girl like you must have had half a dozen men after her. And then what about that doctor fellow—Woolley?"

"What about him?"

"That's what I'm asking you. Something happened to cause the unpleasantness between Mrs. Woolley and yourself, and I've a very shrewd suspicion that I know what it was."

"Then I needn't tell you," said Elsie feebly.

"That isn't the way to speak."

His low voice was suddenly nasty, and she felt frightened. "I'm sorry."

"Yes. Don't do it again, Elsie. How far did Woolley go? That's what I want to know."

"He—he frightened me. He tried to kiss me."

"And succeeded. Anything else?"

"Mr. Williams!"

He gazed at her stonily. "Well," he said at last, "I'm half inclined to believe you. How old are you?"

"Seventeen."

"Seventeen!" he repeated after her, and his accent was covetous. "You should be very innocent, at seventeen, Elsie—very innocent and very pure. Now, my dear little late wife, when we were married, although she was a good deal older than you are, knew nothing whatever. Her husband had to teach her everything. That's as it should be, Elsie."

A certain prurient relish of his own topic, in Williams' manner, affected Elsie disagreeably. Neither did she like his reference to Mrs. Williams.

She was glad that the conversation should at that point be interrupted by the entrance of the austere Mr. Cleaver.

Suspense was beginning to make her feel very irritable. She now wanted Williams to propose marriage to her, but had begun to doubt his ever doing so. He continued to look at her meaningly, and to lay his rather desiccated hand from time to time on her shoulder, or upon the thin fabric of her sleeve, with a lingering, caressing touch. Elsie, however, had inspired too many men to such demonstrations to feel elated by them, and her employer's proximity roused in her little or no physical response.

One day, to her surprise, he brought her a present.

"Open it, Elsie."

She eagerly lifted the lid of the small cardboard box.

Inside was a large turquoise brooch, shaped like a swallow, with outspread wings.

She knew instantly that it had belonged to his dead wife, but the knowledge did not lessen her pleasure at possessing a trinket that she thought beautiful as well as valuable, nor her triumph that he should wish to give it to her.

"Oh, I say, how lovely! Do you really mean me to keep it?"

"Yes, really," Mr. Williams assured her solemnly.

"But I couldn't! It's too lovely—I mean to say, really it is!"

"No, it isn't, Elsie. You must please put it on, and let me have the pleasure of seeing you wear it."

"Put it on for me, then," murmured Elsie, glancing up at him, and then down again.

He took the ornament from her with hands that fumbled. "Where?"

"Just here."

She indicated the round neck of her transparent blouse, just below the collar-bone.

He stuck the pin in clumsily enough, and she stifled a little scream as it pricked her, but remained passive under his slowly-moving, dry-skinned fingers.

"There! I'm sorry there isn't a looking-glass, Elsie."

"Oh, I've got one! Don't look, though!"

She stooped, pulled up her skirt, revealing a plump calf, and in a flash had pulled out a tiny combined mirror and powder-puff from the top of her stocking. She had no other pocket.

Williams did not utter a sound. He only kept his pale grey eyes fixed gleamingly upon her.

"Are you shocked?" Elsie giggled. "I didn't ought to, I suppose, but really it's hard to know what else to do."

She peeped into the tiny looking-glass. "Isn't it pretty!"

"You are," said Williams awkwardly. "How are you going to thank me, Elsie?"

He always seemed to take pleasure in repeating her name.

"How do you suppose?"

"You know what I'd like."

He came nearer to her, and put his hands upon her shoulders. Although Elsie was short, he was very little taller.

She shut her eyes and put her head back, her exposed throat throbbing visibly. She could feel his breath upon her face, when suddenly she ducked her head, twisting out of his grasp, and cried wildly:

"No, no! It isn't right—I oughtn't to let you! Oh, Mr. Williams, I'd rather not have the brooch, though it's lovely. But I can't be a bad girl!"

He had taken a step backwards in his disconcerted amazement. "What on earth——Why, Elsie, you don't think there's any harm in a kiss, do you?"

"I don't know," she muttered, half crying. "But you make me feel so—so helpless, somehow, Mr. Williams."

Purest instinct was guiding her, but no subtlety of insight could have better gauged the effect of her implication upon the little solicitor's vanity.

He drew himself up, and expanded the narrow width of his chest. "You're not frightened of me, little girl, are you?"

"I—I don't know," faltered Elsie.

"I can assure you that you needn't be. Why, I—I—I'm very fond of you, surely you know that?"

Elsie felt rather scornful of the lameness of his speech. She saw that he was afraid of his own impulses, and the knowledge encouraged her.

"Here, Mr. Williams," she said rather tremulously, holding out the turquoise brooch.

He closed her hand over it. "Keep it. Are you fond of jewellery?"

"Yes, very."

"It's natural, at your age. I'd like to give you pretty things, Elsie, but you mustn't be such a little prude."

"Mother always told me that one shouldn't take a present—not a valuable present—from a man, without he was a relation or—or else——" She stopped.

"Or else what?"

"He'd asked one to marry him," half whispered Elsie.

Williams recoiled so unmistakably that for a sickening instant she was afraid of having gone too far.

Genuine tears ran down her face, and she did not know what to say.

"Don't cry," said the solicitor dryly. "I'd like you to keep the brooch, and you can thank me in your own time, and your own way."

"Oh, how good you are!"

She was relieved that he said no more to her that day.

She wore the brooch on the following morning, and fingered it very often. Williams eyed her complacently.

She began to notice that he was taking some pains with his own appearance, occasionally wearing a flower in his coat, and discarding the crêpe band round his arm. She even suspected, from a certain smell noticeable in the small office, that he was trying the effect of a hair-dye upon his scanty strands of hair. Elsie mocked him inwardly, but felt excited and hopeful.

When Williams actually did ask her to marry him, Elsie's head reeled with the sudden knowledge of having achieved her end. He had offered to take her for a walk one Sunday afternoon, and they were primly going across the Green Park.

To Elsie's secret astonishment, he had neither put his arm round her waist nor attempted to direct their steps towards a seat beneath one of the more distant trees. He simply walked beside her, with short little steps, every now and then jerking up his chin to pull at his tie, and saying very little.

Then, suddenly, it came.

70

"Elsie, perhaps you don't know that I've been thinking a great deal about you lately." He cleared his throat. "I—I've been glad to see that you're a very good girl. Perhaps you've not noticed one or two little tests, as I may call them, that I've put you through. We lawyers learn to be very cautious in dealing with human nature, you know. And I'm free to admit that I thought very highly of you after— after thinking it over—for the attitude you took up over that little trip we were going to take together. Not, mind you, that you weren't mistaken. I should never, never have asked you to do anything that wasn't perfectly right and good. But your scruples, however unfounded, made a very favourable impression on me."

He stopped and cleared his throat again.

Intuition warned Elsie to say nothing.

"A young girl can't be too particular, Elsie. But I don't want to give up our plan—I want my little companion on holidays, as well as on work days. Elsie," said Mr. Williams impressively, "I want you to become my little wife."

And as she remained speechless, taken aback in spite of all her previous machinations, he repeated:

"My dear, loving little wife."

"Oh, Mr. Williams!"

"Call me Horace."

Elsie very nearly giggled. She felt sure that it would be quite impossible ever to call Mr. Williams Horace.

"Let's sit down," she suggested feebly.

They found two little iron chairs, and Mr. Williams selected them regardless of their proximity to the public path.

When they sat down, Elsie, really giddy, leant back, but Mr. Williams bent forward, not looking at her, and poking his stick, which was between his knees, into the grass at their feet.

"Of course, there is a certain difference in our ages," he said, speaking very carefully, "but I do not consider that that would offer any very insuperable objection to a—a happy married life. And I shall do my utmost to make you happy, Elsie. My house is sadly in want of a mistress, and I shall look to you to make it bright again. You will have a servant, of course, and I will make you an allowance for the housekeeping, and, of course, I need hardly say that my dear little wife will look to me for everything that concerns her own expenditure."

He glanced at her as though expecting her to be dazzled, as indeed she was.

It occurred to neither of them that Elsie's acceptance of his proposal was being tacitly taken for granted without a word from

71

herself. She wondered if he would mention Mrs. Williams, but he did not do so.

He continued to talk to her of his house, and of the expensive furniture that she would find in it, and of the fact that she would no longer have to work.

All these considerations appealed to Elsie herself very strongly, and she listened to him willingly, although a sense of derision pervaded her mind at the extraordinary aloofness that her future husband was displaying.

At last, however, he signed to a taxi as they were leaving the park, and said that he would take her to have some tea. Almost automatically, Elsie settled herself against him as soon as the taxi had begun to move.

Rather stiffly, Williams passed his arm round her. His first kiss was a self-conscious, almost furtive affair that Elsie received on her upraised chin.

Intensely irritated by his clumsiness, she threw herself on him with sudden violence, and forced her mouth against his in a long, clinging pressure.

Elsie Palmer was married to Horace Williams at a registrar's office rather less than a fortnight later.

Williams had insisted both upon the early date and the quietness of the wedding. He had refused to allow Elsie to tell her mother of the marriage until it was accomplished, and a lurking fear of him, and schoolgirl satisfaction in taking such a step upon her own responsibility, combined to make her obedient.

Irene Tidmarsh and a man whose name Elsie never learnt, but who came with Mr. Williams, were witnesses to the marriage. Elsie was principally conscious that she was looking plain, unaccountably pale under a new cream-coloured hat and feather, and with her new shoes hurting her feet. It also occurred to her that she would have preferred a wedding in church, with wedding-cake and a party to follow it.

She felt inclined to cry, especially when they came out of the dingy office, after an astonishingly short time spent inside it, and found that it was raining.

"Where are we going to?" said Irene blankly. ("My goodness, Elsie, just look at your ring! Doesn't it look queer?) I suppose you'll take a taxi?"

Mr. Williams showed no alacrity to fall in with the suggestion, but after a dubious look round at the grey sky and rain-glistening pavement he signed with his umbrella to a taxi-cab.

"I suppose we'd better. Can I see you to your 'bus first, or do you prefer the Tube?" he added to Irene.

Both girls flushed, and looked at one another.

"Aren't you going to give us lunch, I should like to know?" murmured Elsie.

"I'm sure if I'm in the way, I'll take myself off at once, and only too pleased to do it," said Irene, her voice very angry. "Please don't trouble to see me to the station, Mr. Williams."

"As you like," he replied coolly, and held out his hand. "Good-bye, Miss—er—Tidmarsh. I'm glad to have met you, and I hope we shall have the pleasure of seeing you in Elsie's new home one of these days."

"Oh yes, do come, Ireen!" cried the bride, forgetting her mortification for a moment. "I'll run in and see you one of these evenings, and we'll settle it."

"Get in, Elsie. You're getting wet," said Mr. Williams, and he pushed her into the taxi and climbed in after her, leaving Irene Tidmarsh walking away very quickly in the rain.

"Well, I must say you might have been a bit more civil," began Elsie, and then, as she turned her head round to face him, the words died away on her lips.

"You didn't think I was going to have a strange girl here, the first minute alone with my wife, did you?" he said thickly. "You little fool!"

He caught hold of her roughly and kissed her with a vehemence that startled her. For the first time, Elsie realised something of the possessive rights that marriage with a man of Williams' type would mean. For a frantic instant she was held in the grip of that sense of irrevocability that even the least imaginative can never wholly escape.

Her panic only endured for a moment.

"Don't," she began, as she felt that his embrace had pushed her over-large hat unbecomingly to one side. She was entirely unwarmed by passion, unattracted as she was by the man she had married, and chilled and depressed besides in the raw atmosphere of a pouring wet day in London.

The first sound of her husband's voice taught her her lesson.

"There's no 'don't' about it now, Elsie. You remember that, if you please. We're man and wife now, and you're mine to do as I please with."

His voice was at once bullying and gluttonous, and his dry, grasping hands moved over her with a clutching tenacity that reminded her sickeningly of a crab that she had once seen in the aquarium.

Elsie was frightened as she had never in her life been frightened before, and the measure of her terror was that she could not voice it.

73

She remained absolutely silent, and as nearly as possible motionless, beneath his unskilled caresses. Williams, however, hardly appeared to notice her utter lack of responsiveness. He was evidently too much absorbed in the sudden gratification of his own hitherto suppressed desires.

Presently Elsie said faintly: "Where are we going to?"

"I thought you'd want some luncheon."

"I couldn't touch a morsel," Elsie declared, shuddering. "Couldn't you—couldn't you take me home?"

"Do you mean Hillbourne Terrace?"

"Yes. I've got to tell mother some time to-day, and I'd rather get it over."

"Very well," Williams agreed, with a curious little smile on his thin lips. "But you mustn't think of it as being home now, you know, Elsie. Your home is where I live—where you're coming back with me to-night. No more office for my little girl after to-day."

His short triumphant laugh woke no echo from her.

"Do you want me to come in with you?"

"Of course I do!" said Elsie indignantly. "Why, mother'll be simply furious! You don't suppose I'm going to stand up to her all by myself, do you?"

"Why should she be furious, Elsie? You've not done anything disgraceful in marrying me."

His voice was as quiet as ever, but his intonation told her that he was offended.

"I don't mean that," she explained confusedly. "Of course, mother knows you, and all—it's only the idea of me having gone and been and done it all on my own hook; that'll upset her for a bit. She's always wanted to make babies of us, me and Geraldine."

"You haven't told your sister anything, have you?"

"No fear. She's a jealous thing, ever so spiteful, is Geraldine. You'll see, she'll be as nasty as anything when she knows I'm actually—actually——"

Elsie stopped, giggling.

"Actually what?"

"You know very well."

"Say it."

"Actually married, then," said Elsie, blushing a good deal and with affected reluctance.

When they arrived at Hillbourne Terrace, and the taxi drew up before the familiar flight of steps, she began to feel very nervous. She told herself that she was a married woman, and looked at her new wedding-ring, but she did not feel in the least like a married woman, nor independent of Mrs. Palmer's anger.

74

Elsie's mother opened the door herself. "What on earth——Are you ill, Elsie, coming home in a cab at this hour of the morning? Whatever next!"

"Mr. Williams is here, Mother," said Elsie, pushing her way into the dining-room.

Geraldine was there, a check apron, torn and greasy, tied round her waist, and her hair still in curling-pins.

She was placing clean forks and spoons all round the table.

She looked at her sister with unfriendly surprise. Elsie had worn her everyday clothes on leaving home that morning, and had changed at Irene's house.

"Whatever are you dressed up like that for?" said Geraldine at once.

"Wouldn't you like to know?"

"I'd like to know where you get the money to pay for your new hats," said Geraldine significantly. "First one thing, and then another—I wonder you don't sport a tiara, young Elsie."

"Perhaps I may, before I've done."

Elsie was not really thinking of what she was saying, but was rather listening to a sound of voices in the hall outside that denoted a conversation between Williams and Mrs. Palmer.

She could not help hoping that he was breaking the news of their marriage to her mother. Elsie still felt certain that Mrs. Palmer would be very angry. It astonished her when her mother came into the room and kissed her vehemently.

"You sly young monkey, you! Geraldine, has this girl told you what she's done?"

"What?"

"Gone and got married! This morning!! To Mr. Horace Williams!!!" Mrs. Palmer's voice rose in a positively jubilant crescendo.

"Married!" screamed Geraldine. Her face became scarlet, and then grey.

"My little girl, married at seventeen!" said Mrs. Palmer with her head on one side.

She examined Elsie's plump hand with its wedding-ring.

Horace Williams stood by, quietly smiling. "Then you're willing to trust her to me, Mrs. Palmer? You'll forgive us for taking you by surprise, but you see, in all the circumstances, I could hardly—I naturally preferred—something very quiet. But you and I will have a little talk about business one of these days, and you'll find that part of it all in good order. Elsie will be provided for, whatever happens."

"So generous," murmured Mrs. Palmer.

She insisted upon their remaining to dinner, and sent out Nellie

Simmons for a bottle of wine. Elsie, now that she saw that her mother looked upon her marriage with the elderly solicitor as a triumph, and that Geraldine was madly jealous of her, became herself excited and elated.

Williams went to the office in the afternoon, but Elsie remained at home and packed up all her things.

She made her farewells quite cheerfully when Williams came to fetch her, still thinking of her mother's repeated congratulations and praises.

It came upon her as a shock, as they were driving away, when Williams observed dryly:

"That's over, and now there'll be no need for you to be over here very often, Elsie, or vice versa. You must remember that my house is your only home, now."

PART II

I

The European war affected Elsie Williams as much, or as little, as it affected many other young women. She had been married a little over a year in August 1914.

She was vaguely alarmed, vaguely thrilled, moved to a great display of emotional enthusiasm at the sight of a khaki uniform and at the sound of a military band.

Later on, she sang and hummed "Keep the Home Fires Burning," "Tipperary," and "We Don't Want to Lose You, but we Think you Ought to Go," and was voluble and indignant about the difficulties presented by sugar rations and meat coupons. She resented the air raids over London, and devoured the newspaper accounts of the damage done by them; she listened to, and eagerly retailed, anecdotes such as that of the Angels of Mons, or that of the Belgian child whose hands had been cut off by German soldiers; and after a period in which she declared that "everybody" would be ruined, she found herself in possession of more money than ever before.

Never before had so many clients presented themselves to Messrs. Williams and Cleaver, and never before had there been so much money about. Elsie bought herself a fur coat and a great many other things, and went very often to the cinema, and sometimes to the theatre. She very soon found, however, that Williams, when he could not take her out himself, disliked her going with anybody else.

He was willing enough that she should take Irene with her, or her sister Geraldine, but if she went out with any man, Williams became coldly, caustically angry, and sooner or later always found an opportunity for quarrelling with him.

Elsie was bored and angry, contemptuous of his jealousy, but far too much afraid of him to rebel openly.

She was more and more conscious of having made a mistake in her marriage, but her regrets were resentful rather than profound, and her facile nature found consolation in her own social advancement, her comfortable suburban home, and her tyrannical dominion over a capped and aproned maid.

She very seldom went to Hillbourne Terrace, and had quarrelled with her mother when Mrs. Palmer had suggested that it was time she had a baby.

Elsie did not want to have a baby at all. She feared pain and

77

discomfort almost as much as she did the temporary eclipse of her good looks, and the thought of a child that should be Horace Williams's as well as hers filled her with disgust.

She only spoke of this openly to Irene, and Irene undertook the purchase of certain drugs which she declared would render impossible the calamity dreaded by her friend. Elsie thankfully accepted the offer, and trusted implicitly to the efficacy of the bottles and packages that Irene bought.

Sometimes Horace declared that he wanted a son, and as time went on his taunts became less veiled, but Elsie cared little for them so long as she remained immune from the trial of motherhood.

She spent her days idly, doing very little housework, sometimes making or mending her own clothes, and often poring for a whole afternoon over a novel from the circulating library, or an illustrated paper, whilst she ate innumerable sweets out of little paper bags. She never remembered anything about the books that she read thus, and sometimes read the same one a second time without perceiving that she was doing so until she had nearly finished it.

After a time, Elsie became rather envious of the money that Irene was making as a munitions worker, and the "good time" that Geraldine enjoyed in the Government office where she had found a job. Elsie seriously told her husband that she felt she must go and do some "war work."

"You are not in the same position as an unmarried girl, Elsie. You have other duties. These war jobs are for young women who have nothing else to do."

"I don't see that I've got so much to do."

"If you had children, you would understand that a woman's sphere is in her own home."

"But I haven't got children," said Elsie, half under her breath.

"It's early days to talk like that," Williams retorted, and his glance at her was malevolent. "One of these days you'll have a baby, I hope, like every other healthy married woman, and neither you nor I nor anybody else can say how soon that day may come."

"Well, I suppose till it does come—if it ever does-you've no objection to me doing my bit in regard to this war?"

"I don't know. What is it you propose to do?"

"Oh, get a job of some kind. Ireen says they're asking for shorthand-typists all over the place, and willing to pay for them, too. I could get into one of these Government shows easily, or I could go in the V.A.D.s or something, and take a job in a hospital."

"No," said Williams decidedly. "No. Out of the question."

Elsie, who at home had, as a matter of course, surreptitiously disobeyed every order or prohibition of her mother's that ran counter to her own wishes, knew already that she would not disobey her husband.

She was afraid of him.

On the rare occasions when she saw any of her own family, Elsie always made a great display of her own grandeur and independence. She was really proud of her little suburban villa, her white-and-gold china, fumed oak "suite" of drawing-room furniture, "ruby" glasses and plated cake basket. She was also proud of being Mrs. Williams, and of wearing a wedding-ring.

Geraldine came to see her once or twice, and then declared herself too busy at the office to take the long tram journey, and as Elsie hardly ever went to Hillbourne Terrace, they seldom met. But Irene Tidmarsh came often to see Elsie.

She came in the daytime, when Williams was at the office, and very often she and Elsie went to the cinema together in the afternoon. Irene seemed able to get free time whenever she liked, and she explained this to Elsie by telling her that the superintendent at the works was a great friend of hers.

Elsie perfectly understood what this meant, and realised presently that Irene was never available on Saturdays and Sundays.

The war went on, and Mr. Williams made more and more money, and was fairly generous to Elsie, although he never gave her an independent income, but only occasional presents of cash, and instructions that all her bills should be sent in to him.

He did not rescind his command that she should not attempt any war work, although, as the months lengthened into years, it seemed fairly certain that there was to be no family to give Elsie occupation at home.

At twenty-five, Elsie Williams, from sheer boredom, had lost a great deal of the vitality that had characterised Elsie Palmer, and with it a certain amount of her remarkable animal magnetism. She was still attractive to men, but her own susceptibilities had become strangely blunted and no casual promiscuity would now have power to stir her.

She was aware that life had become uninteresting to her, and accepted the fact with dull, bewildered, entirely unanalytical resentment.

"I s'pose I'm growing middle-aged," she said to Irene, giggling without conviction.

One day, more than a year after the Armistice in November 1918, Irene Tidmarsh came to Elsie full of excitement.

She had heard of a wonderful crystal-gazer, and wanted to visit her with Elsie.

Elsie was quite as much excited as Irene. "I'd better take off my wedding-ring," she said importantly. "They say they'll get hold of any clue, don't they?"

"This woman isn't like that," Irene declared. "She's what they call a psychic, really she is. This girl that told me about her, she said it quite frightened her, the things the woman knew. All sorts of things about her past, too."

"I'm not sure I'd like that," said Elsie, giggling. "I know quite enough about my past without wanting help. But I must say I'd like to know what she's got to say about the future. You know, I mean what's going to happen to me."

"Oh, well, you're married, my dear. There's not much else she can tell you, except whether you'll have boys or girls."

"Thank you!" Elsie exclaimed, tossing her head. "None of that truck for me, thank you. Losing one's figure and all!"

"You're right. Anyway, let's come on, shall we?"

"Come on. I say, Ireen, she'll see us both together, won't she?"

"I hope so. I wouldn't go in to her alone for anything. Swear you won't ever repeat anything she says about me, though."

"I swear. And you won't either?"

"No."

The crystal-gazer lived in a street off King's Road, Chelsea, a long way down.

A little hunch-backed girl opened the door and asked them to go into the waiting-room. This was a small, curtained recess off the tiny hall, and contained two chairs and a rickety table covered with thin, cheap-looking publications. There were several copies of a psychic paper and various pamphlets that purported to deal with the occult.

"I'm a bit nervous, aren't you?" whispered Elsie. She fiddled with her wedding-ring, and finally took it off and put it in her purse. When the hunch-backed child appeared at the curtains, both girls screamed slightly.

"Madame Clara is ready for you," announced the little girl, in a harsh, monotonous voice.

She led them up to the first floor, into a room that was carefully darkened with blue curtains drawn across the windows. They could just discern a black figure, stout and very upright, sitting on a large chair in the middle of the room. A round stand set on a single slender leg was beside her.

Elsie clutched at Irene's hand in a nervous spasm.

The black figure bowed from the waist without rising. "Do you wish me to see you both together, ladies?" Her voice was harsh and rather raucous in tone.

"Yes, please," said Irene boldly.

80

"You quite understand that the charge will be the same as for two separate interviews?"

"Yes."

The little girl advanced with a small beaded bag. "The fee is payable in advance, if you please."

Elsie fumbled in her purse, and pulled out two ten-shilling notes.

"Half a guinea each, if you please, ladies."

"Irene, have you got two sixpences?" Elsie whispered, agitated.

Irene, by far the more collected of the two, produced a shilling, and the little girl with the bag went away.

"Will you two ladies be seated? One on either side of the table, please—not next to one another."

Elsie made a despairing clutch at Irene's hand again, but her friend shook her head, and firmly took her place on the other side of Madame Clara.

Elsie sank into the remaining chair, and felt that she was trembling violently. Her nervousness was partly pleasurable excitement, and partly involuntary reaction to the atmosphere diffused by the dim, shaded room and the autocratic solemnity of Madame Clara.

A sweet, rather sickly smell was discernible.

The silence affected Elsie so that she wanted to scream.

Her eyes were by this time accustomed to the semi-darkness, and she could see that Madame Clara was leaning forward, her loose sleeves falling away from her fat, bare arms, her elbows resting on the little table, and her hands over her eyes.

Suddenly the woman drew herself upright, and turned towards Irene.

"You, first. You have a stronger personality than your friend. It was you who brought her here. Do you wish me to look into the crystal for you?"

"Yes, I do," gasped Irene.

Elsie wondered from where the crystal would appear, and then she noticed the faint outline of a globe in front of the seer, on the little stand.

A thrill of superstitious awe ran through her.

"Make your mind a blank as far as possible, please ... do not think of the past, the present, or the future ... relax ... relax ... relax...."

Madame Clara's voice deepened, and she began to speak very slowly and distinctly, leaning back in her chair, the crystal ball before her eyes.

"Time is an arbitrary division made by man—the crystal will not

81

always show what is past and what is to come. For instance, I see illness here—bodily suffering—but I do not know if it has visited you or is still to come. It may even be the suffering of one near to you...."

She paused for an instant, and Elsie just caught Irene's smothered exclamation of "Father!"

"Hush, please," said the seeress. "The shadow of sickness deepens—it deepens into the blackness of death. A man—an old man—he is dying. You will get money from him. Beware of those who seek to flatter you. You are impressionable, but clear-sighted; impulsive, yet self-controlled; reserved, but intensely passionate. I see marriage for you in the future, but with a man somewhat older than yourself. I see conflict...." She stopped again.

"Perhaps the conflict is already over. You have certainly known love—passion——"

Elsie, from mingled nervousness and embarrassment, suddenly giggled.

The clairvoyante raised an authoritative hand. "It is impossible for me to go on if there are resistances," she said angrily, in the voice that she had used at first, ugly and rather hoarse.

"Shut up, Elsie!" came sharply from Irene.

Elsie ran her finger-nails into her palms in an endeavour to check the nervous, spasmodic laughter that threatened to overcome her.

"The current is broken," said Madame Clara in an indignant voice.

There was a silence.

At last Elsie heard Irene say timidly:

"Won't you go on, madame?"

"I'm exhausted," said the medium in a fatigued voice. "You will have to return to me another day—alone. All that I can say to you now, I have said. Beware of opals, and of a red-haired man. Your lucky stone is the turquoise—you should wear light blue, claret colour, and all shades of yellow, and avoid pinks, reds and purple."

She stopped.

Elsie, though awestruck, was also vaguely disappointed. It did not seem to her that she had learnt a great deal about Irene, and the warnings about colours and precious stones might have come out of any twopenny booklet off a railway bookstall, such as "What Month Were You Born In?" or "Character and Fortune Told by Handwriting."

Then she remembered that she herself had made Madame Clara angry by laughing, and that the woman had said the current was broken.

"Probably she's furious," Elsie thought, "and she won't tell me as much as she told Ireen. And she's got our money, too. What a swindle!"

"What about my friend?" said Irene Tidmarsh. Her voice sounded rather sulky.

"Your friend is a sceptic," said the clairvoyante coldly.

"No, really——" Elsie began.

The woman turned towards her so abruptly that she was startled.

She could discern an enormous pair of heavy-looking dark eyes gazing into hers.

"Make your mind a blank—relax," said Madame Clara, her tone once more a commanding one.

Elsie moved uneasily in her chair and fixed her eyes on the crystal. She could only see it faintly, a glassy spot of uncertain outline.

The seeress bent forward, leaning over the transparent globe. After a moment or two she began to speak, with the same voice and intonation that she had made use of in speaking about Irene.

"The crystal reflects all things, but Time is an arbitrary division made by man—we do not always see what is past, and what is future.... In your case, there is very little past—how young you are!—and what there is, is all on one plane, the physical. You are magnetic, extraordinarily magnetic. You have known men—you are married, if not by man's law, then by nature's law—you will know other men. But you are not awake—your mind is asleep. Nothing is awake but your senses...."

Elsie's mouth was dry. She longed to stop the woman but a horrible fascination kept her silent, tensely listening.

"Now you are bored—satiated. You have repeated the same experience again and again, young as you are, until it means nothing to you. You have no outside interests—and you are ceaselessly craving for a new emotion."

Abruptly the sibyl dropped on to a dark note.

"It will come. I see love here—love that you have never known yet. There will be jealousy, intrigue—letters will pass—beware of the written word——Ah!"

The exclamation was so sudden and so piercing that Elsie uttered a stifled scream. But this time she was not rebuked.

Madame Clara, all at once, was calling out shrilly in a hard voice, an indescribable blend of horror and excitement in her tone:

"Oh, God—what is it? Look—look, there in the crystal—what have you done? There's blood, and worse than blood! Oh, my God, what's this? It's all over England—you—they're talking about you—"

Irene Tidmarsh screamed wildly, and Elsie realised that she

had sprung to her feet. She herself was utterly unable to move, wave after wave of sick terror surging through her as the high, unrecognisable voice of the clairvoyante screeched and ranted, and then broke horribly.

"It's blood! My God, get out of here! I won't see any more—you're all over blood!..."

A strange, strangled cry, that Elsie did not recognise as having come from her own lips, broke across the obscurity, the room surged round her, she tried to clutch at the table, and felt herself falling heavily.

Elsie Williams had fainted.

She came back to a dazed memory of physical nausea, bewilderment, and resentment, as she felt herself being unskilfully pulled into a sitting position.

"Let go," she muttered, "let me go...."

"She's coming round! For Heaven's sake, Elsie ... here, try and get hold of her...."

She felt herself pulled and propelled to her feet, and even dragged a few steps by inadequate supporters.

Then she sank down again, invaded by a renewal of deadly sickness, but she was conscious that they had somehow got her outside the dark, scented room, and that the door had been slammed behind her.

Very slowly her perceptions cleared, and she realised that Irene was gripping her on one side, and the little hunch-backed girl holding a futile hand beneath her elbow on the other.

With an effort, Elsie raised her head.

"Look here, old girl, are you better?" said Irene, low and urgently. "I want to get out of here as quickly as possible. D'you think you can get downstairs?"

Elsie, without clearly knowing why, was conscious that she, too, wanted to get away.

She pulled herself to her feet, shuddering, and staggered down the stairs, leaning heavily on Irene.

"What happened?"

"Oh, you just turned queer. Don't think about it. Look here, we'd better have a taxi, hadn't we?"

"Yes. I couldn't walk a step, that's certain. Why, my knees are shaking under me."

"Go and get a taxi," Irene commanded the hunch-backed child, who went obediently away.

Elsie sat down on the lowest stair and wiped her wet, cold face with her handkerchief.

84

"What made me go off like that, Ireen? That woman said something beastly, didn't she?"

"Oh she's mad, that's what she is. She suddenly started ranting, and you got frightened, I suppose—and no wonder. Never mind, you'll soon be home now."

It struck Elsie that Irene was looking at her in a strangely anxious way, and that she was talking almost at random, as though to obliterate the impression of what had passed at the séance.

Elsie herself could not remember clearly, but there was a lurking horror at the back of her mind.

"What did she say?" she persisted feebly.

"Here's the taxi!" cried Irene, in intense relief. "Here, get in, Elsie. Thank you," she added to the child. "Don't wait, I'll tell the man where to go."

She gave the driver Elsie's address after the little girl had entered the house again, and then climbed in beside her friend, drawing a long breath.

"Thank the Lord! We got away pretty quickly, didn't we? Well, it's the last time I'll meddle with anything of that kind, I swear. I say, Elsie, had we better stop at a chemist's and get you something?"

"Yes—no. I don't care. Ireen, I want to know what that woman said. It was something awful about me, wasn't it?"

"She had a—kind of fit, I think. I don't believe she knew what she was saying—she just screamed out a pack of nonsense. And you gave a yell, and went down like a log. I can tell you, you've pretty nearly scared the life out of me, young Elsie."

Irene was indeed oddly white-faced and jerky. Her manner was as unnatural as was her sudden volubility.

Elsie, still feeling weak and giddy, leant her head back and closed her eyes. She felt quite unable to make the effort of remembering what had happened at the clairvoyante's house, and was moreover instinctively aware that the recollection, when it did come, would bring dismay and terror.

She and Irene Tidmarsh did not exchange a word until the taxi stopped.

"Here we are. You'd better pay him, Elsie. I'll take the Tube from the corner, and get home in half an hour."

"Aren't you coming in with me?" said Elsie, surprised.

"I don't think I will. I'd rather get straight home."

"Oh, do!" urged Elsie, half crying. She felt very much shaken. "I'm all alone; Horace won't be back till seven, and this has upset me properly. Besides, I know I shall remember what it was that awful woman said in a minute, and I'm frightened. You must come in, Ireen."

85

"I can't," repeated Irene, inexorably. "I ... really, I'd rather not, Elsie."

The door opened, and Irene turned rapidly and walked away down the street.

Elsie tottered into the house.

"I'm ill," she said abruptly to the servant. "I fainted while I was out, and I feel like nothing on earth now. I shall go to bed."

"Yes, 'm. Shall I go for a doctor, 'm?" said the girl zealously.

"No," said Elsie sharply. "I don't want a doctor. Telephone to Mr. Williams at the office, Emma, and ask him to come home early. Say I'm ill."

"Yes, 'm."

Elsie dragged herself upstairs and took off some of her clothes. She was shivering violently, and presently pulled her blue cotton kimono round her and slipped into bed. She lay there with closed eyes, shuddering from time to time, until Emma brought up a cup of strong tea. Elsie drank it avidly, lay down again and felt revived. Presently she dozed.

The opening of the door roused her. It was nearly dark, but she knew that it must be her husband, who never knocked before entering their joint bedroom.

"What's all this, Elsie?"

"I felt rotten," she said wearily. "Turn on the light, Horace."

He did so, and advanced towards the bed. His face wore an expression of concern, and he walked on tiptoe.

"I fainted while I was out with Ireen," Elsie explained, "and I was simply ages coming to. We came back in a cab, and I must say Ireen's awfully selfish. She wouldn't come in with me, though she must have seen I wasn't fit to be left—just turned and walked off. I'm done with her, after this."

"Where had you been?" enquired Williams quickly.

"Oh, just out."

"Where to?"

"I suppose you'll call me a fool, if I say it was to see one of those clairvoyante women, someone Ireen had heard of. It was all Ireen's doing—she persuaded me to go."

"Very silly of you both," said the little solicitor coldly. "Did this person upset you?"

"Yes. She had a sort of fit, I think, and called out a whole lot of nonsense, only I can't remember what it was." Elsie moved uneasily.

"Where does she live?"

"Why?"

"She ought to be prosecuted for obtaining money under false pretences. I suppose you gave her money?"

86

"Oh yes."

"You'd better give me her name and address and I'll see that she is properly dealt with."

"I'd rather not."

Horace Williams shrugged his shoulders. "Well, you'd better get up and come down to supper, hadn't you? There's no reason for lying in bed if you're not ill."

"All right," Elsie agreed sullenly.

Her husband never shouted at her or threatened her, but she was afraid of him, and of a certain sinister dryness that characterised his manner when he was displeased.

The dryness was there now.

Elsie spent the evening downstairs. Her husband read the newspaper, and she turned over the pages of a fashion magazine listlessly. Her thoughts, unwillingly enough, returned again and again to the scene in the clairvoyante's room, but still she could not remember the actual words screamed out by Madame Clara before she had lost consciousness. But she remembered quite well other words, that had preceded them.

"You are magnetic ... extraordinarily magnetic.... You are not awake—your mind is asleep.... Now, you are bored, satiated. You are ceaselessly craving for a new emotion...."

Elsie reflected how true this was.

She glanced distastefully at her elderly husband.

The bald patch glistened on the top of his head, and he was breathing heavily as he read his newspaper.

He had always been rather distasteful to her physically, and although the continuous, degradingly inevitable proximity of married life in a small suburban villa had hardened her into indifference, Elsie was still averse from the more intimate aspects of marriage with him.

She wished that she could fall in love, remembering that Madame Clara had said: "I see love here—love that you have never known yet."

"That's bunkum," thought Elsie. "I've been in love heaps of times—I was in love with that doctor fellow, Woolley. It doesn't last, that's all."

She hardly ever met any men nowadays, as she resentfully reminded herself.

The husbands of her married friends were at work all day, and if she occasionally met them at their wives' card-parties, they did not interest her very greatly. Most of the wives distrusted the husbands and gave them no opportunity for flirtation with other women. And Horace Williams himself was a jealous man, always

87

suspicious, and never allowed his young wife to go anywhere with any man but himself.

Elsie had been for a long while in inward revolt against the dullness of her life. She remembered with longing the old days of her girlhood, when every walk had been the prelude to adventure, and the casual kisses of unknown, or scarcely known, men had roused her to rapture.

Nowadays, she knew very well that she would be less easily satisfied. The apathy that had been creeping over her ever since her marriage had to a certain extent lessened the force of the animal magnetism by which she had been able to lure the senses of almost every man she met, and for the first time she was beginning to have doubts of her own attractiveness.

Elsie gave a sigh that was almost a groan.

Williams neither stirred nor raised his eyes.

"I think I'll retire to my little downy," Elsie murmured, drearily facetious.

"It's only a quarter past nine."

"Oh, well, we lead such a deliriously exciting life that I'd better get some rest, hadn't I?" she said ironically. "Just to make up for all the late nights we have."

At last her husband put down the paper and looked coldly at her through his pince-nez. "What is it you want, Elsie? I work hard all day at the office, and you have plenty of time and money for amusing yourself in the daytime—and a strange use you seem to make of them, judging by to-day's performance. What more do you want?"

"I don't know. We might go to the pictures sometimes, or to a play. I hate not having anything to do."

"That's the complaint of every woman who hasn't got children."

"I can't help it," said Elsie angrily.

He said nothing, but continued to fix his eyes upon her, with his most disagreeable expression.

"Good-night, Horace."

"I shall come up to bed before you're asleep," he said meaningly.

She went out of the room.

The thought crossed her mind, as it had often done before, that she had made a frightful mistake in marrying Horace Williams.

"I was only eighteen," she thought, "I ought to have waited. Perhaps he'll die."

As she undressed, Elsie idly imagined a drama of which she herself would, of course, be the heroine.

Horace would be at the office, as usual, and a telephone

message would come through to say that he was ill—very ill indeed—he was dead. Everyone would admire the young widow in her black, with her string of pearl beads.... Horace would leave her quite a lot of money. Elsie knew that he was rich, although he had never told her his income. She would stay on in the villa, but people would come and see her—she would go out and enjoy herself—enjoy life, once more....

Elsie sighed again as she got into bed.

Bored and exhausted, she fell asleep almost at once, to dream vividly.

In her dream, she stood outside a closed door, knowing that something unspeakably horrid lay beyond it. Terror paralysed her. At last she pushed at the door, but it would not yield more than an inch or two. Something was behind it. She looked down and saw a dark stain spreading round her feet, oozing from beneath the resistant door.

Screaming and sweating, Elsie woke up, and as she did so the remembrance came back to her in full of everything that the clairvoyante had said that morning.

II

"Hallo, Elsie!"

"Hallo, Geraldine!"

"You're quite a stranger, aren't you? I think it's about a year since we had the honour of seeing your majesty last."

"Well, now I have come, aren't you going to take the trouble to invite me to come in?" asked Elsie good-humouredly.

"There's a visitor of mine in the drawing-room."

"Who is it? Aunt Ada?"

"No, not Aunt Ada, Miss Smarty. It's a friend of mine, I tell you, who I knew at the office during the war."

"Well, you can introduce me to her, I suppose," said Elsie carelessly.

She noticed that Geraldine's hair was not, as it generally was, in curling-pins, and that she was wearing a new dress, of an unbecoming shade of emerald green. Geraldine always went wrong over her clothes, Elsie reflected complacently. She herself wore a new black picture hat, and it was partly from the desire to show herself in it that she had come to her old home.

"Where's mother?"

"Out."

"What a mercy!"

Elsie walked into the familiar drawing-room, feeling glad that she no longer lived at Hillbourne Terrace, under her mother's dominion, and forced to share a bedroom with the fretful Geraldine.

A young man of two- or three-and-twenty was sitting in the drawing-room, and rose to his feet as Elsie and Geraldine came in.

"This is my sister, Mrs. Horace Williams. Elsie, this is my friend, Mr. Morrison," said Geraldine with pride.

Elsie was immediately conscious of a quickened interest. The young man was of a type that appealed strongly to her; dark and tall, with very brown eyes, and a wistful, ingenuous smile that was the more noticeable because he was clean-shaven.

When they shook hands, she was conscious of the slight, unmistakable thrill of mutual magnetism.

"I thought I was going to find a young lady in here, when Geraldine told me she had a friend!" Elsie exclaimed, laughing.

"Sorry I'm a disappointment," Mr. Morrison replied, also laughing.

"Oh, I didn't say that. Only my sister doesn't have gentlemen friends as a rule," Elsie declared innocently.

Geraldine's sallow face flushed. "You don't know much about it, do you, considering that we never see you nowadays. I'm not one for talking much about my own affairs, either, so far as I'm aware. It's a misfortune, really, to be as reserved as I am. I often wish I wasn't!"

It was unprecedented, in Elsie's experience, to hear Geraldine setting forth a claim, however obliquely, to be considered interesting. Elsie looked at her in astonishment.

"She must be gone on this fellow," she thought, and without the slightest compunction she immediately put forth all her own powers to attract Morrison's notice and admiration to herself.

The task proved to be as easy as it was congenial. In a very little while, Elsie and young Morrison were talking and joking together, and it was only an occasional, spasmodic, and quite evidently conscientious effort from Morrison that from time to time caused Geraldine to be included in the conversation.

Morrison told Elsie that he travelled for a big firm of silk merchants in the City, and was very little in London.

"How did you and Geraldine meet, then? I thought you were in the same office as her during the war," said Elsie sharply.

"Just for six months I was, and then I got this job in the place of a man who'd joined up. I was under age for joining up myself, worse luck," said the youth.

90

Then he must be younger than she was herself, Elsie reflected, surprised. She felt oddly touched by the thought.

She looked at Morrison, and found that he was looking at her with admiration evident in his dark eyes.

Elsie allowed her eyes to dwell for a second on his before she broke the momentary silence. "What about tea, Geraldine?"

"All right," said her sister sulkily. "Where's the hurry?"

It was already half-past four, but Elsie guessed that Geraldine did not want to go and fetch the tea and leave her alone with Morrison.

"No hurry, I suppose," she cried gaily, "but I'm a bit tired, that's all, and I thought I'd like a nice cup of tea. It's a good long way to come, and the Tube was pretty full."

"Where did you come from?" Morrison asked eagerly.

She named the suburb. "You must come and look us up one day, Mr. Morrison. My husband is a solicitor, and he's always at home on Saturdays and Sundays. The rest of the week I'm by myself and ever so lonely," sighed Elsie.

"I'd love to come. I should—er—like to meet Mr. Williams," said Morrison solemnly.

"Here's Mother!" Geraldine announced sharply, as a door banged downstairs.

Mrs. Palmer came in, breathing heavily, her hands full of parcels.

"Elsie! Dear me, this is a surprise. Good afternoon, Mr. Morrison, how are you? Quite well, thank you, but for Anno Domini, that's all that's the matter with me." She dropped into a chair.

"Where's tea?"

"I'll get it up," said Geraldine.

"Go and give her a hand," Mrs. Palmer calmly directed young Morrison. "My gurl is out. They're all the same, nowadays—always out, never in."

"I never have any trouble with servants," Elsie murmured.

She was annoyed that her mother should thus dismiss Morrison, and that he should meekly prepare to obey her.

He opened the door for Geraldine and went out behind her, and Elsie heard her sister talking animatedly as they went downstairs.

"What's come over Geraldine?" she coldly enquired.

"Why should anything have come over her, as you call it? Geraldine's a gurl like you are, I'd have you remember, and a very much better one than you've ever been, to her widowed mother. You mind your own business, Elsie."

"That's a nice way to speak to me, when I haven't been at home for I don't know how long."

91

"And whose fault has that been?" enquired Mrs. Palmer. "Not but what I'm always pleased to see you, Elsie, as I've told you time and time again, and Mr. Williams too—Horace, I should say—if he cares to come. But don't you go interfering with Geraldine's friends."

"Is this fellow a friend of hers?"

"Of course he is. They've been going together for some time now."

"I suppose she's not engaged?"

"No, she's not engaged," Mrs. Palmer reluctantly conceded. "But I'm free to confess that I hope she will be. This Leslie Morrison is a nice fellow, as steady as can be."

Elsie reflected that Leslie was a lovely name.

"Now, Elsie," said her mother warningly, "I know what you are, and I give you fair notice that I won't have any of your goings-on. You'll remember that you're a married woman, if you please, and just behave yourself. Any of your old tricks, my lady, and I shall drop the hint to Horace. Him and me knew one another before ever he set eyes on you."

"All the more reason for not making mischief between us now. He's jealous enough as it is, making a fuss of anyone so much as looks the same side of the room as I happen to be."

"I don't blame him," said Mrs. Palmer curtly. "You're a caution, you are, and always have been. I don't mind telling you that I never was more thankful in my life than to get you safely married. And don't you go casting sheep's eyes at poor Geraldine's fellow, for I tell you I won't have it."

Elsie laughed scornfully. She was secretly flattered at the alarm that was conveyed by Mrs. Palmer's reiterated cautions.

"What should I want with a boy like him? He must be six years younger than Geraldine, at the very least."

"Nothing of the kind. And if he was, it wouldn't matter. It's the first time anyone has looked like business, where Geraldine's concerned, and with you off my hands I can afford to make things a bit easy for her. She's been a good daughter to me, has Geraldine," said Mrs. Palmer with a significant emphasis.

"Well, I'm sure I don't want to stand in her way," Elsie declared contemptuously.

"Anyone less selfish than you are, Elsie, would offer to help things on a bit. I can't be for ever asking him here, and he's not got the money to take her out a great deal. Why don't you get them to meet at your place?"

"Perhaps I will," said Elsie slowly.

She was rather silent during tea, mentally reviewing her mother's suggestion from various angles.

Leslie Morrison definitely attracted her. She asked him how long he was to remain in London.

"Not long, Mrs. Williams. I'm doing Bristol and Gloucestershire next week, and then I'm taking my holiday."

"Where are you going for that?" Mrs. Palmer enquired.

"I haven't made up my mind. Anywhere near the sea is good enough for me."

"My husband and I are thinking of Torquay," Elsie said. "We've been wondering if you'd care to come along, Geraldine. I suppose Mother wants to stew on in London, as per usual."

"That's right," Mrs. Palmer assented complacently. She looked at her younger daughter with approval. It was the first time, actually, that Elsie had ever invited Geraldine to spend a holiday with her.

"Torquay is a first-rate place," declared Leslie Morrison enthusiastically. "I was there once on business, and I quite made up my mind to return one day."

"Thanks very much, Elsie," Geraldine said rather coldly. "It's a long journey, isn't it, and I'm a wretched traveller, as you know."

"Please yourself. Horace wants a thorough change, and we're sick of Wales. We've been there every year ever since we were married."

"Come, I don't suppose that makes much of a total, does it?" Morrison gallantly remarked, looking at Elsie.

"More than you'd think for, perhaps. I was caught young—eighteen, if you want to know."

"Elsie," said her mother abruptly, "have you been to see your aunties lately?"

She directed the conversation so that no more personalities were possible, until Elsie rose and said good-bye.

"Allow me," said Morrison, as he helped her to put on her coat.

Elsie fumbled for the sleeve-hole until she felt the guiding pressure of his fingers on her arm.

"Thanks ever so much. Well, good-bye, Mr. Morrison. Let me know if you come up our way any time."

"I ... I hope you're going to let me see you to your 'bus," he said rather awkwardly.

"Really, there's no need—I couldn't think of troubling you."

Elsie took no pains to hide that her protest was a purely conventional one.

"Put on your hat, Geraldine, and go with them. A walk'll do you good," urged Mrs. Palmer.

But Geraldine, as she frequently did, had turned sulky. "I've got something to do upstairs," she muttered, and disappeared.

It was exactly like Geraldine, Elsie thought, to cut off her nose just to spite her face. Not that it could have made any difference if she had succeeded in preventing that brief walk taken by Leslie Morrison and Elsie Williams.

Elsie knew, beyond any possibility of mistake, the very first moment at which a spark from her own personality had lit the flame destined to burn more or less fiercely in that of another.

But this time she experienced an odd excitement that held in it something new.

She wondered, rather wistfully, whether this was because it was such a long while since she had had any opportunity of talking to a man other than her husband or one of his elderly married acquaintances. Her conversation with Morrison did no more than skirt the edge of personalities that were implied, rather than spoken. Yet when they parted Elsie knew, and knew that Morrison knew, that each was determined to see the other again. She travelled home in a dream, and hardly heard her husband's vexed enquiry as to the reason of her lateness.

Williams had always shown a very strong conviction that it was a wife's duty invariably to be at home in time to welcome her husband's return from business.

"I've been to Hillbourne Terrace."

"H'm. You've made yourself very smart. That hat suits you, Elsie."

He so seldom paid a compliment that Elsie was astonished, and ran to look at herself in the mirror over the dining-room sideboard.

It was the hat, was it?

Her full face was softly flushed, and her eyes looked bigger and darker than usual. Elsie saw her own closed mouth break into an involuntary smile as she gazed at her reflection. She went up to her room singing softly.

Two days later Leslie Morrison came to see her.

"I hope you won't think I'm taking a liberty. Knowing your people so well, it seemed quite natural, like, to take advantage of your kind invitation."

"That's right," Elsie encouraged him.

She hardly knew what she was saying, but already their intercourse seemed to be on a plane where conventional interchanges of words were unnecessary.

Although it was only the second time they had met, Morrison told her a great deal about himself, and Elsie listened, with a growing, tremulous tenderness.

94

He went away before her husband came in, and Elsie underwent a momentary, essentially superficial, reaction.

"I'm getting soppy about that boy—that's what I'm doing! Just because he's got a pair of eyes like—like I don't know what. Him and Geraldine! It's too ridiculous. Why, he's younger even than me."

She reflected that if Morrison, indeed, had been a year or two older, he would certainly have kissed her by this time. But it was quite evident to her that such an idea had never even crossed his mind. He viewed her with obvious admiration, and with great respect.

The next day Elsie bought a book of poems, about which Morrison had told her. She read some of them, and it seemed to her that she had a new understanding of a form of expression which had never made the least appeal to her before.

"I'm a fool!" Elsie told herself in astonishment, but with an ominous sensation of strange, new emotions, softer than any she had yet known, taking possession of her life. She felt that she would like to give the book to Morrison as a present, but they had made no definite arrangement for meeting again, and she could not bring herself to send it by post. Restlessness possessed her.

It was a relief when one evening her husband began to speak of their summer holiday.

"We can start on Tuesday, like we planned. Cleaver gets back on Monday morning, and the sooner we get to the sea in this weather, the better. It won't last."

"It might. September can be a ripping month sometimes," said Elsie dreamily.

"That's your experience, is it? Well, it's not mine. I only hope we shan't have a rainy spell as we did last year, and sit in an everlasting sitting-room without so much as a book to look at."

Elsie shuddered at the recollection. She and Horace had quarrelled incessantly throughout their last holiday.

"Is your sister coming with us?"

"Yes."

"Well, that'll be better than nobody. She'll be somebody for you to go with to those picture-houses that you're so fond of. But it's a pity that girl hasn't got a sensible husband. We might get a decent game of bridge, then."

"It's a pity you haven't got any men friends," Elsie retorted. "I never knew anybody like you for that."

Williams did not answer, but he turned upon his wife a look, peculiar to himself, that always vaguely frightened her. It held not only utter contempt, but something of quiet, unspecified menace.

She hastily spoke again. "Geraldine's got a—a young fellow that she thinks is going with her now. A boy called Morrison."

"Is he coming to Torquay?"

It was Horace Williams' own matter-of-course tone in making the suggestion that suddenly filled Elsie with a frantic determination to see it carried out.

"Yes, most likely he is. So you'll get your bridge, I daresay, and there'll be somebody to take us to the pictures of an evening."

As Elsie said the words, her heart seemed to herself suddenly to leap against her side, as though in anticipation of a joy almost too great to be borne.

She lay awake most of that night, revolving schemes by which Leslie Morrison could be brought to Torquay without letting Williams know that it was Elsie who had originated the idea.

Although formerly she had been as much flattered as irritated by her husband's suspicious jealousy, it seemed to Elsie now to be of the utmost importance that he should not look upon Morrison in any other light than that of Geraldine's friend. She wondered if she could induce Geraldine herself to suggest that Morrison should come to Torquay, but decided that it was unlikely. Finally, after a great deal of deliberation, Elsie next day wrote a note to the young man:

"Dear Mr. Morrison,

"If not otherwise engaged, we shall be pleased if you will come to tea on Saturday afternoon. It will be the last time for some weeks we shall be at home, as we go to Torquay on the Tuesday. My sister, Miss Palmer, is coming with us. Why not join the party, as you say you would like to visit Torquay again?!!!

"Yours sincerely,
"E. Williams."

Elsie thought about this note incessantly after it was written and posted, and awaited the reply with proportionate excitement.

It came by return of post:

"My Dear Mrs. Williams,

"Very many thanks indeed for your most kind invitation to tea. Unfortunately I am not able to avail myself of it, as am already engaged to go to Hillbourne Terrace. The suggestion about me going to Torquay is simply great—that is, if you really meant it! I intend talking it over with your sister when we meet on Saturday.

"Believe me, with kind regards,

"Yours very sincerely,
"Leslie M. Morrison."

Elsie came downstairs earlier than usual in order to conceal her letter before Williams should ask to see it, as he invariably did with his wife's correspondence.

She put it in her pocket, and kept it there all day. On Saturday she wanted very much to go to Hillbourne Terrace, but Williams was at home, and on such occasions he never expected his wife to go out except with him. They spent the afternoon drearily enough, Williams reading the newspaper, and Elsie pretending to sew, and in reality wholly occupied with speculations as to how Geraldine would receive Leslie Morrison's suggestion.

She felt pretty certain that Mrs. Palmer, at all events, would be in favour of it. "If only he has the sense to make it sound as if it came from him, and not from me!" thought Elsie.

She had felt confident of receiving another letter from Morrison before starting for Torquay, but to her dismay there was no word, either from him or from Geraldine, and on the eve of departure she still did not know whether or not her scheme had succeeded. For the first time, she heartily wished that there had been a telephone in her mother's house.

On the morning of their journey the weather changed and became suddenly sultry. The train was crowded and unbearably hot.

Geraldine was to meet them at the station, and the fact that she arrived late made Horace Williams angry, in his own unpleasant, silent way. There was only one empty seat in the railway carriage, which Elsie at once took, and Williams and Geraldine were forced to stand in the corridor, already strewn with hand baggage and full of heated, perspiring people.

The train ran from London to Taunton without a stop, and at the end of two hours Williams forced his way into the carriage and spoke quietly to his wife.

"Here, Elsie, give me your place for a little while. One of my boots is hurting, and I can't stand any longer. Go and take your turn for a bit."

Elsie joined Geraldine in the corridor without demur. There were certain tones in Horace Williams' voice that she had learnt to obey. Geraldine, her face pallid and shiny with heat, her tight blue cloth dress looking as though it constricted even her narrow chest

97

and shoulders, was sitting in an uncomfortable, crouching position on a roll of rugs.

Both she and Elsie had removed their hats, and while Elsie's hair dropped naturally into soft, flattened curls and rings, Geraldine's clung damply in straight, short wisps to her neck and forehead, and she constantly raised her hand to push away, quite ineffectually, a straggling end that immediately fell down again.

"Hell, I call this," she remarked shortly, as Elsie, stumbling over bags and packages and the feet of other passengers, reached her side and propped herself up against the side of the swaying train.

"You're a nice one to take on a holiday, I must say," Elsie retorted, but without acrimony. She felt that nothing would really matter if she could once get the assurance that she craved.

"Horace is in a foul temper. He never can stand the hot weather. I'm sure I hope it'll be cooler at the sea than what it is here. Have you brought a new bathing costume, Geraldine?"

"M'm. A blue one, with a decent skirt—not one of those horrible skin-tight things you see in the picture papers. Improper, I call them."

"You couldn't be improper if you tried," said Elsie cryptically. "Besides, there'll be nobody to go in the water with you except me. Horace never bathes—makes him turn green, or something."

She eyed her sister carefully as she spoke. Something in the wariness of Geraldine's return glance gave her a rising hope.

"I'm sure I wish we were going to have someone we knew there. Horace would be much easier to keep in a decent temper if he had another man to go with sometimes."

Then Geraldine spoke. "That boy Leslie Morrison said something about coming down one day this week, and spending part of his holiday at Torquay. He was awfully keen I should go and stay with his mother, near Bristol, too."

"Was he? Well, you could do that later," said Elsie. She was nearly breathless with triumph, but strove to make her voice sound matter-of-fact. "But I hope to goodness he will come to Torquay. It'll make all the difference to Horace."

Geraldine sneered. "I daresay you think it'll make all the difference to you, too. It's anything in trousers with you, old girl, whether the fellow belongs to another girl or not. But I'm not afraid of anything of that sort while Horace is about. He knows how to keep you in order, as Mother said."

"I'll thank you, and Mother too, to keep your opinion of me till it's asked for." Elsie, however, spoke mechanically.

She had immediately become obsessed by visions of herself and Morrison, walking, swimming, sitting beside one another on the sands, or in the intimate closeness and darkness of the picture palace....

"I'll just tell you this, young Elsie. Leslie Morrison isn't the sort of fellow you've been used to—not like Johnnie Osborne, and that truck. And as for carrying on with a married woman—why, he'd be ashamed to think of such a thing."

Elsie smiled, and said nothing. She hardly heard what her sister was saying.

A hand laid upon her shoulder made her jump violently.

"Are you in the moon, Elsie? I've been making signs to you for ten minutes, I should think. It's more than time we had our sandwiches," said Horace Williams querulously.

"Oh, all right."

By tugging and pulling at piled-up packages, they succeeded in getting hold of the basket in which Elsie had packed ham sandwiches, seed-cake, and bananas.

The train sped onwards....

III

The Williamses and Geraldine stayed in a boarding-house that proudly advertised itself as being situated "right on the front," and young Morrison had a room in an apartment house, much cheaper and more remote, half-way up one of Torquay's steepest hills. He arranged to have all his meals except breakfast at the boarding-house.

The weather was very hot, and sunny, and breathless.

Elsie felt as though she had never lived before. Every morning she came downstairs, her face sunburnt and glowing, but never unbecomingly freckled, her open-necked, short-sleeved blouses and jumpers indefinably smart and well put on, her undependable and essentially variable good looks seeming always to increase.

She was greatly admired in the boarding-house, and Williams for the first time did not appear to resent this.

He had suddenly become absorbed in a new and obscure digestive complaint, and would discuss the subject endlessly with his neighbours at meal-times. An elderly widow without any companion took a fancy to Geraldine, and as she sometimes gave her presents of clothes, or took her for a drive, Geraldine always sat

99

next to her at the long table in the dining-room, and listened to her with a fair pretence of amiability.

Breakfast was a long, hot, abundant meal. The boarding-house knew its clientèle and catered for it according to the views of business men who never allowed themselves to eat as much as they would have liked on week-day mornings during all the rest of the year. Tea and coffee, eggs and bacon, and fish and sausages were provided, toast and jam and marmalade and potted meat.

Elsie, who never ate anything but bread-and-butter with jam, and drank innumerable cups of tea, at her own home, enjoyed the novel fare because it was novel, and because she had not bought and ordered it herself, and because she was living in a haze of happiness that made everything enjoyable.

The prophecy of the clairvoyante had come true. Elsie knew the love that she had never yet known.

Every morning they went down to the sands and met Leslie Morrison there. They sat in deck chairs, and ate fruit from paper bags, and listened to a pierrot entertainment. At midday Elsie and Geraldine ran back to the boarding-house, undressed, and put on their bathing-suits, and came back to find Morrison already in the water and Horace Williams asleep in his deck-chair behind a newspaper.

Elsie's bathing-dress was blue, trimmed with white braid, and she wore a rubber cap with a blue-and-red handkerchief knotted over it. Her bare legs and arms and neck had tanned very slightly; Geraldine's showed scarlet patches of sunburn.

As they joined Morrison in the water, both girls always screamed, clinging to one another's hands. But once the water was high above their waists, Elsie, a naturally strong swimmer, struck out boldly, consciously enjoying the cold water and the exercise of her muscles. Geraldine, of poor physique and defective circulation, only bobbed up and down in the shallows, still uttering staccato shrieks.

At first, Elsie and Morrison would keep near her, swimming short distances, and then returning, or splashing beside her in shallow water, but sooner or later they would both strike out, swimming side by side. They spoke very little.

"I say, you swim simply splendidly, Mrs. Williams. Why, I've never seen a girl swim as well as you do."

"D'you think so? It's nice, isn't it?"

"It's ripping. I've never had a holiday like this one—I mean, one that I've enjoyed so much."

"Neither have I."

"I hadn't looked forward to my holiday a bit this year. I never

100

thought it would be anything like this. I didn't know that anything in the world——"

It was always Elsie who suggested that it was time to go back.

"Geraldine's gone out already. She turns a funny colour if she stays in too long."

Once, when they were rather further out than usual, Elsie said that she was getting tired.

"Put your hand on my shoulder—I'll help you. Yes, do."

"Oh no, I couldn't."

"Yes, you must."

"Well, if you are sure you don't mind...."

"Mind!"

His voice was very eloquent, and Elsie was abundantly satisfied. She laid her hand upon his shoulder, and kept it there after her feet touched the sandy bottom once more and they were almost out of the water.

They raced to the bath-towel cloak that she had left under the wall, and as she put it round her Elsie said, without looking at him and in a peculiar tone:

"Did you enjoy it?"

"I loved it," Morrison replied very low, and after a moment he added:

"Better than any of our other bathes."

Elsie had never before conducted any one of her numerous love-affairs in a key so reticent, and the very novelty of the experience rendered it strange and precious.

Subconsciously, they might both be waiting for the spoken word, but on the surface each was supremely contented in the present.

The presence of Geraldine did not disturb Elsie in the least. Geraldine had been jealous of her intermittently ever since the days of their earliest childhood, and her manifestations of temper were always latent, rather than active. Elsie was used to them, and indifferent to them.

Besides, Leslie Morrison was always very nice to Geraldine. He sat between the sisters at the entertainments to which they went frequently, he gave chocolates and sweets to Geraldine oftener than to Elsie, and he was always ready to talk of Geraldine's favourite topic, the old days in the office.

Only his dark eyes sought Elsie's face with increasing frequency, his pleasant young voice altered slightly and indescribably when he found himself alone with her.

It seemed part of the magic of those enchanted days that

101

Geraldine should make no scene, Horace Williams appear to perceive nothing.

On Sunday evening a band played in the public gardens. They decided to go and hear it.

Then Williams developed his mysterious symptoms, and refused to come out.

"You girls can go with Morrison. I shall take a glass of boiling water with peppermint," he declared, "and go to bed. I'm in agony."

"Would you like me to stay with you?" Elsie asked, her heart sinking.

"No, no, go and enjoy yourself."

"Perhaps you'll feel better in a bit, and come and join us," she suggested, and thankfully made her escape.

The gardens were lit with Japanese lanterns and crowded with holiday-makers. Pale frocks and scarves flickered oddly in and out of the shadows and beyond the bright circle of glaring white light thrown out from the raised and roofed circular platform of the bandstand.

"No hope of chairs, I suppose," said Geraldine disconsolately. "We're late, thanks to Horace. Just look at the people."

Morrison volunteered to try and find a seat, and they watched his tall figure disappear into the throng of people.

"I shall be sick if I have to stand for long, that's certain," declared Geraldine. "I believe the sun was too hot for me this afternoon. My head's splitting."

"Take off your hat, why don't you?"

Elsie's own hair was only covered with a blue motor veil, knotted at either ear, and with floating ends.

"My hair would be all over the place. I like to look tidy, thank you."

"Please yourself," said Elsie indifferently. She was absorbed in watching for the first glimpse of Morrison returning to them.

When she caught sight of him, elbowing his way through the crowd, it actually seemed to her as though the heart in her body leaped forward to meet him.

As usual, his eyes sought Elsie's and held them for an instant before he turned to Geraldine.

"There's one chair there. I've taken it, and a fellow is kindly keeping it for me. I thought you and your sister could take it in turns to sit down."

"I don't know...." Geraldine began ungraciously.

"It's quite a good place, and nice-looking people on either side. The chap that's keeping it for us seemed very decent."

"Oh, go on, Geraldine!" said Elsie. "Hark, they are beginning again."

The band had struck into a selection from a popular musical comedy.

Leslie Morrison put his arm beneath the girl's elbow, and they moved away, Geraldine still grumbling sub-audibly.

Elsie, motionless, waited.

Never before in her life had she known this ecstasy of anticipation, so poignant as to be almost indistinguishable from pain.

When Leslie came back to her, she thought that she must fall, and instinctively caught at his arm for support.

Without speaking, he drew her away from the ring of light, into the deep shadow of a clump of trees. She stumbled against something in the sudden obscurity, and discerned the low railing that separated the ornamental shrubs and flower-beds from the crowded gravel paths.

"Come," said Leslie's voice in her ear, hoarsely. They stepped together over the little railing on to the grass. Another few steps, and they were in an isolation as complete as though a curtain had fallen between them and the seething mass of talking, laughing, swaying people in the gardens.

Even the sound of the band only reached them faintly as though from a great distance.

Leslie Morrison halted abruptly, and they faced one another, their eyes already accustomed to the semi-darkness.

By an impulse as inevitable as it was irresistible, they were in one another's arms.

Neither spoke a word whilst that long throbbing embrace endured.

Through Elsie's whole being flashed the wordless conviction: "This is what I've been waiting for...."

"Elsie," whispered the man. "Elsie ... Elsie ... Elsie ... I love you!"

"I love you," she whispered back again.

They stood clinging to one another, entwined, the hot summer darkness encompassing them.

"What shall we do?" Morrison murmured at last. "I have no right to say a word to you, Elsie—I never meant to."

"What does it matter?" said Elsie recklessly. "Horace and I have never been happy together. I ought never to have married him. It's you I belong to."

"My darling ... my sweetheart."

They kissed passionately, again and again.

103

"What are we going to do?"

Elsie pressed closer and closer against him. "Forget everything, as long as this holiday lasts, except that we can be together. It's been so heavenly, Leslie! We can settle—something—later on, when it's all over."

"I can't let you go back to that man again. It would drive me mad."

"Take me away with you," she whispered.

"Oh, if I could ... if I only could, little girl!"

They spoke as lovers talk, ardently, and tenderly, and with long silences.

A sudden surging movement, and the distant sound of the National Anthem, penetrated at last to them through the darkness.

"It's all over!" Morrison cried, aghast. "Your sister?..."

"I'll manage her," said Elsie. "Leslie ... once more...."

Her mouth found his, and then she tore herself out of his arms.

"Come with me."

Rapidly Elsie found her way to the little pay-desk outside the enclosure, in which the lights were already being extinguished.

"She's bound to come out this way."

They waited, Elsie's eyes at first dazzled, striving to find her sister's form in the crowd. Every fibre of her being was acutely aware of the presence of Leslie Morrison, standing just behind her, so that her shoulder touched his breast.

Without turning her head she put out her hand, and felt it clasped in his and held tightly.

Her senses swam, and it was Geraldine's own voice that first warned her of her sister's approach.

To her relief, Geraldine was talking to a strange young man.

"Good-night," she said amiably.

"Good-night, and thanks so much for a pleasant evening," he returned, raising his soft hat.

Elsie compelled herself to speak. "Have you met a friend?" she enquired, with simulated interest.

"Hallo! Where have you been, I should like to know? Isn't it funny?—that's a fellow who was at our place for nearly a month during the war. Belcher, his name is. He was the very one that kept the chair for me. Did you two get seats somewhere else?"

"Yes," said Elsie swiftly.

"It was good, wasn't it—the band I mean? Horace has missed something by staying at home."

Geraldine was evidently, and contrary to her wont, in high good humour.

They walked back to the boarding-house, Leslie Morrison

between the two girls, Geraldine openly hanging on to his arm. His other hand was out of sight in his pocket, Elsie's warm, soft fingers locked in his.

At the door they parted.

"Good-night and sweet repose," said Geraldine indifferently, but she waited for her sister to precede her into the lighted house.

Elsie moved in a dream. It startled her when Geraldine, looking curiously at her under the glare of the electric light in the hall, said suddenly:

"What's the matter with you, Elsie? You look moon-struck, and your hair's all over the place, half down your back."

"Is it?" Elsie put up her hands and pushed up the soft, loose mass under her veil again. "I'm going to bed," she said, in a voice that sounded oddly in her own ears. "Tell Horace, will you? I've a splitting head."

She felt an unutterable longing to be in the dark, and alone with her new and overwhelming bliss.

"You're a nice one, I must say, leaving me alone all the evening, and then dashing off upstairs the minute we get in. I should think Horace would find something to say to you——"

Elsie neither heard nor heeded.

She ran upstairs and into the small double bedroom. It contained two beds, and for the first time since their marriage she and Horace had occupied separate ones.

To-night Elsie felt that she could never be thankful enough for the comparative solitude that would enable her to feel herself free again.

She tore off her thin summer clothes, shook down her cloud of hair, ran across the room in her nightdress to snap off the light, and then almost threw herself into bed.

In the blessed darkness, Elsie lay with hands clasped over her throbbing heart, and relived every instant of the evening, thrilling to a happiness so intense that she felt as though she must die of it.

She was perfectly incapable just then of looking beyond the immediate present and the glorious certainty of seeing Leslie Morrison again in the morning.

Although Elsie had been attracted, in a sensual and superficial manner, by a number of men, she had never in her life loved before, and the passion for Morrison that had suddenly swept into her life held all the force of a long repressed element violently and unexpectedly liberated.

Body, soul and spirit, she was obsessed almost to madness by this young man, several years her junior, whom she had not known a month.

105

When Horace Williams came up to bed it was nearly midnight, and Elsie, her face half buried under the sheet, pretended to be asleep.

IV

The love-affair of Elsie Williams and Leslie Morrison swept on its course, and in the early days of their madness neither of them paused for an instant to count its possible cost.

It seemed, indeed, as though Fate were deliberately simplifying their way.

Horace Williams appeared unable to give his attention to anything beyond his newly-discovered digestive trouble, and remained constantly indoors through the hottest and finest of the summer days, experimenting upon himself with drugs, and studying tables of dietetic values. He questioned Elsie very little as to her movements, taking it for granted that she, Morrison, and Geraldine formed a trio.

In point of fact, the youth whom Geraldine had met at the Sunday evening concert, and whom she spoke of as Percy Belcher, now almost always made a fourth in the party.

Geraldine monopolised him eagerly, and openly showed her triumph at feeling that she could now afford to relinquish Leslie Morrison.

Elsie and Morrison went swimming together, and lay on the hot, crowded sands, and dropped behind the others when they all went for walks, and sat with locked hands and her cheek against his shoulder in the stifling, thrilling darkness of the picture theatre, watching together the representation of a love that was never anything but the reflection of their own, the eternal triumph of a Man and a Woman, pale representatives on the screen of Elsie Williams and Leslie Morrison.

The golden fortnight drew to its close, and with the end of the Torquay holiday, it suddenly seemed to Elsie as though the end of the world must come.

"What are we to do, Leslie?" she gasped.

"I don't know, darling," he said miserably.

"You're going to be in town for a bit?"

"For a little while. They're sending me off again, pretty soon— abroad this time."

"I can't live without seeing you sometimes. Oh, Les, how can I go back to the old life with Horace after this?"

"Elsie," said Morrison very low, "would he divorce you if——?"

"Not a hope. It costs money, and he's too mean. Besides, he'd never do it if he thought I wanted it. He's cruel, is Horace."

"Not to you?"

"He doesn't knock me about, if that's what you mean—he knows I wouldn't stand it—but of course he doesn't care for me, or for anybody but himself. I was told he gave his first a rotten time—anyway, I know she used to look wretched enough. You know there was a first Mrs. Williams?"

"No, I didn't. Of course, I saw he was much older than you. Oh, Elsie, whatever made you marry him?"

"Oh, I was a fool and I thought I'd like to be married, and get away from home. I didn't know what it was going to be like, that's certain. Oh, Les, fancy if I was still Elsie Palmer, and you and me could get married!" She gave a sob.

"Don't, sweetheart! I'd have asked for your promise, fast enough, if you'd been free, but I couldn't marry any girl till I'm earning a bit more."

"Don't you get a good screw, Leslie?"

"Rotten. But I'm jolly lucky to be in a job at all these days, I suppose."

"Lucky!" Elsie echoed the word drearily. "You and I aren't amongst the lucky ones, boy. I don't see how things are ever going to come right for us, without a miracle happens."

"He—Williams—may ... he may die."

"Not he!" said Elsie bitterly. "There's nothing the matter with him. All this talk about indigestion is stuff and nonsense—just fads he's got into his head. There's nothing wrong with Horace. And it's always the ones who aren't wanted that live on and on. But how am I going to bear it, after this wonderful time we've been having?" She began to cry.

"Elsie, don't, darling! I'll think of a way. There must be some way out."

Leslie took her in his arms and she forgot everything else.

On the last evening they all went to the theatre together, and it was there, for the first time seeming awake to the situation, that Horace Williams, sitting at the end of the row of stalls, suddenly leaned across Geraldine and looked long and balefully at his wife.

She felt herself changing colour.

Morrison, however, observed nothing. He talked only to Elsie, looked only at her during the interval, and whilst the play was in

107

progress and the lights in the theatre lowered, his hand sought and held hers.

"Elsie, we can't part like this. How can I see you alone?"

"We can't—not here. But Horace starts at the office again on Wednesday, and he's there all day. Come to the house."

"It means an age without seeing you. Elsie, can I write to you?"

"Yes ... no...." She was startled. "Oh, Les, darling, I'd love your letters!... But he'd see them. Wait a minute."

She thought rapidly.

"Address them to the post-office—I'll call there. He doesn't know or care what I do all day, so long as I'm always there in the evenings when he gets back."

But Elsie was to find herself mistaken. Her husband, after their return to the suburban villa, displayed a very unmistakable interest in her movements during the hours of his absence at work.

He obliged her to give him an account of her day, and took to ringing her up on the telephone for no acknowledged reason, and always at a different hour.

At first, Elsie cared little. She and Leslie Morrison met daily, and on one occasion spent the afternoon in the country together. Elsie recklessly telephoned to her own house at seven o'clock that evening, and said that she was with Irene Tidmarsh, and should not come home that night.

"You must," said the hollow voice at the other end of the line.

"I can't. Her father's awfully ill, and she's afraid of being left."

"When shall you be home?"

"To-morrow."

"I'll come and fetch you."

"All right," said Elsie boldly. "What time?"

There was no answer. Williams had rung off.

Elsie knew, beyond the possibility of mistake, that her husband suspected her; but in the intense excitement that possessed her she was conscious of nothing so much as of relief that a crisis should be at hand.

She spent the night with Leslie Morrison at a tiny hotel in Essex.

Early next morning they travelled back to London, parting at Liverpool Street station.

"Let me know what happens directly you can, darling," urged the man.

"I'll telephone. Anyway, come round as soon as you can get away. He won't be in before seven."

"Good-bye, Elsie darling. I'll never, never forget...."

He left her, joining a hurrying throng of other young men

wearing soft hats and carrying little brown bags, nearly all of them hastening towards the City.

Elsie proceeded by train and tram to the house of Irene's father.

Her friend opened the door to her. "Hullo! I thought I should see you. That hubby of yours is on the warpath."

"What's happened?"

"Oh, nothing, thanks to me! Come in, Elsie. Have you had breakfast?"

"I've had some tea; I don't want anything else. Tell me about Horace."

"Well, Horace, as you call him, saw fit to come round here at eleven o'clock p.m. last night, and got me out of my virtuous downy by ringing at the front door bell till I thought the house was on fire. He said he'd 'come for' his wife, if you please!"

"I know. I told him I was going to spend the night at your place," said Elsie calmly. "I suppose you didn't happen to tumble to it, Ireen?"

"I've not known you all these years for nothing, old girl," said Irene, grinning. "What do you take me for? I told him you were in bed and asleep, and had been for hours."

"You're a real sport, Ireen! How did he take it?"

Irene pursed up her lips and shook her head. "He asked me to tell you to ring him up first thing this morning. If you ask me, you're in for trouble. And p'r'aps now you'll be so kind as to tell me what it all means, and why on earth you couldn't have given me fair warning before saying you were here. It's lucky for you I didn't give the whole show away on the spot."

Elsie, habitually ready to discuss any of her love-affairs with Irene, had told her nothing about Leslie Morrison. But she saw now that a degree of frankness was inevitable.

Irene listened, sitting on the kitchen table, her shrewd, cynical gaze fixed upon Elsie. "You're for it, all right," she observed dryly. "I thought directly I saw you after you'd got back from Torquay that there was something up. But I somehow didn't think you'd go off the deep end like that, Elsie. Why, you're dotty about him!"

"Yes," said Elsie, "I am."

"And what do you suppose is going to happen?"

Elsie groaned. "I wish to the Lord that Horace would do the decent thing, or go West—and let me have a chance of happiness."

"He won't," said Irene. "Well, whatever you do, don't make a fool of yourself and run off with this fellow. It simply isn't worth it, when he hasn't got a penny, and not very often when he has."

"If I thought Horace would divorce me it'd be different," Elsie said. She was not listening to Irene at all. "Though even then, I don't know what we would live on. Leslie hasn't anything except his salary, and that's tiny, and I'm sure I couldn't earn a penny if I tried. Mother wouldn't help me, either, if I did a thing like that."

"No more would anybody else. And surely to goodness, Elsie, you'd never be such a fool. Think what it would mean to be disgraced, and have a scandal."

"I wouldn't mind that with him."

Irene groaned. "You are far gone! Well, the worse it is while it lasts, the sooner it's over. You'll see sense again one of these days, I suppose. Meanwhile, you'd better 'phone that husband of yours."

Elsie's conversation with Williams over the telephone was brief. She agreed to come home at midday, and neither made any reference to the visit of Williams at eleven o'clock on the previous night.

Elsie anticipated a scene with her husband, and felt indifferent to the prospect. She had not enough imagination to work herself up in advance, and, moreover, her faculties were entirely occupied with the blissful expectation of seeing Morrison again that afternoon.

He came some hours after she had arrived home.

Elsie had done some shopping in the morning. With her husband's money she had bought a gold-nibbed fountain-pen for Leslie, and had paid for copies of a photograph of herself.

She had scarcely ever in her life before given anyone a present, and Leslie Morrison's ardent thanks, and rapture over the photograph, caused her the most acute pleasure.

"Darling, it's lovely, and it's just you! I shall always carry it about with me, done up with your dear letters."

"Don't keep my letters, Leslie," said Elsie suddenly.

"Why ever not?"

A sudden recollection had come to her ... "Beware of the written word...."

The medium to whom Irene had once taken her had said that. She had also said other things; had told Elsie that love would come to her.... Perhaps she really knew....

"I'd rather you didn't, really," she said feebly. "Suppose— suppose Horace ever got hold of them——"

"How could he? Besides, Elsie darling, he's got to know about us some time. I wish you'd let me tell him now. I can't go on like this; it's a low-down game coming to a man's house without his knowledge and—and making love to his wife."

"His wife!" said Elsie angrily. "Don't call me that. I may be his wife in law, but it's you that I really belong to."

"Well, let me have it out with him then," said Morrison

earnestly. "We don't know, after all. He may be ready to do the decent thing, and set you free."

"I don't care if you do. I'm pretty sure he guesses.... Horace has always been jealous, though he's never had any cause before."

"He didn't say anything at Torquay?"

"No, it's since we got back. He asked me once if you were engaged to Geraldine, and I said no. And he asked if you meant to come and see us here, and I told him most likely you would. He didn't say anything much, but he hates a man coming near the place, really."

"I'd far rather have it out with him," young Morrison repeated. His face was resolute, and he stood his ground when Elsie, starting violently, exclaimed:

"I believe that's Horace now! I can hear his key in the door. He's never in at this hour as a rule—the skunk, he's come to spy on me!"

"Darling, it's all right!" said Morrison.

He put the photograph away in his breast-pocket with hands that trembled slightly. Both fixed their eyes on the door as it opened upon the figure of the little elderly solicitor. His face wore a no more sardonic expression than was habitual with him, and Elsie could not deduce from it whether or not he was surprised to see Leslie Morrison.

Neither man made any movement towards shaking hands, but they greeted one another conventionally, and talked a little, as though indifferently, of the holiday at Torquay.

Leslie asked whether Mr. Williams was any better in health, and the solicitor replied coldly:

"No, I am no better. I daresay my case would be a very interesting one, from the point of view of a doctor. But I am not one to give up, and I have no doubt that a great many people do not realise there is anything the matter with me."

He turned his eyes upon Elsie for a moment as he spoke.

At the same instant, the inevitable thought that had flashed through her mind at his words caused Elsie to cast a lightning glance towards Leslie Morrison.

It was that glance that her husband intercepted.

V

They had another evening together before the storm broke.

Morrison took Elsie to a dance.

He issued his invitation boldly, in the presence of Williams, and to Elsie's secret astonishment, her husband made no objection to her acceptance.

She wanted terribly to buy a new dress for the dance, but dared not risk a reminder to her husband, for fear he should suddenly forbid her to go. Finally she decided to wear a black dress, covered with black net, and with black net shoulder-straps. It was not new, but she had seldom had any occasion for wearing it, and she had enough money in hand for the housekeeping to enable her to buy a pair of black artificial silk stockings and slim black satin shoes with high heels.

Round her thick, light hair she tied a black velvet band with a spray of forget-me-nots worked in blue silk across it, but instinct told her to leave her full, beautiful throat unadorned by any of the few cheap ornaments that she possessed. Her smooth skin showed a sort of golden glow that merged imperceptibly into the warm pallor of her round arms and the dimpled base of her neck.

Elsie looked for a long while at herself in the glass, rubbed lip-salve into her already scarlet mouth, and, despite the "Japanesey" effect of lids that seemed half-closed, wondered at the brilliant light in her own hazel-grey eyes.

Leslie Morrison came for her, and they left the house together before Williams arrived from the office.

To both of them it was an unforgettable evening.

Elsie, like all women of her type, was a born dancer. Nevertheless, before the evening was half over, they had left the crowded hall for a screened alcove in an upper gallery, where the reiterated refrain of syncopated airs, and the wistful rhythm of valse-times, reached them through the haze of ascending cigarette-smoke.

It was three o'clock when they exchanged a last close, passionate embrace and Elsie, pale, exhausted, with indescribably shining eyes, crept upstairs to her room, undressed, and lay down noiselessly by the side of her husband to relive the evening that she had spent with her lover.

Williams left the house next morning without waking her, but it was that evening that the inevitable crisis came.

The solicitor returned home nearly two hours before his usual time, and found Leslie Morrison just preparing to enter the house.

112

The two men went in together.

Elsie started violently at the sight of her husband, and then laughed artificially. "Hullo! It's a case of Oh, what a surprise, isn't it? You're back early, Horace."

"Yes," said her husband.

"I hope you're not too tired after last night," Morrison began.

"Oh no, thanks! It was fine. Horace, I haven't told you about the dance yet. It's a shame you weren't there."

The moment she said the words, Elsie knew that she had made a mistake.

"Yes," Williams remarked quietly, "you'd have liked me to be there, wouldn't you? Well, let me inform you that you aren't going to any more dances for the present."

"Whatever do you mean, Horace?"

"Morrison knows what I mean all right, and so do you, you little ——" His low, snarling tone gave the effect of spitting the ugly word at her.

Leslie Morrison sprang to his feet. "Look here, sir——"

The solicitor held up his hand. "That'll do. It's not for you to adopt that tone in speaking to me, you know. Please to remember that I'm Elsie's husband."

"Look here," Morrison began again, "I'm perfectly ready to make a clean breast of it. I do love Elsie. Her and me were just pals at first, and then I suppose I didn't exactly realise where I was drifting. But I'm free to confess that I lost my head one—one evening a little while ago—and I told her I loved her." He glanced at Elsie, as though for a further cue.

"And of course she told you that she was a pure woman, and a loving wife, and you must never speak like that again?" sneered Horace Williams.

"Elsie, don't let him speak like that.... Tell him!" urged Morrison.

"I don't need any telling," Williams retorted smoothly. "She thinks she's in love with you, of course."

"I am in love with Leslie," said Elsie suddenly. "And if you did the decent thing, Horace, you'd set me free to marry him. You and me have never been happy together. I didn't ever ought to have married you, but I was a young fool."

"Understand this, the pair of you," said the little solicitor clearly and deliberately. "I shall never set you free, as you call it. You've married me, and you've got to stay with me. As for you," he turned to Leslie Morrison, "you can leave my house. And understand clearly that I won't have you inside it again. And if I catch you

113

speaking to my wife again, or meeting her, or having anything whatsoever to do with her, it'll be the worse for you."

Morrison took a sudden step forward, his hands clenched, and Elsie screamed, but Horace Williams stood his ground.

"I'm well within my rights, and you know it," he declared. "I could horsewhip you, in fact, and if you were fool enough to bring a case for assault it'd go against you. Clear out! That's my last word to you."

"Will you let Elsie have a divorce?"

"No, I won't."

"Will you let her have a legal separation, then? You've her own word for it that she's not happy with you. I'm not thinking of myself, but you can't have the cruelty to keep her tied to you when she's miserable. Let her have her freedom."

For all answer, Williams pointed to the door. The expression of his face had not altered by a hair's-breadth.

Morrison turned to Elsie, white and tense. "Elsie, you hear what he says. What d'you want me to do?"

Elsie had lost her nerve. She began to cry hysterically. Instead of answering Morrison's appeal, she turned to her husband.

"Why can't you let us just be pals, Leslie and me?" she sobbed. "You bring your horrid, mean jealousy into everything. I s'pose you don't grudge me having a friend of my own age, do you?"

Leslie Morrison instantly and loyally followed her lead. "If Elsie is kind enough to let me be her friend, and—and take her out every now and then, and that sort of thing, I'm willing to forget what's just passed, and simply ask you as man to man if you've any objection to us being, as she says, just pals," he said steadily enough.

"I have every objection. You young fool, Elsie has just said in so many words that she's in love with you. Did you mean that, Elsie, or did you not?"

Elsie sobbed more and more violently, and her voice rose to an incoherent screech. "How do I know what I mean or don't mean, when you make a row like this? But I'll tell you this much, anyway, it's true what he said; I'm wretched with you, and if you were half a man, you'd set me free."

"There, that's enough," said Williams. "Going round and round in a circle won't help any of us, and you ought to know by this time, Elsie, that I always mean what I say. You'll please to remember what you were when I married you—a little fool of a typist, without a penny, whose mother kept a boarding-house and was only too glad of the money I gave her. It doesn't take a genius to say what would have happened to you if you hadn't found a man fool enough to marry you, either."

114

"Stop that!" Morrison shouted.

The solicitor blinked at him quietly. "I've twice told you to get out of my house," he observed. "Don't make me say it a third time. It'll be the worse, if you do—for Elsie."

"Are you threatening her, you—you brute, you?"

"I object to your friendship with my wife. That's all—and enough too. Now go."

"Oh yes, go!" said Elsie suddenly, breaking into renewed sobs and tears. "I can't stand this. You'd better go, Leslie boy, really you had. I shall do myself in, that's all."

"Don't talk like that——" the youth began frantically, but Williams opened the door, and stood silently pointing to it.

There was something strangely inexorable in his little, trivial figure and sinister, passionless expression.

"Elsie," said Morrison brokenly, "if ever you want me, send for me. I'll come!"

He went out of the room, and they heard him go down the stairs and let himself out at the front door.

"That's the end of that," said Williams in a quiet, satisfied voice. "Stop that howling, Elsie. You didn't really suppose that I didn't know what was going on?"

She sobbed and would not answer.

There was a long silence, and at last Elsie, face downwards on the sofa, began to feel frightened and curious. She bore it as long as she could, and then looked up.

Her husband was gazing out of the window, in which a potted aspidistra stood upon a wicker stand between soiled white curtains.

At the slight movement that she made he turned his head. "Elsie, tell me. Did you really mean what you said, that you're in love with that boy?"

To her incredulous surprise, his voice had become hoarse and almost maudlin.

"You only said it to make me angry, didn't you?"

In a flash Elsie saw the wisdom of allowing him at least to pretend to such a belief. "Perhaps I did," she said slowly. "Anyway, it's true enough that we aren't particularly happy together, and never have been. And I meant what I said about a separation, right enough, Horace."

"You won't get one," said Williams, and his voice had become vicious-sounding once more. "And remember what I've said—that fellow is never to set foot in here again, and you and he are not to meet in future."

The following morning Elsie went to the High Street post-office and found there the letter that she had expected.

"My Own Darling Girlie,

"What is to be done? I can't tell you, darling, what a
hound I felt to leave you all alone with that jealous brute
yesterday and yet the awful thing is that he has the right to
you and I have none. Oh, Elsie life is hard isn't it darling? I
wish I could take you away but that cannot be and it is you
that have to bear the brunt of it all except that I am in hell
knowing what you are going through all the time. Perhaps
that is not an expression I ought to use to you but you must
excuse it for I hardly know what I am writing.

"One of our chaps has gone sick, and they are sending
me to the North instead of him which means we can't meet
again as I go off to-morrow. But write to me darling and
tell me what it is best to do now. Would it simplify things if
we were to be just friends and no more?

"Cheer up, Elsie perhaps some day things may come
right for us—who knows? He may die; doesn't he always
say there is something wrong with him?

"A thousand kisses for you, dearie. I have your sweet
photo with me and love to look at it and re-read your
wonderful letters. Write and tell me everything, and what
you think we had better do. Shall we be able to meet when I
come back at the end of the month?

"No more at present, from

"Your own true lover, Leslie,
"Boy."

To Elsie, Leslie Morrison's love-letters were wonderful.

She read and re-read this one, but when she had answered it,
she burnt it.

Certain words of the clairvoyante, whom she had once visited
with Irene Tidmarsh, she had never been able to forget, and of late
they had haunted her anew.

"Beware of the written word...."

Elsie burnt all Morrison's letters to her, and asked him to burn
all those that she wrote him.

Gradually these letters that passed between them grew to be the
most important factor in her life.

Elsie, who had detested writing, now desired nothing so much
as to pour out her soul on paper, and the limitations that she found
imposed upon her through lack of education and the power to
express herself made her angry.

Again and again she asked Morrison in her letters to take her

116

away, and after a time his steadfast refusals bred in her mind the first unbearable suspicion that her passion was the greater of the two. Her letters became wilder and wilder.

Sometimes she threatened suicide, or gave hysterical and entirely imaginary descriptions of scenes with her husband; sometimes she expressed a reckless desire for Horace's death, or asked if she could "give him something" unspecified. These phrases, to a large extent, were meaningless, but Elsie frantically hoped by them to impress upon Morrison the extent of her love for him.

When he got back from the North of England they met surreptitiously.

A certain café in a small street not far from Elsie's home became their rendezvous. Sometimes Morrison was able to get there in the middle of the day, but generally he came at about five o'clock, and they had tea together. Very occasionally they met early in the afternoon and went out together.

Each meeting was entirely inconclusive, save in exciting Elsie almost to frenzy and reducing young Morrison to further depths of despondency.

The months dragged on. Morrison was often away, and then he and Elsie wrote to one another daily. She was entirely obsessed with the thought of her lover, and hardly ever saw Irene Tidmarsh, or went to Hillbourne Terrace. And all the while, Horace Williams said nothing.

He and his wife did not quarrel; indeed, they hardly spoke to one another, but the atmosphere between them, day by day, was becoming more heavily charged with mutual hatred and apprehension.

VI

The tension under which Elsie now lived began at last to affect her health. She slept badly, and was nervous as she had never been before.

Williams watched her without comment—a sinister little figure. Sometimes, utterly overwrought, Elsie tried to force a scene with him, but she only once succeeded in making him evince anger.

Strangely reckless, she suddenly suggested that Leslie Morrison should be invited to lodge in their house, with no slightest expectation that her husband would entertain such a scheme, but

117

with a wild desire to provoke him to a scene that should release some of her own pent-up emotion.

"He's looking for rooms, Geraldine says," she declared, "and we've a bedroom to spare, and might as well use it."

Williams gazed at her incredulously. "Are you aware that I've shown Morrison the door once already?" he asked at last.

"Yes, I'm quite aware of that," said Elsie, with insolence in her voice. "I thought you might have got more sense now, that's all."

"Listen to me, Elsie. I forbade you to speak to that fellow again—and by God, if you've done so, I'll see you never forget it!" His face was livid and he spoke through his clenched teeth.

"I'll speak to whom I please."

"Have you been meeting Morrison?"

"Why shouldn't I?"

Elsie felt a curious pleasure and relief in thus mocking at the furious jealousy that was evident in her husband's face and manner.

"Answer my question."

She remained silent.

"Are you and that fellow in love?"

"I've answered that before. I told you months ago, when you first started to insult me, that he was nothing to me."

"That wasn't true then—and it isn't now. Morrison's in love with you, damn him, and you're in love with him!"

"Am I?"

Elsie laughed derisively in the new and uncomprehended realisation that she was no longer afraid of Horace.

"You little bitch!..."

He caught her by the shoulders and suddenly flung her against the wall.

Elsie screamed, but it was reflex action from the physical shock alone that made her do so. She was neither frightened nor very much startled. There was even an odd exhilaration for her in the sudden release of those pent-up forces that had for so long vibrated tensely between herself and her husband.

However, her arm and shoulder were bruised, and her whole body violently jarred. "You're a coward!" she panted. "Hitting a woman!"

"You drove me to it.... Elsie, get up!... I'm sorry I did that, but you're driving me mad. God, if I had that fellow here I'd wring the life out of him!"

"No, you wouldn't," Elsie taunted him. "He's a great deal stronger than you are—he's a man, he is—you'd never dare to touch him. All you can do is to knock a woman about."

"That's a lie! I've never touched you before, though there's

118

many a man in my place would have beaten you within an inch of your life. I didn't know what I was doing just now."

He took a step towards her, but Elsie pulled herself up from the floor without appearing to notice the movement. She felt slightly giddy, and her head ached.

"Aren't you going to—to forgive me? I oughtn't to have hit you, I acknowledge, but you've done everything to drive me to it. Elsie, swear to me that there's nothing now between you and Morrison."

"Oh, all right," she said wearily. "I swear it." She felt that she no longer cared what happened in a sudden overwhelming fatigue.

"I don't believe you," said Williams bitterly.

Elsie shrugged her shoulders, and turned, moving stiffly, to leave the room.

"Are you—are you hurt?"

"Yes, of course I am. My shoulder will be black and blue to-morrow, I should think."

"Shall I get you anything?" Williams muttered, shamefaced.

She made no answer.

That afternoon Elsie rang up Leslie Morrison on the telephone after her husband had gone out. "Is that you, Les?"

"Yes. How's yourself?"

He had told her never to be prodigal of verbal endearments in their telephone communications, and she knew that he was probably not alone, but it struck her painfully that his tone was a purely casual one, such as he might have used to anyone.

"We've had an awful scene, boy."

"What—who?"

"Him—Horace—and me. The same old thing, of course—jealousy. I stood up to him, and told him I didn't intend to put up with that sort of treatment any longer, and I'd never give up anyone I—I liked."

"I say, Elsie, you were careful, weren't you?" asked Morrison, his voice grown anxious.

"Yes, yes, darling, of course I was, for your sake. But Leslie—this is what happened—he knocked me down."

There was a smothered exclamation that made her heart leap with sudden exultation. Of course Leslie cared....

"Elsie—girlie—he didn't! Are you hurt?"

She could have laughed in pure joy at his sharply-anxious question.

"Nothing bad. Shaken, of course, and I expect there'll be a bad bruise, but I can put up with worse than that, you know."

"You oughtn't to have to! The hound! I'd like to.... Look here, can't we meet?"

119

"Yes, yes!" she said eagerly. "What about tea? I'll come to——"

"The same place," he interrupted quickly, and she understood that he did not want her to mention the name of the tea-shop that had so often served them as rendezvous.

"What time?"

"About half-past five. I shan't get away any earlier."

"All right, darling. I'll be there."

"Sure you're all right?"

"Yes, quite all right now," Elsie declared, laughing happily.

"I must go. See you later, then?"

"Yes. Good-bye, boy."

The answering good-bye came to her faintly over the wires as the final click warned her that he had hung up the receiver.

Elsie looked at the clock on the mantelpiece. Only three o'clock—two hours and a quarter before she could think of starting out.

The telephone rang again, and Elsie, with a joyful hope that Morrison had been unable to resist a further word, snatched at the instrument.

"Hallo, hallo! Who's there?"

"I am—Horace," said her husband's flat, nasal voice. "Look here. How would you like to go to the play to-night, Elsie?"

"What!" said Elsie, disappointed at not hearing Leslie Morrison's voice again, and still dazed from the scene of the morning.

"I said, how would you like to do a theatre to-night? I've got tickets for 'The Girl on the Pier'—good places—for to-night."

She understood at last that he was seeking to propitiate her, and to make up for his violence. "I don't mind. What time does it start?"

"Half-past eight, but we'd better meet in town somewhere for some food. I shan't have time to come home first. What about the Corner House, at about seven o'clock? That'll give us plenty of time to go on to Shaftesbury Avenue afterwards."

"All right. How many tickets have you got, Horace?"

"Just the two. I thought you and I would go by ourselves and have a jolly evening," said the far-away voice rather tremulously.

Elsie laughed drearily as she rang off.

It seemed to her that the time dragged interminably until she could go upstairs and dress herself for the evening's outing. She meant to meet Morrison first and then go on to the Corner House and wait there for her husband.

Elsie put on a dark blue coat and skirt, with a new pale blue

120

jumper of artificial silk, and a big black hat with a blue feather. Round her neck she wore a small black fur.

After her variable wont, she had suddenly recovered her looks, after the sodden, stupefied ugliness that the morning's unhappiness had produced in her. Her eyes seemed more widely opened than usual, her hair fell into thick curls and rings, and a soft, bright colour lay under her oddly prominent cheek-bones. She rubbed lip-stick on to her full, sulkily-cut mouth, and lavishly powdered her straight, beautiful neck. The glow of excitement and gladness transformed her as she went out to meet Morrison, slamming the door of the villa behind her.

"Darling!"

"My own dear little girl!" said Leslie, and held both her gloved hands for a moment in his. "I haven't been able to think of anything but what you told me this afternoon. Are we going for a walk, or will you come in?"

"I'd like to come in and sit down," said Elsie languidly. "Have you had tea?"

"No. I'll order some."

"Not for me, boy. I'm meeting Horace for a meal in about an hour and a half. We're going to the theatre."

"Have you made it up, then?"

"Oh, I suppose so! He telephoned and said he had these tickets. I suppose he thought it'd make up, in a way."

They chose a corner table at the further end of the tea-shop, and Elsie took off her coat and leant against it as it lay folded over the back of her chair.

"Where did he hurt you this morning?" said Morrison intently.

She pulled up the loose sleeve of her silk jumper. "Look!"

Her smooth, soft arm was already discoloured all round the elbow and up to the shoulder.

"It's worse higher up, only I can't get at it now to show you."

"Damn him!" Leslie Morrison muttered between his teeth.

His boyish face was black with an intensity of feeling that Elsie had seldom seen there of late. It sent a rush of joyful reassurance all through her.

"Darling, I don't care about anything while we've got each other."

"But it can't go on, Elsie. He's making your life miserable. Isn't there any hope of a divorce, or even a separation?"

"He says he never will."

Elsie spoke slowly. She was revolving a possibility, that she had often viewed before in her own mind.

121

"Les, can't we go away together? I don't care what happens, or what people think of me. I'd face anything, with you."

Even as she spoke, she knew—and one side of her was relieved to know—that Morrison would negative the suggestion, as he had often done before.

"Out of the question, darling girl. Think what I'm getting—two twenty-five a year and no particular prospect of a rise for years to come. And look at what you've been used to!"

"Not before I married."

"Times were different then. It was before the war. Living has gone up five hundred per cent. since then, and it'll be many a long year before it comes down again. Why, Elsie, we couldn't even live!"

"I don't know whether you think I'm living now!" she exclaimed vehemently. "Existing, I call it. And we shall only be young once, Leslie, and it seems so hard to waste it all."

He groaned, and they sat silent for a time, their hands locked together beneath the table.

"Would you be ready to—to end it all?" she asked suddenly. "I mean for us to go out together, right out of life?"

"Do you mean suicide?"

"Yes—a suicide pact."

She fixed her eyes upon him, anxious to believe that he was startled, and acutely touched, at the lengths to which her love could carry her. The actual idea behind the word—that of suicide—conveyed very little to her. Although she believed herself to be fully in earnest, Elsie never seriously contemplated her own death, nor that of her lover.

She had often thought of Williams's death as the one possible solution of their problem, but she had actually never really abandoned the secret expectation that a way out would be found for herself and Morrison that would secure their happiness.

She had read of suicide-pacts, and seized upon the idea eagerly as one more peg upon which to hang the proofs of her passion for Morrison, and maintain his love, and his interest in herself, at the level of her own ardour. Although never consciously owning it to herself, Elsie knew that his love was a lesser one than hers.

Leslie Morrison, now, did not make the passionate response for which she had hoped. "Don't talk like that. Oh, Elsie, it is hard, isn't it? And you don't know what it's like for me to think of that brute making your life miserable. If only there was anything I could do!... I think about it till I see red sometimes. Why doesn't he die?"

"Because we want him to, I suppose," said Elsie, suddenly listless. "He's always talking about his health failing, and things like that, but I don't see any sign of it myself. Things will never come right for us in this world, Leslie."

"Elsie, I'll make him get a separation; I swear I will. It's the only possible thing. Then at least you'll be free."

She noticed that he did not refer to the separation between herself and her husband as to a means of furthering their own love.

"Haven't your people ever tried to get your freedom for you?"

"Oh, I've nobody much, you know! Only mother and Geraldine, and the old aunties. They don't approve of me either—never did."

"Poor little girl, they don't understand you!"

"I don't care while I've got you, Leslie."

They made love to one another, their voices low, until Morrison reminded Elsie suddenly that it was late.

"You'll hardly get to the West End by seven now. I'm glad you're going to enjoy yourself to-night, anyway."

"I wish we were going together, Les, just you and I. That's how it ought to be. Are we going to meet to-morrow, dearest?"

"Lunch here, can you? One o'clock. And meanwhile, darling, I'm going to think hard what I can do to make things better for you. He's got to stop leading you this sort of life, anyway, and it's up to me to find a way of making him do so. When I think of his knocking you about...."

The blood rushed into his face, and Elsie saw that he had clenched his hand involuntarily. It was balm to her to realise that she still had the power of exciting him to a frenzied anxiety on her account.

"He's hit me before now, you know," she said suddenly, hardly realising, and caring not at all, that she was not speaking the truth.

"You never told me. I've sometimes wondered...."

"I didn't mean to say anything about it. I knew it would upset you.... Never mind, darling, I don't care."

"But I do. I tell you it's driving me mad. Oh, what's the good of talking when one can't do anything! Look here, darling, I'm not fit to talk to you now—and besides, you'll be frightfully late. I shall see you to-morrow."

"One o'clock. Good-night, sweetheart. I wish it was you and me going to this show to-night. Wouldn't it be heaven!"

"Indeed it would. But things may come right for us even yet, darling—don't give up hope. Good-bye."

"Good-bye!" she echoed.

Elsie was late for her appointment with her husband, but he did not complain. He seemed anxious to do everything in his power to conciliate her, and it was characteristic of their relations together

123

that, as her fear of his sarcastic petulance vanished, so her contempt for him increased.

"I got dress-circle places," said Williams impressively. "I know you like them."

The piece, a musical comedy, amused her, and she was pleased at various glances that were cast upon her by their neighbours in the theatre. At the back of it all was a warm inward glow that pervaded all her consciousness at the remembrance of Leslie Morrison's championship of her, his assurance that he would "think out a way."

Perhaps Leslie would make up his mind to take her away. She had asked him to do so, and he had always refused. Elsie, with an ever-latent fear that Morrison was already beginning to tire of an attachment that to her was the one reality in life, told herself passionately that, with him, she would care nothing for poverty.

"It's good, isn't it?" said her husband's nasal voice.

"Rather. Topping!"

For a minute or two she listened to the comedian on the stage, and was genuinely amused by his facial contortions and wilful mispronunciations of polysyllabic words.

"He's so silly, you can't help laughing at him," Elsie declared, wiping her eyes.

Then she drifted back again into the dream wherein she and Leslie Morrison figured as sole protagonists, with complete and unexplained elimination of Horace Williams.

"Look who's here, Elsie!"

She started violently, convinced against all reason that she would see Morrison.

"Isn't that your aunties?"

"So it is," said Elsie without enthusiasm.

Aunt Ada and Aunt Gertie were making violent signs to her, and in the interval Horace, still evidently bent upon doing everything possible to please her, insisted upon going to speak to them, and suggested supper after the play.

"He is going it," Elsie reflected dispassionately, not in the least touched, but a good deal amazed at the lavishness of Horace's amends.

She was in reality very much bored by the company of the two aunts in the little restaurant to which they eventually went.

"Why don't you go and see your poor mother, Elsie?"

"I do see her, Aunt Gertie."

"Not very often, dear."

"As often as I've time for," said Elsie curtly.

"Geraldine's not looking well," Aunt Ada began next.

"What happened to that young fellow she was supposed to be going with last year?"

Horace Williams called abruptly for his bill. "It's after twelve, and I've got to be at work to-morrow, if you ladies haven't. All good things must come to an end, you know."

"It's been most pleasant, I'm sure," said Aunt Gertie.

And when Horace had gone to pay the account at the cash-desk, she added sentimentally to Elsie:

"It's a real pleasure to have seen you and him together—and so happy."

"Thanks," said Elsie sarcastically. "We're as happy as the day is long, of course."

"So you ought to be," said Aunt Ada very sharply.

They exchanged good-byes outside the restaurant, and Elsie and her husband went by Tube to their own station.

The long suburban road was almost deserted when they came out into it.

"We'll go by the Grove, of course," said Elsie, indicating the narrow alleyway that eventually merged into their own street, with a high blank wall upon one side of it and the backs of a rather sordid row of houses upon the other.

A few leafless plane-trees showed above the top of the wall, and an occasional tall lamp slightly relieved the gloom of the long, paved passage-way.

Their footsteps on the stones were clearly audible in the unusual stillness that belonged both to the deserted locality and to the small hours of the morning.

"Who's that?" said Horace so suddenly that Elsie jumped.

Footsteps were hurrying behind them, and they both turned. With a strange sense of foreknowledge, Elsie saw Leslie Morrison.

The two men stopped dead as they came face to face with one another. Elsie shrank back against the high yellow brick wall, her eyes fixed upon Morrison's ravaged face.

"I couldn't rest for thinking of it all. I know what happened to-day, Williams," he said in a high, strained voice. "It can't go on. You're making Elsie's life hell. Give her her freedom."

"Damn you! Who are you to interfere between man and wife?" said Williams, low and fiercely. "I know what you want, both of you, but you won't have it. Elsie's my wife, and I shan't let her go."

"You've got to."

Horace Williams, looking full at the youth, who was shaking from head to foot with excitement, gave his low, malevolent laugh.

Almost at the same instant Elsie heard her own voice

125

screaming, "Don't ... don't...!" and saw the flash of a knife as Morrison raised his arm and struck again and again.

Williams spun round as though to run, and his eyes, oddly surprised-looking, glared, straight and unseeing, at Elsie.

Leslie Morrison stabbed at him again in the back.

"What have you done?" sobbed Elsie to Morrison. "Oh, go!"

She saw Morrison dash away up the passage, and at the same moment Horace Williams took a few steps forward.

"Keep up—I'll help you!" gasped Elsie.

She thrust her arm beneath his elbow, dimly astonished and relieved to find that he was walking, when he suddenly lurched heavily against her, the upper part of his body sagging forward. Then he fell heavily and lay motionless, blood trickling from his mouth.

Elsie, utterly distraught, and her knees shaking under her, felt her screams strangled in her throat. A distant figure showed at the near end of the alley, and she flew, rather than ran, towards the stranger, calling out in a high, sobbing voice for a doctor—for help.

The woman, elderly and respectable-looking, asked what had happened.

"I don't know," said Elsie. A blind horror was upon her, but instinct warned her to make no definite statement of any kind.

A nightmare confusion followed. The alleyway, from being a silent and deserted spot, became clamorous with footsteps and voices. Elsie dimly heard a tall man in evening clothes saying that he was a doctor, and saw him kneel beside the blood-spattered form huddled upon the pavement. It was he, and a stalwart policeman, who finally lifted that which had been Horace Williams on to a hand-ambulance and took it away.

Another man in police uniform took Elsie's arm, giving her the support that alone enabled her to move, and helped her to a taxi.

She almost fell into it, weeping hysterically, and he took his place beside her as a matter of course. In the sick, convulsed terror that shook her, his stolid presence was an actual relief. She thought that he was taking her home until he gently explained that she was coming with him to the police-station.

"We want to get this cleared up, you know, and you can help us by telling us just what happened."

A new and more dreadful fear came over her. If Horace was dead someone would be accused of having killed him. They might suspect her.... Elsie felt as though she were going mad with the horror of it all.

She began hysterically to scream and cry.

VII

It was still early in the day when Elsie's mother came to her at the police-station. Her fat face was white, stained and mottled with tears.

"It seems too bad to be true," she kept on repeating again and again. "That's what I said when I heard about poor Horace: too bad to be true. And you in this dreadful place, Elsie, and such a state as you're in—and no wonder. The whole thing seems too bad to be true."

"Have they—found anything? Shall I be able to go home soon?" asked Elsie.

"I don't know, dearie. They've got to find out who killed poor Horace, you know. Elsie, you've always been a sensible girl. You must tell them all you know, however dreadful to you it is to speak of such things. Or I'll tell them for you, if you'd rather just have it out with mother. Didn't you see anyone?"

"Someone flew past, and as I turned to speak to Horace, I saw the blood coming out of his mouth."

"Who was it flew past?" said Mrs. Palmer.

"I don't know. It all happened in a flash, like," said Elsie.

"You and Horace were happy together, weren't you?"

"Yes, always," said Elsie stolidly. She had made up her mind not to say anything else.

"You didn't quarrel?"

"No, never."

"You'll tell them that, won't you, dearie? The police, I mean."

"It's nothing to do with them," said Elsie childishly.

"Now don't talk that way. That's silly. You don't seem to realise, my lady, the sort of mess you're in."

Mrs. Palmer's voice rose to stridency as she let her fear and her temper get the mastery of her attempt at caution.

"My God, Elsie, can't you see what it means? They may try you for murder. Murder—the same as the horrid common people in the newspapers. Who's to know what happened—you and Horace in that empty street at one o'clock in the morning, and he gets done in, and whatever you may say—and mind you, I'll back you up in it—they'll get hold of the fact that you and poor Horace didn't hit it off together."

"We were quite happy together."

"That's right," said Mrs. Palmer approvingly. "You stick to that."

127

Then she began to cry. "To think it should have come to this! I that have always held my head high—I don't know what your aunts will say! It'll be an awful shock for them."

Elsie hardly heard what her mother was saying. Waves of physical nausea kept on passing over her, and she was conscious of nothing but thankfulness when an elderly woman in uniform came to her with a cup of tea, and suggested that she should lie down and get some sleep.

Elsie followed her, scarcely replying to Mrs. Palmer's voluble farewell and assurances of her own speedy return.

She could not afterwards have told where it was that she was taken, but a small, narrow bed awaited her, and she flung herself on to it and fell almost at once into the trance-like sleep of utter bodily and mental exhaustion.

The same uniformed woman was waiting for her when she woke, after several hours, and the sight of her brought back in a sick rush the horrors of the morning.

"Oh, I must go home!" cried Elsie.

The woman took very little notice of her words, but she conducted her to a lavatory and helped her to make her toilette.

Cold water and the effects of sleep combined slightly to steady the wretched Elsie. "I should like to go home at once, please," she said, in a voice that she tried in vain to render firm.

"Yes. Well, I daresay your mother will take you away as soon as you've answered a few questions," said the woman indifferently and quietly. "They want you downstairs first for a few minutes now."

"Is Mother there?"

"She's in the waiting-room. You'll be able to see her afterwards."

"Afterwards?"

Elsie's agonised perceptions fastened upon that one word. She sought with frantic and irrational intensity to pierce the veiled threat that she felt it to convey.

A man whom she knew to be a police-inspector appeared at an open door, and the uniformed woman went away.

"Now, Mrs. Williams, I'm afraid we must trouble you for a short statement," said the man pleasantly. "Will you follow me, if you please?"

He moved forward, and Elsie saw into the room that he had just left.

Leslie Morrison was within it.

As their eyes met, it seemed to Elsie that the last shreds of self-control deserted her, and she screamed on a high and hideous note

128

words that came incoherently and frenziedly from some power outside herself.

"Leslie, Leslie! Oh, God, what shall I do? Why did you do it? I didn't ever mean you to do it.... I must tell the truth...."

The inspector swung sharply round and gripped her by the arm. "Do you realise what you're saying? It is my duty to caution you that anything you say now may be used in evidence against you."

Elsie burst into hysterical sobs and tears.

The man pushed her gently into another room where another official and a young man in plain clothes sat at a table with papers and pens in front of them.

The interrogatory that followed was conducted with grave suavity by the senior official, but Elsie was conscious only of a horror of committing herself.

She said again and again that she and her husband had always been happy together.

It was a faint relief when at last they came to actual questions of fact, and she could reply with direct statements to the enquiries as to her movements on the previous evening.

(O God, was it only last night that she and Horace had gone to the theatre—only this morning that they had started to walk home from the Tube station?)

"Mrs. Williams, I want you to tell me in your own words exactly what happened in the alleyway just before your husband was struck."

Elsie realised with despair that she must say something.

She was not imaginative, but almost without her own knowledge she had evolved a sort of account by which, it seemed to her, confusedly, that she might safeguard herself.

"We were walking along," she said in a trembling, almost inaudible voice, "and there wasn't anybody in sight, and suddenly someone rushed up from behind and pushed me away from my husband. I was sort of dazed for a moment—I think I must have been pushed against the wall—and when I recovered I saw Horace— my husband—struggling with a man. Then the man ran away."

"Did you see the man's face?"

"No," said Elsie, with ashen lips.

"But you know who it was?"

"It was Leslie Morrison."

The room reeled before her eyes, and she made an ineffectual clutch at a chair.

Through a sort of thick fog she heard the official repeating in a low tone: "It was the man known as Leslie Morrison."

Then she felt herself fall.

129

Her mother was with her when she recovered consciousness, and the woman who had attended to her before, and whom Mrs. Palmer now repeatedly and volubly addressed as "Matron."

Elsie looked round her, but the officials were gone. With a groan she let her head drop backwards again on to the rail of the chair in which she found herself.

"Come along now, don't give way. You're better now," said the matron briskly. "Don't let yourself go, Mrs. Williams."

"Oh, Elsie, Elsie," wailed Mrs. Palmer, "whatever will become of us? Didn't I always tell you——"

"Give her an arm, Mrs. Palmer, and I'll take her on the other side, and we'll get her into the other room. There's a nice couch there, and she can lie down a bit."

They half led, half dragged Elsie away, the matron exhorting her all the time with impersonal, professional brightness to pull herself together.

She was conscious of thankfulness when the woman left her alone with her mother, although leaving the door open behind her.

Mrs. Palmer instantly bent forward and asked with avidity: "What did you say to them, Elsie?"

"Let me alone, Mother, for pity's sake!"

"How can I let you alone, as you call it, you unnatural girl? What a way to speak to your own mother, on whom you're bringing sorrow and shame, and may bring worse yet, if you're not careful! Now you tell me this, Elsie Williams, directly this minute: Did you or did you not tell them that you and Horace were on bad terms together?"

"I said we were quite happy together——"

"Stick to that," said Mrs. Palmer significantly. "Did anyone know—any neighbour or anybody—that you quarrelled? He never made a row, or knocked you about, did he?"

"Only the once," Elsie said automatically.

She pushed up her sleeve, then shuddered violently as she recalled that she had last made use of that same gesture in the tea-shop with Morrison.

"My goodness, did Horace do that? You must have tried him pretty high, I know. How are you going to account for that bruise, young Elsie?"

"Who's to know about it?"

"Oh, they'll find out fast enough! They get to know about everything. Look here, did you say that you'd been pushed against the wall by whoever it was who did in poor Horace?"

Elsie nodded, too much stunned even to wonder how her mother had become possessed of this information.

"Very well, then. Those bruises on your arm are where you fell against that wall. Don't forget. I shall say you showed them to me, and told me about it."

"Say what—when?" Elsie asked stupidly. "I suppose all this'll be over before I'm quite mad, and they'll let me go home to-day."

Her mother's fat face puckered up suddenly, and she began to cry with loud, gulping sobs. "I don't know!" she wailed. "I don't know."

"But what—what—for Heaven's sake, Mother, stop that noise, and tell me what they're going to do. What is it?" almost shrieked Elsie, striving to fight down the panic that threatened to overwhelm her.

"Don't you understand, you little fool? (God forgive me for speaking like that!) Oh, Elsie, I'm afraid—I'm afraid they'll—they'll arrest you—for murder!"

"Don't use that word!" almost screamed Elsie.

"How can I help it? Murder's what's been done, and it lies between you and that fellow Morrison. Elsie, how far have things gone between you and him? But there, I needn't ask. I know you." Mrs. Palmer wept convulsively.

She remained with her daughter until late in the afternoon, and twice during that time Elsie was summoned to a further interrogatory. She learnt that Morrison's knife had been found close to the alley, and that he had been fetched from his office early in the day and taken away by the police.

It was after her mother had gone away, as the dusk was gathering, that Elsie Williams and Leslie Morrison were charged together with the wilful murder of Horace Williams.

"For God's sake, Mrs. Williams, tell me the whole truth!"

Elsie looked dumbly at Mr. Cleaver, too sick with fright to speak.

"Do you understand that you're in the most frightful danger?"

A sound that just amounted to an interrogation forced its way between her dry lips.

"You know what the sentence is for anyone found guilty of wilful murder?"

Elsie screamed and shrank.

Cleaver bent forward, deep dents coming and going at the corners of his nostrils, his white face working with earnestness. She could see the sweat shining upon his forehead.

"Try and understand. You will be committed for trial for the murder of your husband."

"But Leslie Morrison...."

131

"He's in the same boat. His one idea, it seems, is to shield you—to pay the whole of the penalty himself."

"It was him who—who...." Elsie's voice trailed away.

"I know. But who inspired him to do it, Mrs. Williams? I tell you that nothing but absolute frankness can give you a chance."

"Shall I be in the witness-box?"

A bewildered idea that she could still make use of her charm to serve her present cause made Elsie ask the question.

"You will be in the dock," said Cleaver grimly. "Understand that everything—your life itself—depends upon your being absolutely straightforward with me. Don't conceal anything—don't attempt to. I tell you, it's your one hope."

Elsie stared and stared at Mr. Cleaver. "I never meant Leslie to do it!" she cried suddenly and wildly.

"But you knew he was going to?"

"No, no, no!"

"Mrs. Williams, tell me the truth. You and Morrison were madly in love with one another, and had been for over a year?"

She nodded.

"You knew that your husband would never, in any circumstances, set you free?"

"Yes. We asked him, begged him to. He—he was very cruel, Mr. Cleaver."

"You and Morrison would not face open scandal by going away together?"

"It wasn't that."

"What was it, then?"

She hesitated, twisting her handkerchief round and round in her fingers.

The solicitor moistened his lips with his tongue. "Your only hope, your one and only hope in this world, Mrs. Williams, is to speak the truth. I'm powerless to help you if you won't be open. Don't be afraid that everything you say now will come out in the police-court; it won't necessarily be so at all—far from it. But I can judge of nothing unless I know every single thing."

"I'll tell you," said Elsie, white to the lips.

"Why would you and Morrison not have gone away together? Were you afraid?"

"We had no money."

"I see. Morrison's pay was very small, and you had nothing but what your husband gave you?"

"Yes."

"Whereas if you were a widow, you had reason to suppose that Williams would leave you comfortably provided for?"

132

"Yes."

"Did it not occur to you, then, that his death would be a very convenient solution of the whole problem?"

"Oh yes! How could I help thinking that?"

"You not only thought it, Mrs. Williams, you said it, and you wrote it."

"I never——" The denial sprang from her quite instinctively.

Mr. Cleaver put up his hand authoritatively. "Wait! Do you remember a conversation with a friend of yours, Miss Irene Tidmarsh, on the eighteenth of last October, when you made use of the words, 'I wish to the Lord that Horace would do the decent thing or go West, and let me have a chance of happiness'?"

Elsie was terrified at the precision with which her very words were quoted and the occasion known. "I can't remember," she gasped.

"Mrs. Williams, you must speak the truth. Remember that a great deal is known already, and banish any idea of false shame from your mind. This is a question of life and death to you: neither more nor less. If I know the truth from you, I can advise you as to the line you must take under cross-examination. Remember that it will be a terrible ordeal for you, and it's essential that you should be properly prepared for it. And weight will be attached, without a doubt, to that conversation of yours with Miss Tidmarsh."

"But how will they know about it?" she sobbed, forgetting her previous denial.

"Miss Tidmarsh will be called as a witness against you," said Mr. Cleaver gravely. "We've got to account for those words of yours somehow, and what is more serious still—if anything could be more serious—we've got to keep out of sight, if we can, those damning letters of yours."

"What letters?" screamed Elsie, a new and unbearable horror clutching at her.

"The letters, Mrs. Williams, that you have repeatedly written to Leslie Morrison during the past months."

"They're burnt, they're burnt!" shrieked Elsie. "He swore he'd burn them!"

"I wish to God he had, but he never did, Mrs. Williams. Those letters may form the bulk of the evidence against you. You repeat in them, again and again, that Williams ill-treated you, made you miserable, and that you wish he was dead. In one of them occurs the words: 'He's ill now, and taking sleeping draughts. One little mistake in pouring out the mixture, Leslie, and you and I might be free! I'd do more than that for our love's sake, darling.' Do you understand the awful weight that those expressions and many,

133

many similar ones would carry with a jury, Mrs. Williams? We've got to put some construction on them other than the obvious one, if we can't get a ruling that they're inadmissible as evidence, which is what we shall try for. I want to make it very, very clear to you. Everything depends on your co-operation. Are you fit to listen to me?"

Elsie was sobbing and writhing.

"Have you any letters whatever from Morrison?" pursued the relentless voice of the solicitor.

"No."

"What have you done with them?"

"I burnt them all."

He looked at her as though doubting her words. "Very few women burn their love-letters, Mrs. Williams."

"I was afraid to keep them."

"For fear of your husband seeing them?"

She hesitated. "Partly."

In Elsie's mind was a piercing recollection of the haunting fear that had obsessed her ever since the scene at the house of Madame Clara, the medium.

"Beware of the written word...."

But she would not give that reason for having destroyed Morrison's letters to the solicitor. The strange, undying remnant of vanity that finds a lurking-place upon the most apparently trivial and unlikely ground held her back from the truth.

Elsie Williams realised that Mr. Cleaver was in grimmest earnest when he told her that only the absolute truth could possibly save her; she was prepared to tell him the truth in spite of her deadly terror and shame, but she could not bring herself to say that the reason why she had destroyed the letters of Leslie Morrison was because she could never forget the words spoken by the clairvoyante whom she had visited.

"I burnt the letters because I had nowhere to keep them, and I was afraid they might be found," she repeated, her young face grey and ravaged.

It was the only particular in which she lied to Mr. Cleaver, and she did so with blind and irrational persistence.

After the hours that he spent with her, Elsie, physically exhausted, and psychically strung to a pitch of tension that she had never known in her life before, was left alone in her cell, face to face with her own soul.

At first, fragmentary recollections of the past forty-eight hours obsessed her. She went over and over her conversations with the police officials, her own replies to Mr. Cleaver, her mother's

134

hysterical ejaculations. Then she thought of Leslie Morrison, who had backed up her statements to the police, and who, when both were arrested together, had only asked through white lips: "Why her? She was not aware of my movements."

But since her own half-unconscious betrayal of him, Elsie's feeling for Morrison had undergone an extraordinary revulsion.

It had all turned out so utterly unlike anything that they had ever planned. It still seemed to Elsie that catastrophe had fallen, a bolt from the blue, into the midst of their lives without warning. She still felt that none of it could be true, that she must wake as from a hideous dream.

When had she had a hideous dream—something about Horace—something like this?

Dim associations of horror and bewilderment awoke slowly within her, and brought to her the remembrance of her visit with Irene Tidmarsh to the woman who had called herself "clairvoyante." She had talked in a deep, rather artificial voice about love and intrigue; she had bade Elsie beware of the written word. And then all of a sudden the atmosphere had altered, Madame Clara's voice itself had altered, horribly, and she had screamed out terrifying words and phrases. "Blood, and worse than blood ... you're all over blood! O, my God, what's this? It's all over England—you—they're talking about you."

Elsie understood. In a flash of searing, anguished intuition she understood what would happen.

With the appalling rapidity of a vision, there came to her the realisation of all that would come to pass in the near future.

She knew already that the police-court trial was the almost certain preliminary to her committal and Morrison's for trial at the Old Bailey. They would be tried for murder.

She and the man who had been her lover would stand in the dock together as prisoners; lawyers would fight out questions concerning their past relations; people would give evidence against them—evidence in their favour; Elsie would in all probability hear her own letters to Leslie Morrison read aloud in court....

It would be a sensational trial, such as she had often followed with avidity in the newspapers.

"It's all over England—they're talking about you...."

But why ... why?...

Elsie Williams' instant of vision fled from her as suddenly as it had come, and left her agonisedly and wildly rebellious, bewildered at the vortex of terror and shame and misery into which it seemed to her that she had suddenly, without volition of her own, been flung.

135

She could not trace the imperceptibly-graduated stages that had brought her to the pass where catastrophe became inevitable. To her, it seemed that she had swiftly been hurled from security into deadly peril by some agency as irresistible as it was malignant.

Every now and then realisation came to her, when certain frightful words sprang into frightful meaning, as they had never done before.

"Murder...."

"Conspiracy ... and incitement to murder...."

"Principal in the second degree...." The police officials had made use of that expression—so had Mr. Cleaver.

Elsie's mother had fetched Mr. Cleaver, and had wildly repeated, in front of Elsie and the lawyer, that she would grudge no expense, not if it cost her her last penny.

"And the aunties will help, Elsie, they've been ever so good—anything we can get together, says your Aunt Gertie, and her face the colour of the tablecloth. Mr. Cleaver here will tell us the best man, if it—if it comes to—to...."

"You could scarcely do better than Sir Cambourne Trevor, Mrs. Palmer, but his fee, I ought to warn you, is a thousand guineas."

"A thousand guineas!" Elsie and Mrs. Palmer had screamed together.

And Mr. Cleaver, gaunt and haggard and grey-faced, had made answer: "It's her life that will be at stake."

From time to time, Elsie understood. She knew, at those moments, what it all meant. There would be no more concealments, everything would be dragged out into a publicity that could only bring with it dishonour and shameful notoriety, and hatred, and execration.

And she would have to live through it—to suffer through an ordeal of vast, incredible magnitude, of which the climax—she knew it in a prescience that mercifully could not endure—would come in the ghastly dawn of a prison-yard, beneath the shadow of the scaffold....

Inexorable results would be suffered by herself, and she would never know how it was that these things had become inevitable—had happened.

Dawlish, 1923

136

THE BOND OF UNION

(To A. P. D.)

A wide, cushioned seat runs round three sides of the deep fireplace in Torry Delorian's library for the admitted reason that Lady Pamela March likes to face the room when she is talking.

The room, of course, means the audience. Personally, I consider that she could safely—I mean, without spoiling her picture of herself—make use of the very word itself. It is so obviously the only one that applies, when she sits there, smoking one cigarette after another, and we sit there, smoking one cigarette after another, all listening to Pamela, playing up to Pamela, and all more or less sexually attracted by Pamela.

The subconscious mind of Pamela projects on these occasions, I think, something of this kind:

"The girlish figure dominated the room. Magnetism vibrated in every gesture of the slim hands, every glance from the brilliant eyes, every modulation of the rather deep voice. She held them all, by sheer force of personality. The peacock-blue folds of her dress, with its girdle of barbaric, coloured stones...."

The bit about the dress, of course, varies. Sometimes the folds may be saffron-yellow, and the girdle opalescent, or there is no girdle at all; and anyhow, in those particulars, the same effect is never repeated twice. But I imagine that, like all women, she makes a point to herself of the accoutrements, not realising that the audience—almost altogether composed of men—attribute the entire effect to the sheer, smooth slope of her shoulders, the alluring curves of her mouth, the rich swell of her breasts beneath semi-transparencies.

The impression that inwardly she is projecting really does reflect itself on to the minds of most people, I believe.

It is only slightly distorted, even in my own version of it, which runs something like this:

"The girlish figure dominated the room. Animal magnetism vibrated in every gesture" ... and so on—only leaving out the brilliancy of the eyes and the deepness of the voice, both of them rather cheap accessories to a pose that really is quite strong enough without them—to the end:

"She held them all, by sheer will-to-dominate."

Pamela, being a brilliant talker, prefers always to talk personalities.

137

Two nights ago, sitting on that cushioned rail that runs round the fireplace, she recounted an adventure.

"... Only it's the spiritual adventure that I'm telling all of you. Because you'll understand. The other part was all obvious, the danger and all that. You've probably seen it in the papers."

She was right. It had been lavishly paragraphed, with photograph inset. Her flair for publicity is unerring.

"Darlings, how I loathe the Press—if I could only tell you! But the other part of the affair was so utterly wonderful, that it's swamped everything else. It was like a revelation.

"You know how essentially super-civilised I am? A man once wrote a poem about my being like a piece of jade—hard, and brilliant, and polished, and yet with the unfathomable subtlety and agelessness of the East. My civilisation is partly temperamental, I suppose, and of course to a certain extent the result of elaborate education—and then hereditary as well. Look at Anthony. Could anyone have a more utterly civilised parent, I ask you? Elma is less poised, of course, but mercifully for me I've managed to inherit my mother's physique and my father's mentality. Like a sensitised plate, isn't it? It does mean isolation of soul, and those terrible nerve-storms of mine, but in my heart of hearts I know it's worth it.

"Only people are so ghastly. My friends have to rescue me.... You remember what it was like, Torry, the night that woman assaulted me at the Embassy, and talked, and talked, and talked. O Christ! it was all about food, or flannel, or babies—something too utterly indecent, I know. I sat there, helpless, martyred—and darling Torry came and rescued me. I shall never forget it, Torry, you sweet, never.

"Now this is what happened the other day. (Why do you allow me to be discursive, dear people?) You know my car was held up by Sinn Feiners? I, who adore everything lawless! But it was simply for being Anthony's daughter, of course. They hate him so.

"You know how I drive for miles and miles, entirely alone, just so as to feel the air in my face, and my hands—rather small, really, by comparison—controlling that great swift machine. Well, I'd got to such a lonely place that it was like finding God—when suddenly these men appeared.

"I wasn't a bit frightened—I never am frightened—but it was horrible, all the same. And I kept thinking of the people who'd be so sorry if I were killed, and wondering who'd be the sorriest, and who'd remember longest."

(She looked round the room, her dark brows raised in an expression part whimsical, part pathetic.)

"All this isn't the adventure, you know, though they took my

138

jewels, and tied me up to a bench on a sort of heath place. They tied me here, and here."

She held out a slim ankle, and extended both wrists.

"Dear hearts, don't, don't touch me! I'm so dreadfully on edge to-night. Nothing to do with the adventure, though. That was altogether beautiful.

"You see there was another woman on the bench, to whom they'd done exactly the same thing—only she'd been walking, not driving. They left us together, and said they'd come back later and shoot us. Terrorism, of course, but it would be such an ugly way of going out, wouldn't it?

"She and I looked at one another, tied to either end of that bench, and in some way that I simply can't describe, our spirits leapt together. She, it turned out afterwards, recognised me at once—that's the worst of being too weak to refuse sittings when one's pestered by every photographer in London—but I hadn't the least idea who she was, and don't care. Bright red hair, quite distinguished-looking, and altogether rather lovely in a pallid, blanc-de-Ninon way, though no actual physical charm. But I felt it wouldn't have mattered if she'd been a déclassée. By the way, what is a déclassée?

"This still isn't the adventure—besides, you know this part already, all of you—but some of those ruffians came back again, and untied us, and said we could find our own way home. They'd taken my car, needless to say. I gave them one of my looks—the sort that means I'm really, really angry, like when someone kisses me in a clumsy way, or spills something on my frock—and the men melted, literally melted, away. Then she and I began to walk, and this is really when the part that matters started to happen.

"Having come through this shattering episode, and found ourselves unshot, and alive, it was almost like two disembodied spirits communing together. We got into the realities straight away. It was far more wonderful than if one of us had been a man, because then sex must have come into it, but as it was, each of us laid her whole soul perfectly bare, in the way one can never do to a man, if he loves one, for fear it should kill his love, or if he doesn't love one, for fear it should make him think he does.

"But as it was, each of us was perfectly fearless, and in a way perfectly shameless. It was partly violent emotional reaction. You see, we'd both thought we were facing death.

"She told me that she was utterly miserable. Her husband was a brute, and her lover had let her down. He'd fallen in love with a girl, a sort of pure-eyed-baby person, and had just told this woman—

139

who'd been giving him everything, of course, for years—that he wanted to se ranger and get married.

"She was nearly out of her mind, that woman. You see, she wasn't young, and then some skin treatment she'd been having hadn't succeeded, and was helping to break her up. She told me about that, too. Oh, there was nothing she didn't say, but she simply didn't care, we were so utterly intimate for that fleeting moment. Nobody else in the world knew, she told me. She'd always tried to avoid scandal, and no one had ever really known about her liaison with this man. (Women are clever about love.)

"And then I told her every single thing about myself—things that I'd never dream of breathing in this room, nor you of believing, most likely. Foul, filthy, hateful things about myself.... I know now why Catholics go to confession. It releases so much.

"Darlings, words can't ever describe what it was like. I shall never forget it, as long as I live, and neither will she.

"We parted, of course, but we both knew that there was a link between us that nothing could ever break, even though we never met again. It was too utterly perfect and complete as it was."

There was a silence, and then someone said, suitably: "Wonderful Pamela!"

She smiled vaguely, shook her head, and then tragically clasped both hands to her breast. "Please, a cocktail. I'm so tired. Oh, and what's the time? I'm dining with a man at eight, and he's thrown over a most important engagement to take me, and he'd be quite capable of getting angry if I failed him. Sweet, no! Not a quarter past nine! Oh, please, someone, a car, and take me to the little tiny, tiny French restaurant in Wardour Street."

Lady Pamela waved away the cocktail, spilling it, prayed for another one and drank it, and then wafted away on the wings of little distressed exclamations and futile, effective gestures of farewell.

That was two nights ago.

This morning I was in Bond Street, and I saw Pamela March in her father's car, held up by a block in the traffic.

On the other side of the narrow street another car with a solitary woman in it passed slowly. I recognised the woman instantly from Pamela's description, for she had bright red hair, was quite distinguished-looking, and altogether rather lovely in a pallid, blanc-de-Ninon way, and radiated a marked degree of physical charm.

The eyes of the two women who had been as disembodied spirits communing together met in a long look.

And the expression in each pair of eyes was momentarily

identical, and it was with the same effect of immutable determination that each simultaneously administered and received the cut direct.

They knew....

LOST IN TRANSMISSION

I

The Lambes were very rich.

This was all the nicer for Mrs. Lambe, because once upon a time, not so very long ago, when she was still Maude Gunning, she had been poor. From the time she was eighteen to the time she was thirty, she had taught music at the girls' school in Carlorossa Road. She had gone to and from her work four days a week all through term time by tram. Fortunately, the tram took her almost from door to door. She was a bad walker, owing to corns.

During the school holidays Maude had always tried to find private pupils, and as she and her father and mother were well known in the big manufacturing town and its suburbs, and her successes at the L.R.C.M. examinations were a subject of local pride, she had generally succeeded.

And it was odd to think, as Mrs. Lambe quite often did think, that most of the large, comfortable, expensive houses to which she had gone—with a very keen appreciation, on autumn and winter afternoons, of the big fire blazing in the pupil's schoolroom or dining-room, as the case might be—to think that these houses, for the most part, were less large, comfortable, and expensive than the one of which she was now the mistress.

Edgar Lambe, when he first met Miss Maude Gunning at a tea-party, was already a wealthy man, although not as rich as the demand for houses that sprang up during the war afterwards made him.

At the party, Maude played the piano, and played it very well. Mr. Lambe, who was naturally musical, asked to be introduced to her. He had never married, although he was forty years old, and he had recently made up his mind to look for a wife. Maude attracted him, although she was neither pretty nor very young.

Three months after their first meeting they were married.

Mr. Lambe bought the largest corner house in Victoria Avenue.

It was, of course, wholly detached from its neighbours. There was a carriage-sweep in the front, and a long, wide garden at the back, and a high wall all round. There was a tennis-court, two greenhouses, and a vegetable garden beyond the flower-garden.

The inside of Melrose was even more magnificent than the

142

outside, and far more interesting to Mrs. Lambe, who was not very fond of being out-of-doors, having had a great deal too much of it in her tram-journeying days. But she had many ideas as to comfort and elegance indoors, and Edgar was generous with money, and had a standard of his own—and one that secretly rather scared her—as to the way in which a house should be "run."

This standard of Edgar's was principally applied to lighting, heating, food and service. The house was fitted with electric light, of course, and Edgar had had a separate boiler put in for the three bathrooms, so that it was his favourite boast that if anyone wanted a bath in the middle of the night, the water would still come out of the tap almost boiling. There were radiators in all the rooms except the kitchen, offices and servants' bedrooms, and hot pipes in the linen-cupboard.

It took Mrs. Lambe a little while to assimilate Edgar's views as to meals. She quite understood that these must be served punctually, and that the plates must be hot—really hot—and that there must always be a relay of fresh toast towards the end of breakfast; and of course late dinner every night except Sunday, when it was cold supper. But she did find it a little bit difficult, just at first, to realise that Edgar disapproved strongly of twice-cooked meat. At her own home there had been a weekly joint, which was hot on Sunday, cold on Monday, hashed on Tuesday, and cottage-pie'd on Wednesday—and sometimes, if it had been a larger joint than usual, curried on Thursday and turned into rissoles on Friday.

At Melrose, after one, or at the most two, appearances in the dining-room, the beef disappeared into the kitchen and was finished there, while a new joint, or a pair of fowls, took its place on the upstairs menu.

The amount of "butcher's meat" that came into the house amazed and disconcerted its mistress, until she found that her servants took it as a matter of course, and that her husband continually praised her to his friends as a good manager, and that the monthly bills—which at first had appalled her—by no means exceeded the sum which he had himself suggested that he should allow her for the housekeeping.

By the time that Mrs. Lambe had a nursery, with two little girls in it, and a nurse, and a nursery-maid to wait upon them, she took it quite as a matter of course that there should be yet a third list of items to consider in the ordering of meals—weekly chickens, and special dairy produce, and a regular supply of white fish, for the nursery. This question of food for the household was, of course, immensely important, and she gave a great deal of conscientious thought to it, thankful when the cook suggested a new variety of

143

sweet for the dinner-parties to which Edgar so much enjoyed inviting his business friends and their families.

On these occasions he himself selected the wines with the utmost care, and instructed the two parlour-maids minutely and repeatedly in the proper formula to be employed with each course.

Mrs. Lambe was always relieved that this great responsibility did not in any way rest upon her. A mistake, she felt, would be altogether too terrible.

The parlour-maid and the waitress who always came in for the evening when the Lambes entertained, never made mistakes.

Mrs. Lambe was very "good" with servants, and never had any difficulty in finding and keeping thoroughly satisfactory domestics. The little girls' nurse, who received far higher wages than any of them except the cook, was the only one with whom there was sometimes a little trouble.

She occasionally hinted that Ena and Evelyn were rather spoiled, and inclined to come up to the nursery disposed to be fretful and out of sorts after too much notice in the drawing-room, and far too many expensive chocolates from the pink and blue and gilt boxes that were always being given to them.

Mr. Lambe was a lavish and indulgent father. He thought his fair-haired, pretty little daughters wonderful, and took the greatest delight in associating "Dad's" return from the office with new toys or "surprises" of sweetmeats.

Mrs. Lambe never had the heart to disappoint him by suggesting that his munificence was making the little girls rather critical and capricious, even at six and four years old. Edgar only roared with appreciative laughter when they told him, seriously and rather crossly, that they always wanted the chocolates to come from Blakiston's—which was the best, and by far the most expensive, confectioner's in the city. They did not care for any other kind.

Edgar repeated this story to a great many of his friends, who were as much amused as he was himself at such an instance of early discrimination.

Mrs. Lambe was amused herself, and could not help thinking that Ena and Evelyn were smart and original children.

They were also very pretty; rather pallid, sharp-featured little things, always beautifully dressed, exactly alike. Neither she nor Edgar regretted in the very least that neither of them had been a boy.

Every night Maude Lambe, who had been brought up to be thoroughly religious, knelt at the side of her enormous bed, with its opulent pink satin duvet, and humbly thanked God for all that He had given her—Edgar and the children, and Edgar's wealth and kindness, and her beautiful, comfortable home.

144

There was only one fly in the ointment—Aunt Tessie.

Edgar had told her all about Aunt Tessie before they were married. He had explained that she would live with him always, in spite of the undeniable fact that she was Not like Other People, and that he would never allow her to be sent away to an institution, whatever the other Lambe relations might say.

Aunt Tessie had been very good to him when he was a little boy, and this Edgar never intended to forget. He had had a very unhappy childhood, with a mother who drank and a stepfather who beat him. Aunt Tessie, who had actually made a living for herself in those days out of painting pictures, had done everything that she could do to induce them to let little Edgar come and live with her, and when they would not agree to that, she had still sent him presents and surreptitiously given him pocket-money, and when he had been sent away to school, she had come regularly and taken him out, and invited him to her flat whenever she could. She was the only person who had ever shown him any affection when he was a child, Edgar had once told his wife.

Maude had been very much touched, and thought it noble of dear Edgar to remember so faithfully, in his great prosperity, the good old aunt who had long ceased to be able to paint even bad pictures, and who had become terribly, almost dangerously, eccentric about ten years earlier. Edgar had then immediately taken her to live with him, declaring Aunt Tessie once and for all to be his charge.

All this he had explained to his wife before they were married, and her generous and even eager acquiescence had met him more than half-way.

Maude, indeed, had been ready to accept Aunt Tessie as her charge, too. She had felt nothing but a tender compassion for the probably frail, half-childish invalid, towards whose garrulousness she would never fail of kindly semi-attention, and to whose bodily weakness every care should be extended. But Aunt Tessie had turned out not to be that sort of invalid at all.

To begin with, her physical health was robust and powerful. She was only fifty-five, and her hair was not grey, but a strong, virulent auburn.

Her complexion was sanguine, her large, harshly-lined face suffused with colour and disfigured by swelling, purplish veins.

Her voice was very loud and hoarse, and she laughed with a sound like a neigh. As for Aunt Tessie's appetite, it was simply prodigious. Even had expense been a serious consideration at Melrose, Mrs. Lambe would never have grudged anyone a hearty meal—she had too often gone semi-hungry herself for that—but really, Aunt Tessie, with her second and third helping of beef, and her two glasses of claret, and her frank eagerness for dessert chocolates, was not decent.

She always had her meals in the dining-room, and it was really on that account that Ena and Evelyn had their midday dinner upstairs, and only came downstairs when the starched and mob-capped maids were handing round coffee. Their mother would have liked them to come to the dining-room for luncheon, at least on Sundays, but they both hated Aunt Tessie, and made faces and laughed at each other when she uttered any of her loud, inconsequent remarks, or pushed her food into her mouth with her fingers.

Maude, and even Edgar, had tried to persuade Aunt Tessie that it would be more comfortable for her to have all her meals in the large upstairs sitting-room that they had given her, but Aunt Tessie had been first angry and then hurt. They wanted her out of the way, she said angrily, they were ashamed of her, and did not like her to meet their friends.

Mrs. Lambe could not help thinking that it was rather ungrateful of Aunt Tessie to say this, after all that had been done for her. However, they would not vex and disappoint the poor old lady, and so she continued to appear downstairs, even when there was a party, and to embarrass and disconcert everybody by her ineptitudes and her uncouth manners at the dinner-table.

II

By the time the Armistice was signed, Mr. Lambe had become richer than ever.

He entertained his friends even more often to dinner, and gave them better wine, although it had always been so good before. He increased Mrs. Lambe's allowance for the housekeeping, and frequently gave her presents of money to be spent upon herself or the little girls. He would have given Aunt Tessie money too, but she had grown even queerer in the course of the past year, and it was only too evident that what had been called her "eccentricity" was now becoming something much more serious. For the very first time, there was trouble with the maids.

They did not like waiting on Miss Lambe. It was no wonder, either, poor Mrs. Lambe was forced to admit.

Aunt Tessie was untidy, even dirty, and as the housemaid once pertly remarked, her bedroom only needed three gold balls over the door. She kept things to eat upstairs, and scattered crumbs everywhere.

The parlour-maid, speaking for herself and for the housemaid, declared that it was quite impossible to do the proper work of the house and to clear up after Miss Lambe as well.

In another moment she would have given notice.... Mrs. Lambe could see it coming.

Hastily she sent for Emma, the little between-maid, and informed her that in future she would have the sole care of Miss Lambe's bedroom and her sitting-room, and would wait upon her, instead of the housemaid. She at the same time raised Emma's wages by two pounds a year, for she always tried to be very just.

Emma was only seventeen, and a very childish little thing, and Mrs. Lambe had not expected her to raise any objection to the new scheme; but it was surprising, although satisfactory, to find that Emma seemed to be actually pleased by it.

She said "Yes'm," a good many times, and smiled at her mistress as though joyfully accepting a form of promotion.

Mrs. Lambe was relieved, the parlour-maid and the housemaid did not give notice, and even Aunt Tessie—very difficult to please nowadays—appeared contented and satisfied.

But she was getting worse all the time.

It became more and more embarrassing when visitors came to Melrose.

The old lady always found out when anyone was expected, and the more people were coming the noisier and more excited she became.

One dreadful Sunday there were guests for luncheon—two of Edgar's important clients, and little Ena's godfather—a rich old bachelor cousin—and two unmarried ladies, friends of Mrs. Lambe's maiden days. She was always very faithful to her friends.

Aunt Tessie actually pranced downstairs and met some of these people in the hall as they arrived, and greeted them boisterously, and so incoherently that really they might almost have been excused for thinking that she had been taking too much to drink.

Mrs. Lambe, hastening downstairs from her own room, could hear it all, although she could not see it, and it was thus that she afterwards described it to Edgar.

"So glad—so glad to see you!" shouted Aunt Tessie. "This fine house—always open, and my nephew is so generous and hospitable. They take advantage, sometimes—there are bad people about, very

147

bad people. Sometimes they make attempts ... one's life isn't as safe as it looks, I can assure you...."

She had thrown out such ridiculous and yet sinister hints once or twice lately. But what could the poor guests think of it all?

They were very polite, and soon saw that the best thing to do was to ignore Aunt Tessie as far as possible, and pretend not to hear when she talked, and not to see when she shuffled about the room, upsetting ornaments here and there, and every now and then whisking round suddenly to look behind her as though she expected someone or something to be following her. Once she shouted very loud, "Get out, I tell you! I can smell the poison from here!..." But after the first involuntary, startled silence, everyone began simultaneously to talk again, and very soon after that, luncheon was announced.

Mrs. Lambe saw that her husband, talking to his principal guest and smiling a great deal, kept on all the time turning an anxious eye towards Aunt Tessie, and this emboldened her to do what she had never done before.

She put her hand on the old lady's arm, and detained her whilst the others were all going into the dining-room.

"Dear auntie," she said, speaking low and very gently, "I'm sure you're not well. You look so flushed and tired. All these people are really too much for you. Do let Emma carry your lunch upstairs on a tray and have it comfortably in your own room."

But it was of no use.

Aunt Tessie, her looks and her manner stranger than ever, vociferated an incoherent refusal, mixed up with something about Emma, to whom she had taken a violent fancy.

"A good girl—the only one you can trust. She never plots against people!" Aunt Tessie shouted, nodding her head with wild emphasis, and rolling her eyeballs round in their sockets.

Mrs. Lambe could do nothing. She dared not let Aunt Tessie sit next to any of the visitors, and of course she herself had to have one of the important clients upon either side of her, but she made Ena and Evelyn, who were lunching downstairs in honour of the godfather's presence, take their places one on each side of their extraordinary old relative.

Evelyn, who was very little, began to whine and protest, but Mrs. Lambe pretended not to hear. She knew that Evelyn's attention was always very easily distracted. She felt much more afraid of Ena, and her heart sank when, out of the corner of her eye, she saw Aunt Tessie officiously trying to put Ena's long curls away from her shoulders.

The little girl's fair, pretty face turned black with scowls in an instant, and she twitched herself away from the big, heavy, mottled hand fumbling clumsily at her neck, and sat with her back as nearly as possible turned to Aunt Tessie.

One couldn't really blame the poor children for disliking her so much, but it was very bad for them ... it made them naughty and ill-mannered....

Poor Mrs. Lambe could only give half her attention to her guests, and she saw that Edgar, too, underneath his geniality and his urgent and repeated invitations that everyone should have more food and more wine, was anxious and ill at ease.

Every now and then Aunt Tessie's strident tones rose above all the other sounds in the big, hot dining-room.

"Not any more—no. They put things into one's food sometimes, and then they think one doesn't notice. But the one who waits on me—Emma, her name is—she's all right. You can trust her."

Aunt Tessie's words, no less than her emphasis on Emma's trustworthiness, would of course be noticed, and bitterly resented, by the other two servants, waiting deftly and quietly at the table. But neither of them moved a muscle, ·even when she went on to something worse.

"Never put any confidence in upper servants," declared Aunt Tessie, leaning across the table and almost shouting. "They may be civil enough, but they plot and plan behind people's backs. There's cases in the newspapers very often ... it's ... it's murder, really, you know. They call it accidental, but sometimes it's poisoning. One can't be too auspicious—suspicious, I should say."

She paused to laugh vacantly at her own slip of the tongue, and to let her eyes rove all over the table as though in search of something.

Mr. Lambe clumsily wrenched at the conversation: "Talking about newspaper reports, that was a curious case in Staffordshire...."

The visitors seconded him gamely, and Aunt Tessie's voice was overborne and heard again only in snatches.

Mrs. Lambe, however, was very much upset, and she ordered coffee to be brought to the drawing-room so as to make a move as soon as possible.

Things were a little better in the drawing-room. Ena and Evelyn were soon screaming and romping round Ena's godfather, and one of Maude's humble friends, perhaps feeling that she owed her something in return for the splendid luncheon and lavish hospitality, sat in the bow-window with Aunt Tessie and kept her away from the rest of the room. This was a great relief, although it led to an uncomfortable moment when the party was breaking up, and Aunt Tessie, vehemently taking leave of her kind companion, actually caught up a little gilt trifle from Maude's knick-knack shelf and tried to press it upon her acceptance.

Miss Mason was very tactful, pretending with rather an embarrassed look to accept the impossible gift, and secretly slipping it on to a table near the door as she went out.

Aunt Tessie did not see, but Maude did. She was nearly crying by the time it was all over and everyone had gone away. The children had been sent upstairs again, and Aunt Tessie's heavy footsteps had taken her to her own part of the house.

Curiously enough, she and Edgar hardly spoke to one another about the disastrous subject, but Maude Lambe knew very well that he now, as well as she, fully realised the discomfort and humiliation entailed upon the whole household by his too-generous treatment of Aunt Tessie.

III

Soon it was no longer possible to pretend that Aunt Tessie was not getting worse and worse. Her constant, irrelevant allusions to plots, and poisonings, and wicked people, had become a fixed delusion.

She really thought that everyone at Melrose was conspiring against her life, and she would allow no one, except Emma, to do anything for her.

It was a mercy, Mrs. Lambe often told herself, that Emma was such a good little thing. She was so willing, and never seemed to grudge the time and trouble that she was obliged to spend over cleaning Aunt Tessie's apartments and tidying up after her. She would even listen, respectfully and yet compassionately, to Aunt Tessie's long, rambling denunciations and accusations.

"Poor old lady!" Maude once overheard Emma saying to another servant. "She's a lady just the same, for all she's gone queer, and I behaves towards her like I would to any other lady, that's all."

"Funny kind of a lady that makes a face at a servant, as she did at me this morning."

"She never done that to me, nor nothing the least like it," said Emma stoutly.

It was only too true that Aunt Tessie was very rude to all the maids except Emma, and sometimes to Edgar and Maude as well.

150

As she grew worse, she seemed to forget all their kindness and generosity, and to look upon them as being her enemies.

Mrs. Lambe would not let the little girls go near her any more, and the nurse had orders to keep them away from Miss Lambe "until she grew better."

Aunt Tessie, however, did not grow better.

The doctor, an old friend of Edgar Lambe's, advised them to have a nurse for her, if they were still determined to keep her on at Melrose, instead of sending her to one of the many excellent establishments that he could have recommended.

"Nothing in the least like an institution or—or asylum. Simply a nursing home where Miss Lambe would have entire freedom and every possible comfort, but would yet receive the constant medical supervision that her unfortunate condition renders necessary."

But Edgar Lambe remained obstinate. Aunt Tessie had been very good to him in the past, and he had always said that she should be his special charge. He would not send her away to any nursing home, however highly recommended.

He was, however, quite willing that a professional nurse should be installed at Melrose. The expense, he said, was nothing, if it would make things easier for Maude and be of advantage to Aunt Tessie.

The presence of Nurse Alberta certainly fulfilled both these requirements.

She was an intelligent, pleasant-looking woman of five- or six-and-thirty, with none of the pretensions so often associated with her class. She had meals with Aunt Tessie, in the latter's big, comfortable sitting-room, and slept in a little room adjoining hers. Both of them were waited upon by Emma.

Aunt Tessie nowadays made no difficulty about not coming to the dining-room. Her crazy old mind had fastened upon the idea of poison, and Emma and Nurse Alberta were the only people from whom she would accept food or drink.

The nurse told Emma, with whom she became quite friendly by dint of constant association, that the "persecution mania" was a very common symptom amongst those who were mentally deranged.

"They always think that everybody's against them," she declared cheerfully, "even those who do most for them. Look at this poor old lady, for instance! She thinks Mr. and Mrs. Lambe are plotting against her, and I'm sure they're goodness itself to her, and have been for years, I should think. No expense grudged, and everything done to make her comfortable. Why, most people would have had an own mother sent away by this time and put under restraint—and Miss Lambe is only an aunt. No real relation at all, as

151

you may say, to Mrs. Lambe. Really, I do think Mrs. Lambe's behaved wonderfully, and I'm sure she finds it a strain."

Nurse Alberta was quite right. Mrs. Lambe did find the presence of Aunt Tessie in the house a great strain, even now.

In her heart, she was terribly afraid that the old aunt, who had so rapidly passed from one distressing stage to another, might suddenly become a real danger to those around her.

She thought of Ena and Evelyn and shuddered. Very often, she woke in the night and crept out to the landing, trembling, to listen at the night-nursery door.

One day, when Nurse Alberta had been in the house for some time, Mrs. Lambe felt so wretched and so much unstrung by her state of now chronic nervousness, that she detained the doctor after his habitual visit to Aunt Tessie, and timidly spoke to him of her own symptoms.

He listened very attentively, asked her several questions, and finally made a suggestion which Mrs. Lambe saw at once ought to have occurred to her earlier.

She was going to have another child.

It was over five years since Evelyn's birth, and she had somehow never expected to have any more babies, but both Mr. and Mrs. Lambe were honestly pleased.

They hoped for a son.

It was this discovery that led to the modification of Edgar Lambe's views about Aunt Tessie. Obviously, the presence of the unfortunate old lady subjected Maude to a continual strain that might easily become more and more severe as time went on.

The doctor, privately consulted by Mr. Lambe, admitted that in his opinion it was not quite fair on Mrs. Lambe, in her condition, to keep the aggressive, turbulent invalid in the house with her. And it wasn't as if Aunt Tessie herself really benefited by it, either. She was far past appreciating any kindness or attention shown to her now. Her idée fixe was that everyone at Melrose excepting poor little Emma, the maid, was plotting against her in some way, and seeking to poison her.

Mr. Lambe listened, nodding his head, his red, heavy-jowled face puckered with distress. It went against the grain with him to invalidate the boast of years—that Aunt Tessie should always share his home—and yet in his heart he felt that the doctor was right.

Aunt Tessie was past minding or knowing, poor soul—and Maude and their unborn son must come first.

When once he had fairly made up his mind to it, Edgar Lambe could not help feeling a certain relief. He, too, in his own way, had suffered on those dreadful occasions when Aunt Tessie had insisted

152

upon appearing downstairs, and had made his friends and his family uncomfortable by her strange, noisy eccentricity. Even nowadays his daily visit to her room was a miserable affair. It gave her no pleasure now to see the nephew for whom she had once done so much, and who had done so much for her in return. She classed him with her imaginary enemies.

It was very difficult for Edgar Lambe, who was not at all an imaginative man, not to feel irrationally wounded by those wild accusations of enmity. He could scarcely be brought to understand that poor Aunt Tessie's floods of foolish vituperation had, in themselves, no meaning at all.

"But she was always devoted to me," he said, half resentfully and half piteously. "I can't make it out at all. You'd think that even now she'd be able to—to distinguish a bit between me and the wretched cook or charwoman. But no, she abuses us all alike, and seems to think we're all in league to do her in."

"It's part of her illness, Mr. Lambe," said Nurse Alberta soothingly. "You know, she really is quite cracky, poor old lady."

The "arrangements," as the doctor called them, were made as speedily as possible, since they were naturally distressing to everybody, and Mr. and Mrs. Lambe went themselves to see Aunt Tessie's new quarters, and to talk to the charming lady at the head of the establishment, and get special permission for Nurse Alberta, to whom Aunt Tessie was used, to take her there and remain with her for some time until she grew accustomed to it all.

"Fires in her room, of course, and any extras that she may fancy," said Mr. Lambe impressively. "Expense is of no consideration at all. I shall send round a comfortable couch for the sitting-room this afternoon."

He did so, and Mrs. Lambe added two or three fat cushions, and a decorated lampshade and waste-paper basket, such as she liked in her own drawing-room.

When Aunt Tessie was told that she was going away from Melrose for a time, she was delighted.

"Then I can relish my food again," she said rather coarsely. "There's never any knowing what they're all up to here."

That remained her attitude up to the very last. She dumped them all together as objects of her aggrieved resentment. Edgar, Maude, the two little girls, the impassive, well-behaved servants.

But when she said good-bye to Emma the night before she was to go away, Aunt Tessie squeezed her hand hard, and gave her some money and several ornaments and little trinkets from her own possessions.

Soft-hearted Emma cried, and hurried away to the sitting-room to find Nurse Alberta. "I just can't bear to listen to her, poor old lady, saying I'm the only one as never tried to do her a mischief," she sobbed.

"You're a silly girl to take on so," said the nurse good-naturedly. "Why, she'll be ever so well looked after where she's going, and there's good money being spent on her comforts, I can tell you, and Mr. Lambe won't let that be wasted. It isn't like some poor looneys, that get put away and not a soul of their own people ever goes near them to see how they're getting on. She'll be kept an eye on, you may be very sure, and it'll be best for all parties to have her under another roof, really it will."

"Oh yes, I know!" said Emma.

"It isn't even as if she wanted to stay, you know, Emma. She's turned dead against them, like cases of her sort often do. Look at the way she spoke to you about your being the only one that didn't want to poison her, or some such rubbish."

There was a pause.

"Nurse," said Emma suddenly, "do mad people know as they're mad?"

"They say not," indifferently returned Nurse Alberta, biting a thread off her piece of needlework. "Why, Emma?"

"Because—well, me and Cook got to talking last night about poor Miss Lambe, and—I can't say it how I mean," Emma rambled on confusedly, "but Cook would have it that people as go off their heads—well, they are off their heads. They don't look at anything like we do any more—it's sort of all upside down to them. But I didn't think it was like that—well, at any rate not with Miss Lambe."

"Why not?" said Nurse Alberta.

She looked interested and Emma was encouraged.

"I thought, perhaps," she said timidly, "that the inside of her poor mind is still like everybody's else's, in a way, only she can't get the thoughts to come out right. And I thought, perhaps, that when she said all that about them wanting to poison her, it was only her—her mad sort of way of saying that she'd felt, all along, they really wanted her to go away. And that would be why she said I was the only person that she was safe with. Because I never did want her to go away. The master and mistress and the young ladies may have felt like that. Of course, it's been ever so trying for them, I know, having her here like that—and the girls downstairs, they wanted her to go. But I never did, and I wondered if perhaps that was what she sort of felt, only she couldn't explain it right, and so it came out that way—in all her talk about being poisoned, and that."

Emma stopped and looked rather wistfully at the nurse.

"You'll think I'm balmy myself, talking like that. And I can't

154

explain what I mean a bit well. It's not as if I'd been educated like you——"

"Oh, I don't know," said Nurse Alberta, smiling. "I think I understand what you mean, Emma. According to your notion, the poor old lady feels and thinks pretty much the same as we do, but she's lost the trick of communicating her feelings and her thoughts. They—they get lost in transmission, so to say."

"You do put it well, Nurse!" said Emma admiringly.

Nurse Alberta looked gratified. "I don't know," she said modestly. But she was herself rather pleased by the sound of the phrase that she had used, and could not resist repeating it.

"It's a bit far-fetched, perhaps, but there's certainly something in what you say, Emma," she observed, biting off another thread. "Lost in transmission—that's the idea—lost in transmission!"

TIME WORKS WONDERS

I

"You funny little thing!" he said patronisingly.

Adela resented the term violently, but because he was the only man who had ever attempted to talk personalities with her, she accepted it smilingly.

"I must read some of those books of yours. Tell me what the names are."

"Oh, it doesn't matter! Never mind about my books," she said hurriedly.

Adela could not imagine Willoughby reading anybody's books, unless definitely of that class which deals with a fictitious Secret Service or the intrigues of an imaginary kingdom.

Her own books were small masterpieces of psychology, subtly ironical. A shudder, half-humorous, half-despairing, came over her at the idea of Hal Willoughby, bored and mystified, ploughing his way through one of her books.

"Never mind about my books," she repeated. "I'd rather you thought of me as a girl than as a writer."

She felt wildly daring in so speaking, partly because she had called herself a girl, although she was thirty, and partly because it was the first time that she had ever attempted what she supposed to be a flirtation.

Her reputation for cleverness had always been so great and so terrible that young men had never dared to approach her.

She supposed that must be the reason for their aloofness, since she had always been passably pretty; and even now, by artificial light, she looked five years younger than she was.

Her hair and her colouring were charming in a subdued and unvivid way, her features straight and very clean-cut. She hardly realised how much too thin were the lips of her tiny mouth, how intense and over-prominent her large hazel eyes.

"I never can imagine how anybody can write a book," said Willoughby.

Adela moved uneasily. She could tell what was coming.

"Do you think of a plot first, or do you just make it up as you go along?"

"It all depends."

156

She made the meaningless reply that had so often served her before.

"I should never know what to make the people say next. Aren't conversations awfully difficult?"

"Sometimes."

"I suppose you are always on the look-out for people to put into your books—under invented names, of course."

"I don't think I am."

"Oh, but I expect you are! I expect really you sit there, taking it all in, you know."

Why did people always think it necessary to talk to her like this?

"You ought to write a play. They say it pays like fun."

"But, you see, I'm not a dramatist."

"Oh, rubbish! If you're clever enough to write books, of course you could write a play. I should, if I were you—really I should." His voice was charged with encouragement.

"No, I couldn't. Don't let's talk about that."

"Why not? I want to hear about these books of yours. I've never met a literary lady before."

It was of no use. He would not talk to her as she was almost sure that he would have talked to any other woman in the room, given those distant sounds of music from the ballroom, that hazy moonlight above the bench beneath the syringa-bushes.

Adela grimly sacrificed her art, perjuring her soul away. "I expect you think it's very funny of me to write books," she said, desperately adapting her vocabulary to his own. "I really do it mostly—a good deal—because it brings in money." She tried to laugh, and hated herself for the artificiality of the sound.

"I suppose girls are always glad of extra pocket-money," he assented indifferently.

A girl—that was how he thought of her.

She was pleased at that, but she struggled for a more serious recognition of her capabilities, too. "It's not only pocket-money. I can really get a living from my writing, though I'm always at home with my mother. But I could be independent to-morrow if I liked."

"Oh, come now!" The words might have expressed remonstrance, incredulity, astonishment.

"The advance royalty—that's the money the publishers give me in advance—on my last book was two hundred pounds," she said calmly.

She had never gone away to work, never had to pay for her food or for a roof over her head, never tried her strength or the strength of her resources in the struggle for livelihood amongst unsupported women.

Two hundred pounds for her year's work was a large sum, with no calls upon it.

Willoughby repeated after her: "Two hundred pounds! I say! You don't expect me to believe you get that just for writing a story?"

"Yes." She was uncertain of the reason for his disbelief, and even whether he really did disbelieve her.

"But was it a serious book, or just a novel?" He really sounded perplexed.

"Oh, 'just a novel'!" she said bitterly.

"Good Lord! How many do you write in a year?"

"That last one took me over a year. My first one I worked at, on and off, for five years."

"I suppose it doesn't matter to you, taking your time, but it would be quite worth scribbling them off one after the other, if you can get money like that without working for it, so to speak," said Hal Willoughby.

He fingered his thick, fair moustache, and Adela looked up at him furtively in the moonlight.

He was very big and good-looking; and when she danced with him, and met his full, bold gaze, Adela could almost forget about such conversations between them as the present one.

Besides, he had not always talked like this. Once he had pretended not to know what colour her eyes were, and once he had told her about his life in India. She wished intensely that the conversation now would shift to some such topic.

The moonlight and the heavy scent of the syringa seemed to mock her.

"And what are your books about?" said Willoughby laboriously. "Love, I suppose?" He broke into a roar of laughter. "Does the heroine fall fainting into the hero's arms in the last chapter, eh? That's the style, isn't it?"

Adela stood up, trembling. "I think I want to go in now, please. The—the dance must be finished now."

He stood up also. "But I say! What's the matter? You're not ratty, are you?" He pulled unceremoniously at the prim velvet ribbons that hung from her waist. "Sit down again. Don't you know I'm going away to-morrow? You might be a little bit nice to me, I do think."

"I didn't know you wanted me to be," she said swiftly.

He laughed, and pulled her on to the bench again.

Adela's mother, with whom she always lived, had told her very often that men never really respected a woman who let them "take

158

liberties." Adela, never before put to the test, recklessly determined to disregard the parental axiom.

When Willoughby caught hold of her chilly little ringless hand, she made no movement of withdrawal.

He looked down at her and laughed again. "What an odd little thing you are! I don't believe you've ever been kissed, have you?"

She was silent.

"Has anybody ever made love to you, now?"

"Yes," she said defiantly and untruly.

He laughed quite openly, and declared, "I don't believe it!"

Still laughing, he put his hand under her chin, tilting up her face, and kissed her.

II

Hal Willoughby's careless parting kiss remained the only one that Adela was destined to receive.

For ten years more she lived with her mother, and heard her say proudly to other mothers, coming with the news of Mollie's engagement, or Dolly's beautiful new baby:

"Ah, I still keep my Adela, I'm glad to say. She's almost too fastidious, I sometimes think. She's never made herself cheap with anyone. And then there's her writing, too."

Adela had slowly been making a name for herself, but her great success only came after her mother's death. A long novel, at which she had been working for several years, made her reputation in the world of letters.

She had inherited money from her mother, and her books brought her in more.

Adela was able to indulge in artistic necessities.

It became imperative that she should retire, whenever she wanted to write, to a Yorkshire moor with an atmosphere of ruggedness and strength, and very few trees.

So many journalists, so many fellow-writers, such a number of the new-born coterie that "followed the Adela Alston method" had inquired so earnestly in what peculiar setting Adela found it necessary to enshrine her inspiration, that the need of the Yorkshire moor had suddenly sprung, full-grown, into being.

She built a two-roomed cottage, engaged a caretaker, and wrote in a small summer-house, wearing knickerbockers and sandals, and smoking violently. This was in the summer. In the winter, inspiration was obliged to content itself with Hampstead, and Adela had to wear shoes and stockings and a skirt.

At forty she had gained greatly in assurance, and knew herself for the leading spirit in a small group of intensely modern women writers, by whom she was devoutly worshipped.

Adela became accustomed to being the person who was listened to, in the society of her fellows.

They were not only interested in her work, but deeply, intensely interested in herself.

"You know almost too much of human nature, Adela. It's not decent."

Adela enjoyed being told that.

"I've seen all sorts in my time," she said musingly.

It would no longer have pleased her to be thought younger than she was. On the contrary, she was apt to emphasise in herself the aspect of a full maturity.

"That last study of yours is simply magnificent. Dear, I don't wonder you've never chosen to marry. No man's vanity could survive your insight."

A newcomer to the group leant forward eagerly. Her characteristic was lack of self-restraint, which she acclaimed in herself as fearlessness.

"But you've known the great realities—you've known passion," she urged foolishly. "You could never write as you do, otherwise."

Adela gazed at her new disciple from under drooping eyelids. "I am not ashamed of it," she said quietly. "I am proud of it."

The girl nodded with grotesque, unconscious vehemence.

The two other women-friends of Adela who were present, exchanged a meaning look with one another. Each had heard Adela's story before, had shown loyal pride and understanding. There was no need of further demonstration from them. Adela was looking at the girl.

"There was one man in my life," she said low and deeply. "There is never more than one—that counts. And a woman who has never loved, never been loved, never met her mate—has never lived."

The room was tensely silent.

"It was more than ten years ago, and I have outlived the poignancy of it. I have never seen him since—I never shall. But I make no secret of having known fulfilment."

Her voice was low and rich with intense enjoyment of her own effect.

"Even now, though, when all the storm and stress is long, long

160

past—it's odd, but the scent of a syringa in bloom can still hurt me. You see—I was swept right off my feet."

She paused before concluding with the words that she had unconsciously learnt by heart, so significantly did they always round off her retrospect.

"I had waited for him all my life. He asked everything, and I gave—everything."

"Ah!"

"You splendid woman!"

Adela leant back again, her large eyes gazing abstractedly into the past, full of a brooding satisfaction. Her lips exhaled a sound that was barely audible.

"Hal Willoughby!"

Time works wonders.

THE GALLANT LITTLE LADY

I

"I hope you are using all your influence to prevent the marriage?" said Clyde, in the impersonal tone that he always adopted when speaking to his wife of her only daughter.

"Why, Charles? They're madly in love."

"That is why," said Sir Charles.

"What do you mean?"

Lady Clyde had not the slightest desire to know what her husband meant, and had already made up her mind that she disagreed with it root and branch, so she said, "What do you mean?" in a tone of indignation, and not one of enquiry, and gave him no time to answer.

"Richard is a gentleman, he's earning a very good salary, and he adores Rita. The only possible objection is their having to live in the East, but everyone says the Malay States are quite healthy, and she's very strong, thank heaven. If she's plucky enough to face it, I don't see how we can object."

"My objection has nothing to do with their living in the Malay States. It is simply concerned with the fact that they will have nothing whatever to depend upon except Richard Lambourne's salary. He is a young man, he has saved nothing, and he has no expectations from anybody."

"Rita has her own small income."

"It might keep them from starvation, certainly, but it wouldn't be enough for a family."

"No one expects it to be. Richard will save if he has a wife, naturally, and he hopes to become a part owner of the rubber estate, later on. After all, it's very creditable for a man of his age to have been made general manager already."

"Very."

"Then what have you against him?"

"Nothing at all," said Sir Charles mildly.

"A minute ago you were telling me how you hoped I should use my influence to prevent this marriage. If you have nothing against him, why shouldn't they marry?"

"Perhaps I have 'something against' Rita, as you express it."

"Rita is only your step-daughter, Charles, and I know very well that your own children——"

162

"Our own children——"

"That they come first, and always have. But I have an unprejudiced eye," said Lady Clyde warmly, "and I don't pretend that Rita isn't a greater deal cleverer, prettier, and more attractive than all the others put together. And as for talking of having anything against her, it's the sheerest nonsense, as even you must know."

Sir Charles looked at his wife with an expression which she had long ago summed up, not inaptly, as "Charles looking as though he couldn't decide if one were worth explaining the alphabet to or not." On this occasion, Sir Charles appeared to decide in favour of the modicum of intelligence required.

"My case is simply this, Catherine. If Richard Lambourne and Rita marry now, they are entirely dependent upon Richard's job. Say he loses it, or loses his health—which amounts to the same thing—or falls off his horse and breaks his neck, Rita may be left with a child, or children, and nothing whatever to live on except a yearly sum which she has hitherto spent upon her clothes, largely supplemented by presents from you."

"As though Rita wouldn't always have a welcome from me, and as though I wouldn't share my last crust with her!"

"On the contrary, I should expect you to divide your last crust into equal parts between Rita and your four other children," said Sir Charles with coldness. "But apart from last crusts, which is a rhetorical way of speaking, you had better understand once and for all, my dear Catherine, that my sons and daughter are not to be sacrificed to Rita. If she marries this man, he must keep her. This house is her home, and has been so for twenty years or so, but once she is married, it ceases to be her home. I am sorry if I hurt your feelings, but if Rita is to take the risk of marriage with a man who has nothing to depend on but what he can earn for himself, she had better understand exactly what she is doing. Personally, I consider her entirely unfitted to take such a risk."

"She is more than ready to take any risk. You are perfectly incapable of understanding Rita, Charles, and what a generous, ardent nature she has. And she is very, very much in love, for the first time in her life. You know as well as I do that plenty of people have wanted to marry Rita, and I think it's wonderful that she should have refused so many offers, to give herself to a man who isn't rich, simply because she loves him."

"You look upon it as being decided, then?"

"Of course I do. She is absolutely determined to marry him and go out with him at once. I can't refuse my consent—and I shan't—and they're not dependent upon yours, Charles."

She looked at him with a rather nervous defiance, but Sir Charles said with great calm:

"Certainly they're not. I shall therefore consider the subject closed, so far as my objections go."

He kept his word, as he invariably did.

The wedding of Rita and Richard took place six weeks later.

Rita was little and very pretty, with big dark eyes, a pathetic baby face, and, in rather quaint contrast, a very erect little figure and a decided bearing.

Unlike her stepfather, the majority of her friends and relations fully realised the beautiful recklessness of Rita's love-match.

"A very gallant little lady!" said an old friend of Lady Clyde's, and she reversed an opinion which she had hitherto held as to his senility. He used the same phrase, which had evidently caught his ancient fancy, when the bride was making her farewells, and it oddly suited her appearance, in a velvet dress and a three-cornered hat with a long plume, vaguely recalling pictures of cavalier heroines.

"So she's marrying all for love, and going eight thousand miles away from home!" said Rita's aged admirer. "None of your mercenary, modern, ideas there. A gallant little lady, I call her."

II

The same phrase was repeated, and by many people, when Rita and Richard Lambourne came home again, three years later. The great rubber slump had come, and Richard had lost his job. He said that he hoped to find something to do in England.

"Professional men of all classes are hoping exactly the same thing at the present moment, all over the country," said Sir Charles Clyde.

The Lambournes stayed with the Clydes for a little while, then they and their baby and their nurse moved into a tiny house on the outskirts of a large neighbouring town, and then it was that such a number of people took to making use of the apt descriptive phrase first employed when Rita married.

Many of them had known her in her girlhood, the spoilt and favoured child of Lady Clyde, at home in her stepfather's house.

They could fully appreciate the contrast with her present position.

Richard could not find any work, although he answered

164

advertisements and wrote to influential friends. He was not a strong man, and very soon showed signs of great discouragement and anxiety.

Rita, on the contrary, was always cheerful, and discussed the situation very frankly, laughing merrily at her own struggle with unaccustomed privations.

"It's so lucky I've got a little money that my own father left me. By managing very, very carefully, we're living on that. Poor Richard hadn't a penny beyond his salary, and now of course that's all gone—poor darling!"

She was drolly confidential with her numerous friends.

"It's so funny to have to think before I take a second helping of pudding, even, and yet I suppose I really ought to. But I don't think I've got a very large appetite, have I, Richard?"

"No, you haven't."

"What a good thing!" She laughed as she spoke, but Richard remained unsmiling and miserable, and gradually it became evident to Rita's friends that one of Rita's trials was her husband's inability to face their position with a gallant laugh, as she did.

As time went on, and there appeared to be no hope of a salary for Richard, she sent away the little girl's nurse.

"I think I ought to be able to manage. Lots of poor women have to, only it's a great pity I was brought up to play the piano, and dance, and play tennis, instead of learning to cook. One somehow never thought of it's being necessary."

"It oughtn't to be necessary now," said Richard violently, "if you'd married a fellow with money, or brains enough to make some."

"Why, I might have been a millionairess, if I'd married the first man that ever proposed to me," she said brightly. "Doesn't it seem odd?"

He made no answer.

"D'you know, darling, I saw a really lovely jumper in Colson's window to-day. It was real old rose, the colour that suits me. It was one of the sale things and marked down to half a guinea. I had a frightful struggle—it is such ages since I had anything new. I wouldn't even let myself go into the shop, though I had to get some things for baby. I went somewhere else. I felt I couldn't bear to come out of Colson's without that jumper. It was so lovely—and really marvellously cheap. It's been haunting me ever since."

"Surely we can find half a guinea," said Richard, his face flushing.

"Richard!" She gave a little laughing scream. "Why, I work out every penny of my income on paper before I spend it, and do you

165

know what's left over for my clothes, when I've paid the wages and the rent, and rates and taxes, and the housekeeping books? Just—exactly—five pounds a year!"

She held up five fingers, laughing.

"I know."

"I can't believe that I once spent five pounds a year, or thereabouts, on gloves, but I suppose I did. I don't really know how I could manage now, if mummie didn't still give me so many presents."

She looked at him with her head on one side, rather like a very pretty squirrel.

"I do manage rather well, don't I, dear? I have to work pretty hard, you know."

"Of course you manage well," he said ungraciously. He hardly ever encouraged her with praise nowadays, although she was doing wonders. He only gave way to violent outbreaks of despair and self-reproach, when she assured him that she could do without things that she had had all her life, and that she wasn't really so very tired after two bad nights with the baby.

"Isn't it lucky I'm so strong?" she sometimes asked her friends. "I do a lot of the housework myself, you know, because we can only afford one servant, of course, and she's a rough sort of girl. It was so funny at first, I couldn't understand that class of servant at all. At home, of course, the maids were all quite different. Ellen means very well, really, though I've had to learn cooking, so as to do a certain amount myself. Will you forgive me now, if I run to see that Richard's supper is all right—not burning?"

She tripped away, still laughing, in spite of the tired lines that were beginning to show beneath her sparkling dark eyes.

"Rita is too wonderful, poor darling!" said Lady Clyde. "As she says herself, she's never in her life been used to poverty. And look at the way she makes the best of things! You know they're living on her tiny little income, that she manages too wonderfully for words. You can't say now, Charles, as I remember you once did, that Rita, of all people, wasn't fitted to take the risk of poverty."

Whether Sir Charles could, or could not, have repeated his axiom, was not destined to be made clear, for he said nothing at all.

He did, however, make many attempts to find a job for Richard, and went to see the originator of the phrase that described Richard's wife so well—"a gallant little lady"—who was connected with some highly-remunerative business.

The old man shook his head.

"I'm on the point of retiring, Sir Charles. Times are bad, though

I've made my pile, but it was done by hard work at one job all my life. I'll see if there's anything for your—stepson, is it?"

"He is no relation of mine," said Sir Charles very distinctly. "He married my wife's only daughter by her first husband. He is now obliged to live upon her—very small—fortune."

"I've heard something of that. Poor little lady—she's doing wonders, I hear. Well, well, I'll see if they've anything to offer the lad, but we don't want men without experience these days, you know. But I'd like to do something, for the sake of that gallant little lady."

III

"Richard dear, I would like to ask mummie and Sir Charles to dinner—supper, I mean—one night. I've got a little cash in hand, so I shouldn't feel too extravagant. You know I got rather more than I expected, for the sale of that old bracelet of mine."

Richard did know, because Rita had told him this already, quite gleefully, although admitting that the bracelet had been a legacy from a specially beloved grandmother, and that it cost her a pang to let it go.

"I loathe your selling your jewellery. It makes me feel such a cad for having got you into this mess, though God knows I never foresaw anything like this. Rita, must you do these things?"

She looked at him with a face of piteous, childlike surprise. "Oh, aren't you at all pleased that we've got an extra pound or two, Richard? I'm sure you've no idea what a difference it makes."

He groaned impatiently.

"Of course, if you think I've no right to suggest entertaining anybody, even on a tiny scale, now we're so poor, I won't do it. It was silly of me, I daresay, but I haven't really properly got used not to having an occasional little party, I suppose. It's all right, Richard darling. Never mind."

She smiled bravely.

"Rita, I shall go mad if I can't find a job, and take you out of this sort of thing," said Richard, and he began to pace up and down the little room.

When Lady Clyde and her husband did come to dinner, Rita told her mother privately that poor darling Richard was becoming almost hysterical sometimes. It did make things so much, much

167

harder when one was doing all one could to keep up under the strain, and be always bright and ready to make the best of it.

"No one can say you're not doing that, my dearest child," said her mother.

Tears of mingled admiration and compassion rose to her eyes when Rita apologised gaily for the poverty of the fare, when she corrected herself every time that she mentioned the word dinner instead of supper, and when she laughingly excused herself for having to run away and help with the washing-up, because the servant now was only a daily one, and went home early.

"It seemed so funny at first, mummy, and I was always ringing the bell and expecting it to be answered, like when I used to ring for Cooper or Ellis or Mary, at home. I really can't believe that I had a maid all for myself, just to do my hair and keep my clothes tidy, not so very long ago."

"What a plucky little thing she is!" said her mother in a choked voice.

She glanced resentfully at Richard, who sat silent, moody and haggard, without endorsing her tribute to his wife in any way.

He looked very ill, but Lady Clyde at the moment could only realise to what straits he had brought Rita, and with what surly unresponsiveness he seemed to confront her courageous acceptance of poverty.

Lady Clyde asked her husband that night if he could not, as man to man, give Richard Lambourne a hint that his ungracious attitude to his wife, whilst living on her money, was the final crown of the wrongs that he had done her.

"I was going to suggest, personally, that you should give Rita a hint," said Sir Charles.

"Rita! Why, when I think of that poor child's gallantry——"

"Exactly. My own impression is that a very little more of it will drive Lambourne into a mad-house, or worse."

Sir Charles spoke in his usual level accents, and Lady Clyde did not attempt to attach any meaning to his words. Neither did they recur to her when Richard Lambourne disproved her assertion that he had placed the crown upon the wrongs done to his wife, by the final ignominy of suicide.

"Coward, coward!" sobbed Lady Clyde. "Can you deny that he was a coward, Charles?"

"No. Richard was a coward," said Sir Charles gravely.

"After all that poor little Rita had done!"

"And said," added Sir Charles, not flippantly, and half under his breath.

The old magnate who had admired Rita at her wedding made use of almost the same words as Lady Clyde.

"After all that his wife had done, and was doing, to quit like that, and leave her to face the life he'd brought her to! What a brute!"

A little while afterwards he proposed to Rita, diffident, in spite of his wealth, because of the great difference in their ages.

She accepted him, and this time it was Sir Charles, looking at the bridegroom's bald head and infirm gait beside the pretty bride at the quiet wedding, who repeated to himself the old man's catchword, with an ironical emphasis of his own:

"A very gallant little lady."

THE HOTEL CHILD

(To Y. de la P.)

I

The first time that I saw her was in Rome. I was governess to the children at the British Embassy, and every morning before breakfast I took them out into the Borghese Gardens.

They were very good, insignificant little children, and never gave me any trouble. Whilst they played tame little games between the grey-green olive trees, I used to watch the more amusing Italian children in the Gardens, the biggest groups consisting of pupils from the great white Convento dell' Assunzione, on the corner of the Pincio.

But the little girl in whom I took the greatest interest was always by herself. An enormous grey limousine would leave her at the entrance to the Gardens, and fetch her away again at the end of an hour. Sometimes the limousine, which was always empty except for a liveried chauffeur, appeared to have forgotten her, and then I was obliged to take my children away, leaving her serious and solitary, and quite undisconcerted, sitting on her bench. I judged her to be about eight years old, and the child of rich people. Her white embroidered dresses, far too elaborate, were expensive, and she always wore white shoes and stockings.

At first, her nationality puzzled me. Her quite straight hair was black, cropped short round her beautifully shaped little head in a fashion that was then very unusual, and her lashes were as long and as black as those of any Roman-born child. But her grave eyes were of a deep grey, and her skin, fine and colourless. Perhaps she was scarcely pretty, but her poise, her erect gracefulness, above all, her unmistakable air of breeding, made her remarkable. It was that air of aristocracy that made me feel sure that, in spite of her independence, she was not American. One gets to know, after seven years spent in the best families. The American children are well-drilled, well-dressed, well-behaved—sometimes—but they never achieve that look of distinction. Some of the French ones have it, but then those are the children of the old Catholic families, and so they are poor, and generally badly dressed. On the whole, it is to be seen amongst the English as often as anywhere—and then, it is

170

almost always accompanied by the expression that denotes, to an experienced governess, either stupidity or adenoids—and sometimes, indeed, both.

My little aristocrat of the Borghese Gardens spoke Italian perfectly. I heard her greet the chauffeur when he came for her, and those were the times when she was most childlike. The man very often let her take the wheel, after he had started the car, and I used to watch, not without misgivings, the great car sliding away, with the small erect figure in the driving-seat, her straight black fringe blowing back from her forehead, her tiny hands gripping the big wheel.

My charges, it need hardly be said, might never speak to strange children, but one day the unknown little girl restored to me a toy that one of them had dropped the day before.

"I found it, after you'd gone," she said very politely and distinctly.

I knew then that she must be English, at least in part.

My children were playing at a distance, and after thanking her for returning the plaything, I sat down on the stone bench that she had made her own.

After an instant's hesitation, she sat down there, too.

We entered into conversation.

I asked whether she lived in Rome.

"No. My papa is here on business for a little while, and then we are going to Paris again."

"Your home is in Paris, then?"

She looked rather puzzled. "I don't know Paris well," she observed apologetically. "We were only there once before, when mama was with us. It was a nice hotel, I thought, but noisy. This one—the Grand—is better. Have you been much in Paris?"

"Not since I was at school there. My French was acquired in Paris," I added, automatically.

One says that kind of thing so often, to please the parents.

"Mademoiselle aime parler francais, hein?" she enquired, with a little smile.

Her French was as perfect as her Italian, or her English; and it was evidently natural to her to speak either language.

"Are you English?" I could not refrain from asking her.

"My papa is Italian—mama was half English, and half French."

Was? Then her mother must be dead. That would account for the empty limousine, and the strange independence of the child.

"Mama is in New York, now, we think," she remarked. "I am to join her when I am ten; that was arranged for, in the deed of separation."

171

"Separation?" said I.

"There is no divorce in Italy," said the little creature, shrugging her shoulders. "Papa is a Catholic, though not, of course pratiquant. They have been separated since I was seven."

"Then who—who——" I wanted to ask who looked after her, but such a form of words seemed singularly inappropriate. "Who looks after your papa's house?" I found at last.

"We are in hotels, most of the time, papa and I, and my maid, Carlotta, but in the holidays—les grandes vacances—we go to the country somewhere—villegiatura—and there is a lady then, always."

Her grave eyes looked at me. "A different one," she explained, "each time."

Her very complete understanding of the status held by the "ladies" was implicit in her manner, but that struck me less poignantly than did her philosophical acceptance of all that they stood for.

The grey limousine came into sight, and she made an amiable little sign to the chauffeur.

"I must go now. It doesn't do to keep the auto waiting."

In her grave little voice, was all the circumspection of the child that has learnt to fend for itself, that knows by experience that it will only be tolerated so long as it gives no trouble, runs counter to no prejudices, is guilty of no indiscretions.

"It has been so pleasant to talk to someone English. Good-bye Miss——?"

Her little pause was exactly that of a grown-up person, before an unknown or unremembered name. And what precocity of discernment had told her that "Miss" was the suitable prefix?

"Miss Arbell," said I. "Tell me your name before you go."

"Laura di san Marzano."

She pronounced Laura in the Italian way—Lah-o-ra.

When I held out my hand, she kissed it, as Italian children do, and after she had climbed to the driving-seat, she waved to me, before turning the grey car down the hill.

I looked for her every morning after that, but she never came to the Borghese Gardens again.

II

The second time that I saw Laura di san Marzano was nearly four years afterwards, in the hall of the Majestic Hotel, at Lucerne.

I had thought of her, at intervals, and had no difficulty in recognising her, in spite of the difference between eight years old and twelve.

She was tall and very slim, and the set of her dark head on her straight shoulders was just the same. Her black hair now fell in a long plait to her waist, but she still wore the straight, short fringe that suited her du Maurier profile.

It was late afternoon—tea-time, and the hall was full of people, and noisy.

Laura sat motionless, but somehow, one felt, very attentive, beside a beautifully-gowned and jewelled and painted woman, who was talking to half a dozen men.

Mama?

She looked very young to have a child of Laura's age.

Then I saw that Laura's green silk frock was absurdly short, and made in a babyish style, that matched the huge bow of green satin ribbon unnecessarily fastened over one ear.

My pupil, a nearly grown-up one, was late, and as I waited for her, I watched Laura.

Presently our eyes met. At once recognition leapt into hers, and she smiled at me, and bowed.

I returned the salutation—with infinitely less grace, as I knew in my middle-class British self-consciousness—and wondered whether she would come and speak to me.

Later on she did so, when the group round mama was at its noisiest.

"How do you do, Miss Arbell?" There was not the faintest hesitation over my name. "I used to see you often in the Borghese Gardens, in Rome, and once we talked together. I hope you remember?"

"I remember very well," said I, "but I am surprised at your doing so. You were so very young then, and you must have met so many people since."

"I never forget people," said Laura simply.

"You left Rome suddenly, didn't you?" I continued. "I was there for nearly a month after our meeting, but I never saw you in the gardens again."

Laura shook her head slightly.

"I can't remember," she admitted. "Very likely we left suddenly. One does that so often. The management of the hotel becomes intolerable, or tiresome acquaintances appear—and then the simplest thing is to pack up and go elsewhere."

She spoke so evidently from experience that one could but accept her strange, rootless, attitude as part of her natural equipment.

We talked for a little while, and she told me, or I deduced, that since the Roman days she had been a great deal in Paris—("I adore the Opera there, but the theatres not much")—and then in New York, with mama. She was to spend the next few years with mama.

173

Where?

Laura's shoulders indicated the faintest of shrugs. Anywhere. Mama liked New York as well as most places, but personally Laura thought that the rooms in the hotels there were always too hot. They went to London a good deal. Delightful—she smiled at me politely— but one missed the sunshine. Her point of view, inevitably, was one of great sophistication. It did not, to my mind, detract from her charm, which had never been of a direct, childlike kind, but rather of a description so subtle that amongst the many it might easily pass for mere oddity.

"I hope we shall meet again," she said to me, when a certain nervous movement in the group of mama's admirers had culminated in the detachment of a tall, fair youth, who was coming now towards Laura herself.

"I am afraid that I leave here to-morrow. My pupil and I are on our way to rejoin her parents in Italy."

"We may be gone ourselves to-morrow. I meant for later on— any time, anywhere." She smiled charmingly, but her unchildlike eyes remained serious and rather weary.

I heard the fair youth say something to her, with a burst of meaningless laughter. She did not laugh in return, but her clear, well-bred little voice was raised to a sympathetic tone of interest.

"Mama likes an olive in hers, always, but for me I prefer a sweet Martini—with two cherries, if you please."

I saw Laura twice again before leaving Lucerne, but we did not speak to one another.

The first time, at seven o'clock the evening of that same day, was in one of the gigantic hotel corridors, on the first floor, where I was waiting for the lift that was to take me to the fifth.

The hotel hairdresser, in a white coat, with an immense head of curled and discoloured yellow hair, stood before a shut bedroom door. It flew open suddenly, and then closed sharply behind Laura di san Marzano.

"Vous voila donc! Eh bien, il est trop tard."

Her voice was ice, her face scornful and unbelieving as she listened to the man's torrent of excuses for his tardiness.

"Assez," said Laura. "Madame est fort mécontente. Elle ne veut plus de vous."

"Mademoiselle——"

"C'est inutile. Madame se passera de vous."

And as the hairdresser turned away, grumbling and disconcerted, she added superbly:

"J'arrangerai la chose. Soyez exacte demain. Mais pour ce soir, c'est moi qui coifferai madame."

174

Much later in the evening, when I had long ago despatched my pupil to the bedroom opening out of mine, I returned for a moment to the hot and strident lounge in order to make certain enquiries at the office.

Mama was in a white wicker armchair, with crimson and orange cushions overflowing upon either side of it, and showing up the elaborate waves of her hair, as black as Laura's own. The paint that I had seen on her face earlier in the day was now concentrated into one scarlet curve upon her mouth, her white lace dress was held up by narrow black velvet straps cutting across the opulent creaminess of her shoulders, and the electric light above her head had fastened upon the diamond butterfly bows of her satin shoes, so that they winked and flashed right across the hall.

One hardly saw—certainly did not distinguish—the figures that composed her numerous entourage, but the prevailing black and whiteness, the glitter of continually raised small glasses, gave a general impression of unrelieved masculinity.

Laura sat beside her mother, on an upright chair. She was dressed in rose colour, a frock even shorter than the green one that I had seen before. Her straight hair had been somehow persuaded into a semblance of long curls; the green silk bow over her left ear had been replaced by a pink one with fringed ends.

She did not see me. Her eyes, indeed, were glazed with fatigue, and every now and then her head fell forwards and was jerked upwards again.

The hall was unendurably hot with a breathless, artificial heat, and the orchestra was playing an American rag-time that every now and then succeeded in out-sounding the medley of raised voices and high-pitched laughter and clinking glasses.

It was long after eleven o'clock.

As I looked at Laura, I saw that her slim, silk-clad legs were swinging gently to and fro between the bars of the high-backed chair. Her feet, in bronze-coloured dancing slippers, could not quite reach the floor.

For the first time, I saw her as the child she really was—the efficient, helpless, cosmopolitan, traditionless, hotel child.

III

It is a far cry from the family of a British Ambassador—collectively distinguished, if individually dull—and the blue wonders of Italy, to an English Girls' School and the grey horrors of an east coast town.

The post that I filled temporarily at Lundeen School was not one that I should have considered, but for personal and family reasons of convenience. They are long since past, and matter nothing to the story.

But it was at Lundeen School that I saw Laura di san Marzano for the third and last time.

It was the most inappropriate setting imaginable.

She was left there by mama, in mid-term, because a continental doctor had declared that she needed bracing air and companionship of her own age, and also—this I learnt later, quite incidentally, from Laura herself—because mama and a cher ami had suddenly planned a visit to Monte Carlo for the express purpose of visiting the Casino, to which Laura, being under twenty-one, could not have been admitted.

Laura, as the hotel child, had been pathetic, but her dignity had been safeguarded, if not actually enhanced, by the kaleidescopic background of her surroundings.

At school, she was pitiful—and out of place. The girls, without ill nature, despised her from the first.

She arrived amongst them in the short, fanciful, ultra-picturesque silk frocks and infantile bows of hair ribbon that I had seen her wear abroad. Those unimaginative, untravelled English schoolgirls had seen no one like her before, and what they did not know, by experience or by tradition, they distrusted and disliked.

Lundeen School made demands upon the pupils' physiques, upon their powers of conformity, and upon each one's capacity for assimilating wholesale a universally applied system.

Laura di san Marzano had no chance at all.

The child who "never forgot people" could not remember her multiplication table, and although she spoke perfectly at least three languages besides English, she had never learnt syntax, nor read a line of any history. She had seen the Guitrys play in Paris—(and from her crisp appreciations and criticisms I deduced that no finest nuance of their art had been lost upon her)—but she had memorized no standard selections from the poets. And she did not know how to learn.

176

No one, not even the head mistress, was very much disturbed by Laura's educational deficiencies, because it was so evident from the first that her stay amongst us would only be a very temporary affair.

Mama would certainly swoop down again, probably without warning, and resume Laura as suddenly as she had discarded her.

That was how mama always did things, one felt sure.

Laura herself, although evidently aware of her shortcomings, accepted them with a grave, but unexaggerated, regret. She seemed, quite without arrogance, to know that, even educationally, there were other standards than those of Lundeen, and that her connection with these latter was after all merely transitory.

What really distressed her, and shocked her too, I think, was the attitude of the other girls.

Compared with the hotel child, there was only one word that adequately described these daughters of so many excellent English homes—and that word was uncivilised.

They played unbeautiful games violently, they spoke in hideous slang, they were rudest when they intended to be most friendly.

Towards Laura di san Marzano, indeed, they did not wish nor attempt to display friendliness. They were simply contemptuous.

And I saw that the hotel child minded that, both from pride and from ultra-developed social instinct.

My work was entirely amongst the elder girls, and I saw very little of Laura during her brief stay, but towards the end of it, something happened. The rumour arose and spread like wild-fire, even to reaching the Common Room of the teaching staff, that Laura di san Marzano was in disgrace with her fellows for cheating over an examination paper.

The tradition of Lundeen was that of the public-school code. Cribbing was permissible: 'copying' or peeping at the questions set for an examination, was impossible.

They were already prejudiced against her; the accusation was accepted on the instant by her contemporaries.

The Prefectorial system was in full force at Lundeen, and in any case, I could not have made the affair my business. But it so happened that I was present when Laura uttered what I believe to have been her one and only specific denial of the charge against her. I came unexpectedly into the room, and saw the semi-circle of self-righteous inexpressive, young faces that confronted Laura, who stood, rather pale and with her head held proudly high, and spoke very softly and clearly.

"I didn't cheat. Those who thought they saw me, made a mistake. You are being very unjust and cruel, all of you."

She was looking the head of her class straight in the eyes as she spoke, and the girl, giving her back look for look, made a sound that unmistakably expressed contemptuous incredulity.

"What is all this?" said I sharply.

They were taken aback, all of them. There was an instant of confused silence, and it was, after all, only the hotel child who possessed enough of savoir faire to reply to me.

"Miss Arbell," she said courteously, "it was a—a necessary conversation. It is over now."

She crossed the length of the room, very composedly, and went out quietly.

Her ostracism, after that, was complete. It lasted for a week, and then, just as one had always surmised would happen, mama, in sables and violets, drove up in a blue Lanchester car, and said that she and Laura (who looked so much stronger and better for the change) would at once go straight to Paris, give themselves enough time to find some clothes, and sail for New York the following week.

The hotel child, her face radiant, came to find me and say good-bye to me. She was incapable, for all mama's imperious haste, of forgetting or omitting the courtesy.

"Do you actually leave this evening?" I asked her.

Mama had been even more impetuous than I had anticipated.

"Yes. I need never see any of them again."

"It has been an experience, at least," I reminded her.

"Yes—but——" she shrugged her shoulders.

"Expensively bought?" I suggested. And, since she was leaving, I thought that I might add: "At least, my dear, you have kept your colours flying. These last days have been very trying, I am afraid, but you come out of them better than our friends of the Fourth Form, to my thinking."

"Thank you," said Laura. She looked at me with her grave, straightforward eyes.

"It would have been much easier, though, if only I really hadn't cheated."

There is a postscript to the story of the hotel child. A very few years later I heard of her marriage to the Prince d'Armaillh'ac-Ambry, the representative of the noblest, and one of the wealthiest, of French families. I believe that they live almost entirely on his estates in Brittany, and that the Princess interests herself personally in the numerous peasantry around them.

Her two children, a boy and a girl, are brought up in great simplicity, and to the strictest and most orthodox Catholicism.

IMPASSE

(To S.M.A.)

Two, three, five Dedicated Virgins. They stood before their Reverend Mother, ponderous black folds of serge sweeping the boards round each flat-soled pair of black list slippers.

"The orphans must go to the dentist," said Reverend Mother, mournfully, yet with determination. "Here we are in a Protestant country. We must adapt ourselves to the conditions of our exile. The orphans will have to be taken to the dentist's house."

The nuns looked at one another, and at Reverend Mother, and solemnly nodded.

It was an innovation, but if Reverend Mother said so, it must be right.

"Sister Clara and Sister Dominic, you will take three orphans to the dentist to-morrow."

Sister Clara drew herself up a little. Her throat swelled beneath the white swathings that bound her head and neck, and her double chin momentarily became three.

"Yes, Mother dear," she said proudly.

Her Irish voice was rich and deep, compared with the thin, nasal tones of the Frenchwomen.

"Shall I order a cab for them, Mother?"

That was Sister Caroline, the sœur econome.

"No, no. They must walk ... holy poverty.... You will put on the heavy travelling veils, Sisters, and the big cloaks, just the same as for a journey."

The heat of that would be stifling, in this weather and on foot! An unmortified thought.... Sister Clara stuck a pin in her sleeve. She would remember to confess a slight yielding to sensuality of thought.

There had been similar yieldings, once or twice, within the last year.

"Yes, Mother dear. Sister Dominic'll sit in the waiting room with two of the dear orphans, and I'll be looking after the one that's in with the dentist. I'll not take an eye off of her, on any pretext whatever. I quite understand, Mother dear, that's the way it'll be. Make your mind easy."

One had to be knowing, and careful, going out into the world.

There was a sense of adventure in setting out, the additional veil hanging swart, and straight, and heavy, pulling a little so that one's head jerked slightly backwards every now and then.

179

Sister Dominic held a stout umbrella in one black-cotton-gloved hand, whilst the other one grasped the wrist of the youngest orphan. The other two orphans, obscured in blue serge and hard, dark, straw hat-brims, each held on to a fold of Sister Clara's habit.

One thing, Reverend Mother had promised that the community should recite the Litany of Loretto after office just as they did to ensure anyone from the convent a safe journey.

So they'd be protected, even scurrying, a row of five, holding on to one another, across the streets, in front of those frightful honking motor-cars, that looked like they'd take the heads off of you, give them a chance.

"This'll be it, Dominic dear. No. 3."

A maid in a cap and apron to open the door—and the smartness of her! All grey-and-white, and showing her shape the way a modest convent-bred girl would never have done.

And the waiting-room, with a carpet, and padded chairs, and a fine pot-plant—putting worldly ideas into the orphans' heads, as likely as not. As for the pictures and books on the table....

"Don't be casting your eyes about that way, children dear. Sit quiet now. Dominic, the hats'll have to come off of them, we may be sure of that. We'll pile them this way, on the chair, and you'll keep an eye on them, for fear someone else'll be coming in and perhaps making off with them. It's not as though we were in a good Catholic country."

The hats of the orphans were stacked upon a chair, and Sister Dominic sat upon the edge of another chair, facing them. She held her umbrella.

"If he does well by the children, the sisters'll go to him. The Infirmarian says there's some of them with teeth in a terrible state."

Sister Clara's tongue sought familiar cavities, and her hand went to the particular fold of serge sleeve in which were imbedded two large pins, one of which was taken out at the end of meals, and replaced after use in the exact same place, so as to save making a fresh hole.

"If you'll step this way, Sister——"

Mother of Mercy! What a start she'd got! It was the man himself, and smiling, too, standing holding the door open. Awfully young-looking, with dark eyes that might have been Irish, and a queer white coat on him.

And the gentleness of him, when he'd got the orphan into that chair of his! She'd only to stir, and him stopping the machine, and saying, with that smile, that he was afraid it was hurting her.

As if one didn't go to the dentist to be hurt, and the pain to be offered up for all Reverend Mother's intentions!

Look at the hands of him!

She watched them, moving softly and skilfully. Presently he talked to her, at first friendly, joking, little questions, then at more length, telling about himself. He was a stranger in the town, too.

"It'll be the grand thing for you, if Reverend Mother sends the orphans regularly. I'll put in a good word for you," she ventured, and he looked at her, screwing-up his eyes, and laughing.

She'd not spoken to any man, not counting the good holy priests which was a different thing altogether, for many years.

But if they were all like this, where would be the harm in them at all? She'd make the orphans start a novena for his conversion to the Faith, that very night.

"Now the next child, please."

He spent half an hour on each orphan, and the last one, he said, would have to come again.

"I'll be bringing her along."

He entered the appointment in a little book.

"I've no secretary, you see, Sister—can't afford one yet!" and then he shook hands with her. "Good-bye."

The feel of his hand was just what she'd imagined it'd be, gentle, and yet strong. There were funny little dark hairs all down the back of it and along the wrist. And although it was such a hot day, the palm of him was cool and dry.

Sister Dominic spoke to her, humbly, on the way home.

"Well, you're a wonderful woman of the world, Sister Clara dear, getting us all safe there and back and talking to the man just as though it was the gardener at dear old Noisy-le-Grand. It won't be so hard, next time, if Reverend Mother sends us again."

Reverend Mother did send them again, with relays of orphans, and then Sister Clara alone, with old Mother Seraphina who spoke no English and whose cheap râtelier appeared to need endless adjustments.

And he was always kind, and he always smiled, with that screwing-up of his eyes, and talked to Sister Clara.

One day she said that she had toothache, and received Reverend Mother's leave to make an appointment for herself after Mother Seraphina's session. She had, for days, been devoured by an intense curiosity to know what it would feel like to have those hands hovering about one's face. Once, he had had to put his arm right round the back of Mother Seraphina's old head....

"No, it's not hurting me at all, at all." She smiled up at him; a smile that she felt to be beatific, half-hypnotised.

"Would you like to see what I've been doing?"

"I would."

181

"There—on the left—that big molar——"

He put a little mirror into her hands. And she that hadn't looked in a glass, hardly, since the day of her final vows, twelve years ago!

Gracious, what a colour she had! Plum-colour, that was her face. And the smile that had felt beatific, looking foolish and uncertain, as though she were ashamed of something. The glass turned dim as her heavy breathing struck it.

Would she perhaps have been breathing into his face that way all the time, and she never thinking of such a thing?

The face in the glass looked redder than ever. Mother of Mercy, this weather! The heat of it! And the holy habit no less than five smelly thicknesses of serge, and not wearing thin yet, though on the back of her year in and year out.

"That's the last stopping, Sister. I shan't have to trouble you again."

"Amn't I to come to you any more then?"

"It won't be necessary. What I've done should last you for a long while. But if you have pain, come to me at once. Any time."

What'd it be like, at all, not seeing him any more? Could it be that she'd become inordinately attached, the way the Imitation said was so wrong? And to a man, too.

She was a wicked creature, not worthy of the holy vocation.

"Is there nothing more needs doing?"

"Nothing at all. You have excellent teeth, Sister. There'll be no more trouble, now those fillings are in."

The smile he gave her! So that one hardly heard what he was saying....

"If the Reverend Mother wants anyone else seen to, I shall be very pleased to do what I can. Good-bye, Sister. I should like to have persuaded you that there's plenty of good work to be done outside, too. Take a capable woman like yourself, now. It seems a shame you should be shutting yourself up inside four walls. Why, you—you might have been my secretary, if I could only afford to have one!"

That was a grand laugh of his, it made one want to laugh too, only that one might start crying somehow.

It seemed there'd be nothing left to look forward to in the whole world after the shake of the hand meaning good-bye. There was still that....

It was the queer way to feel entirely, and her forty years old.

Touching the hand of him for the last time, and it strong and yet gentle at one and the same time, quite different to the hand of any woman....

It was over now, and one hurried away, scared that old Seraphina'd see something strange in the face of one.

"Will any more of the sisters be going to him, Mother Seraphina?"

"No."

"Nor any of the dear children?"

"No."

Mother of Mercy, there was no sleeping in this heat! But it wasn't the heat. It was the way one was fretting and crying after what couldn't be. Though what for couldn't it be, when he'd said himself that it was a sin and a shame for the like of her to be shut up inside four walls, and himself wanting a secretary and not able to pay one? There'd be some glad enough to work for him without any pay.

Day after day it went on, and night after night, till the pain in one's head was past bearing, and still there was no getting to sleep.

The things one thought of!

There was the door, giving right on to the street, and then only a bit of a walk, and oneself knowing every step of the way, and then the sight of him, and the feel of those hands of his—it was that would put everything right, and take the spell off of one.

On the hottest night of all, Sister Clara made up her mind. She'd break her holy vows, that were already broken in the heart of her, and go back into the world.

In the morning she dressed and went downstairs.

She'd not be taking anything with her. After Mass the nuns'd be going to the refectory, and they'd not be missing her for awhile, and they keeping the custody of the eyes the way the Holy Rule enjoined.

Oh, it was the fine nun she was, to talk about the Holy Rule.

The door was unlocked. Once outside on the pavement, there was nothing to do but pull it to again.

The slam of it!

There'd be no getting in again now, without a great ringing of the bell, and the portress coming to answer it, and the giving of scandal to the whole of them.

If it hadn't been for that slam of the door....

The weather had broken. It wasn't hot any more, but raw and chilly.

The way he'd laugh, and look at you, so interested in any little thing you said! It was wonderful.

What time did people in the world get up and start their day? Later than this, no doubt. But there'd be the waiting-room, where she'd sat with Sister Dominic and the orphans that first time of all. (Maybe she'd never set eyes on Dominic again.)

What for did that maid of his take so long to come to the door?

But it wasn't the maid who opened the door at last.

It was a person in a blue apron, with a man's cap pulled down over her eyes, and her sleeves rolled up, and a bucket with a mop in it at her down-at-heel feet.

"'E ain't come yet. Won't be 'ere, not for a hower, but if it's the toothache, you can come in and wait."

"Does he not live here, then?"

"Ho no,'e don't live 'ere. But 'e comes reg'lar, and 'e'll be along by-and-by. You go in and sit down. You won't mind me going on with the cleaning-up? Turned cold all of a sudden, ain't it?"

The rolled-back carpet in the waiting-room, the chairs piled, seat against seat, round the walls, the broom that presently chased into all the corners, made it seem colder.

It grew colder and colder as the hour went by.

That was the sound of a key in the lock outside.

"'Morning, Mrs. Hatch. A nasty change in the weather, isn't it?"

Mumble, mumble, mumble.

"Oh Lord, already!"

He came into the room where Sister Clara shuddered and cowered inside her folds of enveloping black serge.

Look at the face of him! Different, somehow.

You could see how he felt the sudden chilliness in the air, and he was rubbing his hands together, hard. They were different, too— all mottled with cold.

"You in pain, Sister?"

"I—I've come."

"M'm? I don't attend to anyone till nine o'clock, you know, as a rule, but if it's a question of pain.... Well, what can I do for you? By the look of you, it's an abscess, isn't it?"

THE APPEAL

This isn't a story. It's an attempt at reconstruction. Given my knowledge of the principals—Mary Jarvis, and her mother, Mrs. St. Luth—I think I can do it.

Mary Jarvis was my mother, and Mrs. St. Luth, of course, my grandmother. Thank god, I'm a modern and can look at them impersonally—judge each on her own merits, as it were.

My mother and my grandmother made scenes as other women make jumpers. It was their form of self-expression. I imagine— although I never knew for certain—that it was my father's inability to maintain himself à la hauteur, in the perennial melodrama that was my mother's idea of life, that led to my grandmother being invited to live with them.

She came when I, their only child, had barely reached the stage of exchanging my baby frills for first knickerbockers. (I am certain, although I don't remember it, that my mother wept and said she felt that she had lost her baby for ever.)

Already my parents were unhappy together. Mary—I call her so here for convenience, but she would never have tolerated it in reality—Mary, although really affectionate and impressionable, was fundamentally insincere, with herself and with everybody else. She lived entirely on the emotional plane, and when genuine emotions were not forthcoming she faked them by instinct. Her mother, who belonged to the same type, although with more strength of character, and far less capacity for affection, had always played up to her. They had their violent disputes and violent reconciliations— neither could have been happy without—but they did respect one another's poses.

But my father never played up.

He couldn't. Worse still, if he could have done so, he wouldn't— on principle.

Again I can't remember, but I can imagine, almost to the point of certainty, short and searing passages between my parents.

"Robert, I want you not to ask me to play the piano to-night."

(He so seldom gave her an opening, that she had to force them.)

"Off colour?"

"It isn't that. I heard to-day that Mrs. Thorndyke's child is dead. It—it upset me."

"But you didn't know the child."

"I know Katherine Thorndyke."

"You've met her once or twice, I remember. And didn't we hear that if the poor child had lived, it must have been an idiot?"

185

Probably, at that stage, my mother burst into tears. She'd been heading for that, of course, although she didn't know it consciously. But my father did, and had made her aware that he did, in a rather brutal fashion.

That was the way they reacted on one another.

It was better, after grandmother came. Curiously enough, my father liked her, although she and Mary had so many of the same characteristics. But I think he regarded her as a sort of lightning conductor.

For Mary herself, however, it was different. Like so many people who manufacture continual unhappiness for themselves, she had a frantic craving for happiness, and an irrational conviction that happiness was her due.

She told me herself, long afterwards, that she never had any thought of infidelity towards my father, nor did she ever meet any man who could or would have caused her to break her marriage vows. But—and this she didn't tell me, it's part of the reconstruction—she was constantly obsessed by a vague and romantic expectation of some such encounter. I imagine that she could not believe the world to have been created without a special application to her yearnings.

And then undoubtedly the nervous wear and tear that she imposed upon herself, and upon us all, told on her spirits. Her scenes with grandmother, although they may have served as a safety-valve, were too frequent. They may also have served to throw into painful contrast her husband's stolid opposition to any form of emotional stimulus.

However that may be, grandmother had formed part of our household for rather less than a year, when Mary suddenly ran away.

It was, I suppose, the only dramatic thing that she could think of, in a wet and dreary February, and I have no doubt at all that she did it on impulse. That is to say, she gave herself time to write an immensely long letter to my father—in which perhaps she set forth that view of herself which he never gave her adequate opportunity for putting into words—but she gave herself no time to pack up her things. She simply took her dressing-case, and I am sure that that was mostly filled with photographs in folding frames, and packets of letters tied up with ribbon, and little manuals of devotion heavily underscored in several places.

Then she walked out of the house, and to the station, and eventually got to Assisi. And they traced her there almost at once, partly because she took no pains to cover up her tracks, and partly because my grandmother—who understood the processes of her

186

mind—found a copy of a Life of St. Francis on the drawing-room sofa, face downwards, with one page all blistered, as though tears had fallen upon it.

My father, for his part, found the long letter that no doubt told him how little he had understood a sensitive nature, and possibly to what point their life together had become intolerable.

And this had the strange effect of making him resolve, and declare aloud, that nothing would induce him to try and get her back again. There must have been a stormy scene between him and my grandmother, who had all the conventionally moral instincts of her day, and was genuinely shocked and disturbed at her daughter's abrupt and violent casting off of her obvious responsibilities.

"For the child's sake, at least, Robert ..." she must have repeated many times.

(Neither she nor my mother ever understood the futility of repeating, again and again, words which had already failed of their appeal.)

"A child whose mother can leave him, at four years old, is better without her."

"It was madness, Robert, but you know she's not a wicked woman—my poor Mary. If you go and bring her back now, no one will ever know what has happened, and you can start a new life together, and try again."

"It would be useless."

"Don't, don't say that." The tears must have been pouring down her old face by that time. "Oh, Robert, give her another chance. This will have been a lesson to her—won't you forgive her and take her back?"

Well, in the end she prevailed to a certain extent—that is to say, my father would not seek out the culprit himself, but he would allow grandmother to do so, and if she brought Mary home again properly repentant he would not refuse to receive her and give her the "chance" of starting their married life afresh. "For the boy's sake."

My grandmother must have repeated that phrase a hundred times at least, and it was certainly her pièce de resistance in the scene at Assisi with Mary.

I've had a version of that scene from each one of them, and on the whole the accounts tally, although of course each viewed it—as they viewed everything—exclusively from the personal angle.

My mother saw only a young, beautiful, misunderstood woman, goaded to frenzy in the grip of an uncongenial marriage, taking a desperate step in search of freedom. And then, even stronger and more touching in her relinquishment, finding the courage, for love of her child, to return to the house of bondage.

And my grandmother, with equal inevitability, saw only a sorrow-worn woman, no longer young (but infinitely interesting), courageously undertaking a solitary journey, on a mission that should restore sanctity to a shattered home. And even as her urgent plea had shaken Robert's defences, so her eloquence, her boundless influence and unfaltering understanding, must prevail with the slighter, more trivial personality of her daughter. The achievement of persuading Mary to return to her husband and child was, my grandmother told me, the ultimate justification of her existence, in her own eyes.

As a matter of fact, I doubt if she, any more than the rest of us, felt her existence to be in any need of justification whatsoever—but she was addicted to phrases, and this one at least served as an indication to the magnitude of her effort.

For Mary did not capitulate without a struggle. And it is in the details of that struggle that my reconstruction work comes in, for although each of the protagonists has quoted to me whole sentences, and even speeches, of brilliant oratory from herself and inadequate rejoinder from the other, I do not believe either of them. Accuracy, with that type, can never co-exist with emotion—and emotion, real or imaginary, is never absent.

But this, I imagine, is more or less what took place in the sitting-room of the tiny albergo at Assisi:

"I've come to fetch you home, my child. You shall never hear one word of reproach—Robert only wants to begin again—a new life."

"Never, mother. It's impossible. I've borne too much. I can't ever go back to it. I must live my own life."

(Probably Mary had been reading The Doll's House. People were discovering Ibsen in those days.)

"Mary, it's not five years since you and Robert were married, in the little country church at home, by our dear old vicar, who held you at the font when I took you, a tiny baby, to be christened."

It may have been at this stage that Mary began to cry. Anyway, I'm certain that my grandmother did. Any allusions, however irrelevant, to little country churches at home, and Mary as a tiny baby, were always apt to bring the tears to her eyes—and I'm sure that neither of them had thought for an instant of steadying their nerves by sitting down to a solid meal. So that tears must have been easier, even, than usual.

"Robert doesn't understand me—he never will."

"Darling, don't you remember your early days together? The little things—little jokes, and allusions, and happinesses shared together? Does one ever forget?"

188

"No."

Mary sobbed. "But I can't go back to him."

I think that here, if my grandmother gave her a chance, she probably did make one—or part of one—of the speeches that she long afterwards quoted to me.

She was intensely unhappy. Robert did not understand her, and she could not live in an unsympathetic atmosphere. She should go mad. All that she had ever asked of life was peace, beautiful surroundings, and the ideal companion.... If she went back to Robert now, after having found courage to make the break, it would be a repetition of the misery that had broken her heart during the past three years.

(The hearts of my mother and grandmother both suffered innumerable breakages throughout their lives, neither of them ever seeming aware of the physiological absurdity of the expression.)

"It's braver to stay away than to go back and try and patch up something that can never be anything but a failure," quavered Mary, with a momentary flash of insight.

But of course grandmother couldn't leave it at that. She had the justification of her own existence to think of, for one thing. I am quite sure that a fortuitous street-musician, rendering "Santa Lucia" or "Silver Threads Amongst the Gold" in the distance, would have broken down Mary's frail barrier of honest thought, and have materially assisted my grandmother to her victory. Accessories were so absolutely essentials, to them both.

But so far as I know, grandmother had to win on points, as it were, and received no extraneous help in the shape of sentimental appeals from without.

She made her supreme effort.

"For the boy's sake, Mary ... your little, little boy. Is he to be motherless?"

"Wouldn't Robert let me have him?"

"No, my dear. How could he? I myself—the mother that bore you, Mary—I couldn't think it right that a woman who had deliberately deserted her husband and home should have the care of a little, innocent child."

"Oh, my baby!"

She sobbed and cried, but she had not yet capitulated. Grandmother, however, had gauged pretty accurately the force of the baby-motif.

"Before I came away, on my long, lonely journey," she said slowly, "I went up to the nursery, to say good-bye to Bobbie. He had on his blue overall—the one you embroidered for him last summer,

189

Mary—was it only last summer?—and he was playing with his engine, on the nursery floor, his dear, round face was so solemn...."

"Oh, don't—don't——"

But grandmother, the tears streaming from her eyes, relentlessly continued: "Darling, his big blue eyes looked up at me, and his little voice asked: 'Where's Mummie?'"

Did grandmother's—even grandmother's—conscience misgive her, at the quotation? That it was verbally correct, I have no doubt—but what of the intonation?

My grandmother's poignant rendering of "Where's Mummie?" no doubt contained all the pathetic appeal of bewildered and deserted childhood throughout the ages....

But mine—the original "Where's Mummie?..." I have no recollection of it, of course, but I do remember myself at four years old—a stolid, rather cynical child, utterly independent by temperament, and reacting strongly even then against a perpetually emotional atmosphere. And one knows the way in which small children utter those conventional enquiries which they unconsciously know to be expected of them ... the soft, impersonal indifference of the tone, the immediate re-absorption, without waiting for a reply, in the engrossing occupation of the moment....

Mary held out for a little while longer, but the heart went out of her resistance after the pitiful sound of that "Where's Mummie?" as my grandmother rendered it.

She gave in "for the boy's sake."

And my grandmother had justified her existence.

They travelled home together, and Mary averted anti-climax by quite a real nervous breakdown, that overtook her after she got home, before my father had had time to forgive her in so many words.

So they began again—literally.

It wasn't, in fact, possible for them to be happy together, and they never were so. I grew up in the midst of scenes, tears, and intermittent periods of reconciliation. There was no stability about my childhood; and no reality. Undoubtedly I was the victim—far more so than my father, who presently sought and found consolation elsewhere, or than Mary, whom he thus provided with a perfectly legitimate grievance that lasted her until he died, fifteen years later. After that, she was able gradually to forget that there had ever been unhappiness between them, and to assume the identity of a heart-broken widow.

Mrs. St. Luth, my grandmother, lived to be very old.

"But useless old woman though I am, God gave me the

190

opportunity of justifying my existence, when He let me bring a mother home to her little child...."

I wonder.

Thank god, I'm a modern.

THE FIRST STONE

A Play in One Act

Characters:
Mrs. Lloyd-Evans   *Members of the local Welfare*
Committee
Mrs. Ballantyne
Mrs. Akers
Miss Miller   *Secretary to the Committee.*

Scene

A committee-room on the top floor of a house in a small provincial town. Back of the stage, centre, there is a door, opening inwards on to the stage. To the right of the door, a few pegs are on the wall for hanging coats, etc. Right of the stage, is a good-sized window, showing distant views of chimney-pots outside. Left of the stage, a small gas-fire burns. Near it, a table and chairs have been formally arranged for the meeting.

The whole atmosphere of the room is cold and dreary. Time: a winter afternoon in 1917.

Miss Miller discovered. She is cold and tired-looking, mechanically arranging blotting-paper, etc. on the table.

Mrs. Ballantyne enters. She is prosperous-looking and clad in warm furs, and is out of breath from ascending the stairs.

Miss Miller: Good afternoon, Mrs. Ballantyne.

Mrs. Ballantyne (out of breath): Good afternoon. Oh dear, those stairs! I'm out of breath.

Miss Miller: They are trying, aren't they? Four flights!

Mrs. Ballantyne: Oh, you oughtn't to find them trying, at your age. Tell me, have you any idea why we've all been asked to come here to-day, Miss Miller? It's not the day for our regular meeting, at all.

Miss Miller: No, I've got the notice for that all ready to send out as usual. This is a special meeting that Mrs. Lloyd-Evans is calling.

192

She only sent me a note about it last night, telling me to get the room ready.

Mrs. Ballantyne: She wrote to me too, but she didn't say what it was all about. I suppose she'll have written to Mrs. Akers, as well.

Miss Miller: Here they are.

(Enter Mrs. Lloyd-Evans and Mrs. Akers. Mrs. Lloyd-Evans is mysterious and melancholy, and Mrs. Akers lively and full of undisguised curiosity. Both wear heavy coats, furs, etc. They shake hands with Mrs. Ballantyne, and nod and say how d'ye do to Miss Miller. Whilst they talk they loosen or take off their wraps, and place them on the pegs near the door.)

Mrs. Lloyd-Evans (to Mrs. Ballantyne): How d'ye do. We're all a little before our time, I think, but then as I always say, it's better to be too early than too late. (This she says with an air of originality.)

Mrs. Ballantyne: Of course, the minute I got your note I quite saw that something must have happened, or you wouldn't have asked us to come out in this dreadful cold, and up those awful stairs. I do think, when we're doing the whole of this Welfare Committee business gratuitously, that they might have found us a room on the ground floor. Isn't there any hope of getting better premises?

Mrs. Lloyd-Evans: They pretend that any accommodation is difficult to find nowadays, but I should like to know why some building shouldn't be done? What I always say is, that there wouldn't be half this unemployment trouble, if people were given work.

Mrs. Ballantyne (bored): Yes, indeed.

Mrs. Lloyd-Evans: It's just Bolshevism, you know, all this talk of unemployment. There's always work for those who are willing to work. Now I can't help thinking it would put a stop to all this labour unrest, if they could only send a few of the leaders to Russia, to show them what Bolshevism has resulted in, there.

Mrs. Ballantyne: Yes, of course. It really would be a lesson. (She is arranging her dress, etc., as she speaks, and tidying herself at a little pocket-mirror.)

Mrs. Akers (seating herself, to Mrs. Lloyd-Evans): Well, I'm all agog to know what's happened. Your note was most mysterious. What's been happening at the School? Really, the present generation is the limit—always giving trouble. It seems to have come in with bobbed hair.

Mrs. Lloyd-Evans: Girls are often very artful.

Mrs. Akers: Well, we ought to be able to cope with the artfulness of mere schoolgirls, surely. Now do let's sit down and get to business.

Mrs. Ballantyne (to Mrs. Lloyd-Evans): As you see, I haven't brought my daughter. I'm sure it was very thoughtful of you to warn me in your note, but I gather it means that we have something—painful—to discuss?

Mrs. Lloyd-Evans: One hardly likes to put things into words—but your Phyllis is a young girl, after all, and I always feel there ought to be something sacred about a young girl.

Mrs. Ballantyne: I had to pretend to Phyllis that you wanted to speak about some very dull question of finance. It was deceiving her, perhaps, but I do so agree with you about how one ought to treat young girls as something sacred, as you say. So I told her the whole thing was going to be very formal, and only members of the actual Committee allowed to be present. I'm afraid it was rather in the nature of a pious fraud.

(They all laugh, and draw slightly closer together.)

Mrs. Lloyd-Evans: Before we begin, I should like to say that this must all be in absolute confidence.

Mrs. Ballantyne (looking at Miss Miller): Excuse me a moment. (She whispers to Mrs. Lloyd-Evans. The other ladies try to hear what is said, and at the same time to look as though they were doing nothing of the sort.)

Mrs. Lloyd-Evans (aloud): I am sure Miss Miller will be discreet. Charity sometimes forces one to face very painful things, and one must be brave and hear about various tragedies that one would far prefer never to mention at all. (Pause.) One hardly knows how to word certain things. (Pause.)

Mrs. Ballantyne: Really, if it's anything of that sort, I think we ought to ask Miss Miller to leave us. (Aside): she's only a girl.

Mrs. Akers (eagerly): That sort? What sort?

Mrs. Ballantyne: Well, you know what I mean. But I'm sure I hope I'm mistaken.

Mrs. Lloyd-Evans: I'm afraid you're not, Mrs. Ballantyne.

Mrs. Akers: Call a spade a spade. Is it the usual thing?

Mrs. Lloyd-Evans: I should be sorry to call it the usual thing. But I'm afraid that's what it is.

Mrs. Akers: I've worked in a district, and my husband has a large medical practice amongst poor people. I suppose some girl has got into trouble?

(Mrs. Lloyd-Evans bows her head in assent, and once more all three ladies draw their chairs closer together. Miss Miller covers her face with her hands for a moment.) From now onwards, the three ladies are all much more animated, and full of barely-disguised enjoyment of a subject which they all regard as a delicate one.

Mrs. Ballantyne: We're all married women here, and I think we can discuss this better without Miss Miller.

194

Miss Miller (quickly, and with suppressed agitation): If it's a formal meeting, you'll want the minutes entered.

Mrs. Akers: Yes. She'd better stay.

Mrs. Ballantyne (aside to Mrs. Akers): I don't agree. I'm the mother of a girl myself, as you know, and to me girlhood is sacred. We have a most painful subject to discuss.

Miss Miller: Please let me stay. I—I might help.

Mrs. Lloyd-Evans: How could you help, Miss Miller? And even if you could, it would be most unsuitable in an unmarried girl like yourself. Please wait in the next room until we call you to take down the results of the conference.

(Exit Miss Miller, and shuts the door.)

Mrs. Lloyd-Evans: I don't know that I altogether like that girl. Rather horrid of her to be so curious, wasn't it?

Mrs. Ballantyne: Any young woman with a nice mind would have been only too thankful to be spared the embarrassment of staying in the room while such a thing was being discussed. (Her tone changes to eagerness.) Well, this is too dreadful! Which of the girls is it?

Mrs. Akers: I'm certain it's one of those twins! They really are pretty—you know what I mean, pretty for that class. Which of them is it?

Mrs. Lloyd-Evans: It's nothing to do with the twins. (Though I daresay it'll be them next—one never knows, when once this sort of thing begins.) No, it's the girl from London, the daughter of that widowed Mrs. Smith who has been taking in washing in West Street.

Mrs. Akers: Fanny!

Mrs. Ballantyne: That child! But she can't be more than sixteen.

Mrs. Lloyd-Evans: Fifteen. But one knows what London girls are, at any age.

Mrs. Akers: How did you find out? Is it absolutely certain?

Mrs. Lloyd-Evans: Absolutely. It ought to have been found out months ago, if the girl hadn't been so artful. Even her mother says she had no idea, till just the other day.

Mrs. Akers (decidedly): That's impossible.

Mrs. Lloyd-Evans: She pitched a long yarn about the girl herself not having known what was happening. They pretend it came to light by accident, through something Fanny said to her mother, which made her suspicious.

Mrs. Akers (eagerly): What was that? If we're to help at all, we'd better know everything.

(Mrs. Lloyd-Evans whispers to her, and Mrs. Akers whispers in her turn to Mrs. Ballantyne.)

195

Mrs. Ballantyne: And when do they expect——

Mrs. Lloyd-Evans: In three months' time, actually.

(The members of the Committee, in silence, make rapid movements upon their fingers, in evident calculation.)

Mrs. Akers: Then it must have happened after they got down here, that's clear.

Mrs. Lloyd-Evans: I think it's much more likely it was in London. There'd just be time. Londoners are always immoral. Besides, as I said to her, in our town these things don't happen.

Mrs. Ballantyne: How did they take it?

Mrs. Lloyd-Evans: The girl herself seems absolutely callous. I couldn't get a word out of her. The mother says she hasn't been able to, either, and she's been trying to force her to tell her when it happened. The grandmother was there, as well, and you know what an odious old woman she is. I shouldn't be at all surprised if she'd been in the plot the whole time.

Mrs. Ballantyne: When did all this conversation take place, if I may ask?

Mrs. Lloyd-Evans: Only yesterday. I happened to go in there, and found the mother in tears, so of course I got the whole story out of her. I felt it was a question for the Welfare Committee—married women, like ourselves—and I've done absolutely nothing, except ask Dr. Akers to see the girl and make certain.

Mrs. Akers: Well! He's never said a word to me about it. I must say, he was out late last night and early this morning, but I do think he ought to have given me a hint.

Mrs. Lloyd-Evans: Gentlemen are so odd, about anything to do with their business. I've often noticed it. One has to probe for hours, sometimes, to get the simplest piece of information.

Mrs. Akers: Look here, we shall have to settle something. Of course the girl must go away.

The Others: Of course.

Mrs. Akers: The question is, where?

Mrs. Ballantyne: Surely some Sisterhood would take her in.

Mrs. Lloyd-Evans: One doesn't want to be hard on her. I told the mother that we should discuss it all quietly amongst ourselves before settling anything.

Mrs. Ballantyne: I think we ought to send for the girl, and see if we can get anything out of her. Of course, it would be very trying and dreadful, but I'm sure that's what we ought to do. I, for one, shouldn't shrink from it.

Mrs. Lloyd-Evans: You wouldn't get a word out of her. They were all in league together, it seemed to me. Thoroughly artful and determined to stick together, I thought them, all three of them.

196

Mrs. Akers: I can't see why the grandmother should have any say in the matter at all. Pray what has she to do with it?

Mrs. Lloyd-Evans: She talked a great deal of nonsense about wanting to keep Fanny at home. As I said to her, if keeping Fanny at home results in this sort of thing, then the sooner Fanny goes away from home the better. She was thoroughly nonplussed at that, as you may imagine, and couldn't answer anything at all, though of course she chattered away, but I took not the slightest notice.

Mrs. Ballantyne: But, Mrs. Lloyd-Evans, do you mean to say that they won't tell who the man is?

Mrs. Lloyd-Evans: The girl won't say a word. As I said to her myself, it must have been somebody in London before they came away, and it's no use telling me it happened here, because I simply shan't believe it.

Mrs. Akers: Well, what about a Home, or some other place where the girl could go till it's all over? It had better be as far away from here as possible, of course.

The other two as before: Oh, of course.

Mrs. Akers: I have two or three addresses of that kind—one place is near London.

Mrs. Ballantyne: The very thing. I'd gladly take her up myself, if necessary. She's very young and one doesn't want to be hard on her. What line are the mother and grandmother taking up?

Mrs. Lloyd-Evans: The mother cried a good deal, and said how ashamed she was that the girl should make such a return for all that's been done for them down here. People have been very kind about employing her—I've sent washing there myself. (She charges less than the steam-laundry.) She was thoroughly upset, and one could have managed her all right. It's the grandmother that's so impossible, and the girl looks as though she could be thoroughly obstinate. I'm bound to say she was looking very ill, so one didn't want to frighten her.

Mrs. Akers: Well, that doesn't apply to the old woman. She must be squashed. Leave the grandmother to me if necessary. If there's any difficulty about their letting Fanny go, I can say we shall inform the police. These people are perfectly ignorant of the law, and would probably believe anything. (She laughs in a slightly shamefaced, way.) After all, it's for the girl's own good.

Mrs. Ballantyne: Certainly, and besides, for their own sake they want to avoid exposure. The mother can be told that the Committee is taking the whole expense and trouble off her hands, and she'll be only too thankful to let the girl go. She can come back when it's all over, and if they're careful, people needn't know anything about it.

Mrs. Ballantyne: But what will happen—when——

197

Mrs. Lloyd-Evans: What?

Mrs. Ballantyne: What will be done with the—with the little——

Mrs. Akers: The results, you mean?

Mrs. Lloyd-Evans: Oh, the baby. In these sad cases, one almost hopes that it may not live, dreadful though it sounds to say such a thing.

Mrs. Akers: My husband tells me that in his experience, illegitimate children are often particularly strong and healthy infants.

Mrs. Lloyd-Evans: God's ways are not our ways.

Mrs. Akers (to Mrs. Ballantyne): But in this case, of course, the child will be taken away the minute it's born, and the mother will probably never set eyes on it at all. It's taken to some Institution where they look after it, and that gives the mother a chance of living it down. Especially when she's so young.

Mrs. Lloyd-Evans: The grandmother said something about the baby, as she called it, but of course I stopped that at once. They can hardly earn enough to keep themselves, as it is, and if there was any question of Fanny being allowed to keep the child, it would simply amount, as I told her, to putting a premium upon immorality. Of course, if one knew who the man was, pressure could be brought to bear on him, but I don't believe for an instant that it's a case of the girl having been seduced. She's probably a thorough little bad lot. Quite likely she doesn't know who the father is. I'm told that some of these London girls are frightfully—promiscuous.

Mrs. Akers: I don't know how to believe that—at fifteen! I'm afraid it may have been somebody down here, you know.

Mrs. Lloyd-Evans: Oh please don't suggest such a thing. It's the last thing we want to have established. Just think of the talk! As it is, if we don't press the question, we can get the girl away quietly and nothing be known about it.

Mrs. Ballantyne: You think we shan't get anything out of her?

Mrs. Lloyd-Evans: Nothing, nor her mother either, according to her own account. The old grandmother began some story about an assault having perhaps been made on the girl, and she too frightened to tell; but as I said, if that sort of thing was new to her, a girl's first impulse would be to rush to her mother with the story, and if she didn't, it only showed that she thought nothing of it.

Mrs. Akers (thoughtfully): I wonder if I could get anything out of her? I've a very good mind to go home that way. One dreads having to deal with this sort of sad case, but after all, it's charity. I could put the old grandmother into her place once and for all, as you say she's disposed to be tiresome, and make Fanny herself

198

understand that we only want to help her. After all, we've all read our Bible, I hope: "Which amongst you shall cast the first stone?"

Mrs. Ballantyne: As the mother of a girl myself, I was wondering if I ought not to talk to Fanny, perhaps. Goodness knows, it's a miserable affair, but the world is what it is, and it's no use shrinking from these things.

Mrs. Lloyd-Evans (displeased): As it was I who made this very sad and perplexing discovery, I think I had better be the person to see the business through. Naturally, one consults the Committee, but I can't help feeling that there had better be only one intermediary between the Committee and the girl's family. It's more business-like, and one must be business-like.

Mrs. Ballantyne: Oh, certainly!

Mrs. Akers: But this isn't an official meeting, is it? We've had no notes taken, or anything. And we haven't passed any resolution. Now, I should like to propose that I write to-night to St. Mary Magdalene's Home and try and arrange to get Fanny taken in there as soon as possible, and kept till after the birth of the child.

Mrs. Ballantyne: I second that.

Mrs. Lloyd-Evans: Proposed and seconded. Those in favour— (they each lift up a hand). Those against.... Carried unanimously, I think.

Mrs. Akers: Now, is there anything more we can do?

Mrs. Lloyd-Evans: I don't think so. If there are any further developments, I will let you know, of course. I mean, if one can get any admission out of the girl, for instance. She seemed to me perfectly stolid and bewildered, but one doesn't want to risk upsetting her, naturally. It would be extremely annoying if anything happened before we can get her away.

Mrs. Ballantyne: What did they say about her health? Is she all right?

Mrs. Lloyd-Evans: Perfectly all right. Why shouldn't she be—a young, healthy girl like that!

Mrs. Akers: After all, it's nature.

Mrs. Lloyd-Evans: I don't call it nature at all, at fifteen. I call it sin. (Rises, and goes to put on her coat. The other two remain seated.)

Mrs. Ballantyne (shuddering): Fifteen! Just think of it! My Phyllis is only two years older. Thank heaven, I've been able to keep her as innocent as a baby. She knows nothing—absolutely nothing.

Mrs. Akers: Innocence is such a safeguard.

Mrs. Ballantyne: What I shall tell her about this meeting, I really don't know. Unfortunately, she knew where I was coming, and I shall have to invent something to tell her in case she asks any

199

questions about it, as she's certain to do. Luckily, I think she trusts me absolutely.

Mrs. Akers: Come home to tea with me, dear Mrs. Ballantyne. It will help to take both our minds off the whole sad subject.

Mrs. Ballantyne: How very kind of you! I should love to. We must try and forget all about it for the time being.

Mrs. Akers: I can't help wondering how Fanny could have managed to deceive her mother for so long.

Mrs. Ballantyne: I must say, I should have thought any woman with eyes in her head——

Mrs. Akers: Yes, and besides, why didn't the girl, if she was a respectable girl, go straight to her mother when——

(Mrs. Akers and Mrs. Ballantyne, lean across the table, talking busily about Fanny's behaviour, both at once. Meanwhile Mrs. Lloyd-Evans, who has now got her furs on, stands as though listening to some sound outside the door, unnoticed by the other two. She tiptoes rapidly to the door and flings it open. Miss Miller is crouching outside, having evidently been listening. One side of her face is scarlet where it has been pressed to the door, the other white. She rises awkwardly as the door opens, but not before they have all seen her.)

Mrs. Lloyd-Evans: I thought so!

Miss Miller (wildly): What did you think, Mrs. Lloyd-Evans? That I've been listening at the door? So I have! That I've overheard all your charitable plans for Fanny Smith and her illegitimate child? So I have!

Mrs. Akers: You should be ashamed of yourself.

Mrs. Ballantyne: What's the meaning of this?

Miss Miller: I'll tell you. You said just now that the world is what it is—there's no use in shrinking from things—shrinking from them! Ha, ha, ha! (she laughs hysterically). You're a great deal more likely to jump at them. But if you want to have my explanation, you shall have it.

Mrs. Lloyd-Evans (pointing to the door): Miss Miller, leave the room.

(Miss Miller looks at her, still laughing, then turns the key in the door, shutting and locking it.)

Miss Miller: I shan't leave the room, nor you either, till you've heard what I've got to say.

Mrs. Akers: Good heavens, she's mad!

Mrs. Lloyd-Evans (advancing resolutely): Give me that key this moment (putting out her hand for it).

(Miss Miller, too quick for her, dashes to the window, throwing up the sash, and flings out the key. During the rest of the scene she

200

stands with her back to the open window, while the three other women are grouped together behind the table, at the further side of the room.)

Miss Miller (her voice has grown cunning, and bitterly and vehemently ironical both at once. She gives the impression of dementia): I knew what you were going to talk about. She (pointing to Mrs. Akers) gave it away when she said it must be "the usual thing." Of course I listened, to hear what you'd do for Fanny—poor Fanny, who's going to bring a little baby into the world, and who's been ill and terrified and unhappy, all these months. And you (to Mrs. Lloyd-Evans, bitter mockery in her tone) found it out, and you asked these other kind, charitable, rich ladies to come and meet you here, so that you could all talk it over, and make plans about Fanny. (Suddenly and viciously): And oh, how you all enjoyed it—didn't you—telling each other how painful it was, and how sad, and how you could hardly put it into words!

(Fiercely): Why, you nearly scratched one another's eyes out for the fun of going to Fanny's mother, and "putting the old grandmother into her place" and putting Fanny through the Third Degree, nagging and nagging at her to tell, so that you could hear more shocking details, and come and gloat over them.

(Mimicking): "Oh, but we want to help her," and "girlhood is so sacred." (To Mrs. Ballantyne): Yes, you said that several times, didn't you, you who are so thankful that your girl trusts you—so that when you cheat her and tell little lies for her own good, the poor little fool swallows it. She won't always swallow it, you know—she'll find you out one day. Just like I've found out, what charity means and what's done to girls who sin and get found out. I had to know, you see, because—I've done what Fanny did——

(The women cry out, below their breath.)

Miss Miller: You needn't be frightened—it isn't anyone down here. That's what you're afraid of, isn't it—that it may all end up tamely after all, with a hasty marriage, and nothing left to talk about! You'd like to hustle me away, like Fanny, to somewhere that will take your money, and make you feel all nice and glowing and charitable—and where they'll "take away the baby, and the mother probably never sets eyes on it at all." To be allowed to keep it, would "put a premium on immorality" wouldn't it? Ha, ha, ha! I've been frightened all these weeks, but I'm not frightened any more now. Something went snap inside my head, I think, all in a minute, while I was listening to all of you. I'd thought of appealing to you, you see—such kind ladies, all given over to works of charity! If you're the charitable (laughing wildly) what would other people say? No, no,

201

no—I'll not be like Fanny, I've thought of a better plan than any of yours!

(She springs on to the sill of the open window. Mrs. Akers cries "Stop her!" and they dash forward, but the table impedes them, and Miss Miller, still laughing, throws herself out.

The curtain falls as Mrs. Lloyd-Evans, screaming, pulls at the locked door, and the other two women throw themselves against the window and look downwards.)

THE END

Ingram Content Group UK Ltd.
Milton Keynes UK
UKHW041107050623
422888UK00004B/75/J

9 798888 305690